In the Shadow of SILVER LAKE

By James Schneider

ISBN-10: 0615468853
EAN-13: 9780615468853
LCCN: 2011926155

This book is dedicated to
Glenn, Grunt, and Spike

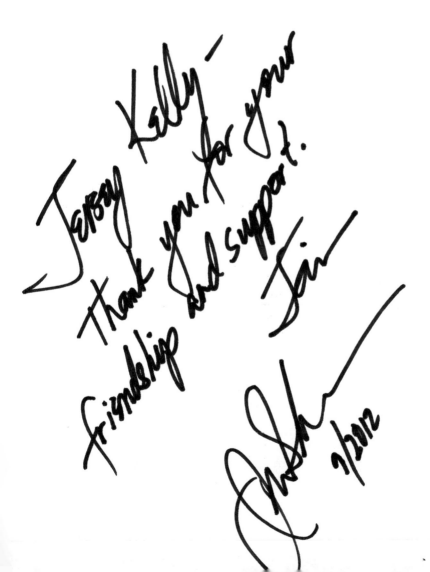

Chapter 1

Sometimes, particularly on one of those bleak winter days so common in our town, wind blowing in off the Atlantic Ocean in a northeastern direction tearing at the sand dunes and beach grasses, the sea spray battering at the roofs and windows, I feel myself drift back to my father's world, my own youth, in a seaside village he loved and in which I still live. I glance outside my office window and see the side street known as Baltimore Avenue in the town of Rehoboth Beach as it once was some forty-plus years ago—a scattering of summer cottages and boarding houses, a ghostly parade of antique cars with their convertible tops down back when they were known as rag tops.

In my mind, the dead return to life and assume their earthly shapes. I see old Mrs. Stanton delivering her basket of peaches to Lingo's Market; Mr. Askin walking toward the beach with his surfboard under his right arm, like a fixture of my youth. He waves as he goes by, a man on a daily mission to tackle the strong late summer waves of the Atlantic.

Standing once again upon the threshold of my youth, I feel sixteen again, with a head of curling locks and no middle-age paunch. Heaven far away and no thought of hell. I even sense goodness at the core of this life.

Then, from out of nowhere, I think of my art teacher Mr. Baldwin again. Not as the young man I'd known so long ago, but as a boy standing with his father many years before, watching a miniature sailboat glide by on the Central Park pond waters of his childhood home, his father telling him what fathers always told their sons—that the future is open to them just like a field of grass, harboring no dark wood nearby. In my mind I see him as he stood in his cottage that day; I hear his strong baritone voice as he speaks. *"Take as much as you want, Robbie. There's plenty."*

In those days, the Epworth Church stood at the western entrance to Rehoboth Beach, immaculately white save for its tall, dark cedar shake spire. There was a bus stop at the corner in front of the church, marked by a stubby white column along the whitewashed picket fence where old Mr. Hazard had his lot of classic used cars from the forties and fifties nestled behind. At this site, the Greyhound buses from Washington, Baltimore, and Philadelphia deposited and picked up passengers.

On that August afternoon in 1966, I'd been sitting on the far bench, nearest to the canal, reading some work of science fiction, my addiction at the time, when the bus pulled to the stop yards away. From this distance I watched as the bus door opened, the doors hinges creaking in the hot, late-summer air. A large woman with three plump children emerged first, followed by an elderly woman with a floppy hat and flowing flowery dress to her calves, a sort of "Henlopen lady" as we called them, many having been married to the "old salts" in the village back in those days.

Then there was a moment of suspension when no one emerged from the shadowy interior of the bus, so that I fully expected it to yank the door inward and pull away, swing an awkward U-turn, and head north to the town of Lewes, with a trail of sand and pine needles following behind it like an old, used feather boa.

But the bus stayed in place, its engine rumbling softly as it idled by Hazard's Classic Cars. I could not imagine why it remained so until I saw another figure rise from a seat near the back of the bus. It was a man, moving slowly, a dark silhouette. Near the door he paused, his arm raised slightly to shield his eyes, his other hand in midair as he reached for the metal rail that would guide him down the stairs.

At the time I couldn't have guessed the cause for his sudden hesitation. But in the years since then, I've come to believe that it was precisely that moment he must have realized just how fully separate our world was from the one he'd lived in with his late father during the many years they had traveled from their home of New York City to foreign lands, the things he had seen with his father—Tuscany in its summer splendor, the lavender fields of Provence, London from the fountain of Trafalgar Square. How could anything in Rehoboth Beach ever compare with that?

Something at last urged him forward. Perhaps necessity, because his father's recent death meant he had no other choice. Perhaps the hope that, in the end, he could make this new place, make his life with us. I will never know. Whatever the reason, he drew a deep breath, grasped the metal rail, and made his way down the final steps of the bus into the afternoon stillness and heat of this beach village where no famous person had ever lived, where no great event ever happened, save for those meted out by sudden storms or the tortuous slow movement of summer days.

It was my father who greeted him when he stepped from the bus that hazy afternoon. My father, Gregory Elliott, was the headmaster of Tidewater Academy, a man of medium height, but whose manner, so expansive and full of authority, made him seem much larger than he was. In one of the old photos I still have of my father from the time, probably from that summer of '66, he held that look of a stern man.

In the photo he is sitting in a white wicker chair on the side porch of our home on Annapolis Street, a large wrap-around porch, overlooking massive hydrangea which bloomed every year since my grandparents owned this home in the 1940s. He is seated with a book in his lap, his hands resting on the hard binding, legs crossed, and a glass of lemonade on the table next to him, hydrangea blooms brushing against the white spindles of the porch behind him.

It was the usual pose of a respectable and accomplished man in those days, one that made him appear quite stern, perhaps even a bit hard, though in his final years he was nothing of the kind.

Indeed, when I remember him in those days, it was usually as a cheerful, ebullient man with an energetic and kindly manner to others outside his family; yet within, he was quick to anger, but also quick to forgive, his feelings always visible in his blue eyes.

"The heart is what matters, Robert," he said to me not days before my mother's death, a principle he had voiced many times through the years, but never for one moment truly lived by. For surely, of all the men I have known he was the least likely enslaved by passion. Now a middle-aged man myself, it is hard for me to imagine how I loathed him so much.

But I *did* loathe him. Silently. Sullenly. Giving him no hint of my lowly regard, I must have seemed a perfectly obedient son, given to moodiness, perhaps, but otherwise quite normal, rocked with nothing darker than the usual winds of adolescence. Considering my father, as I often do, I marvel at how much he knew of Cicero and of Thucydides yet how little of the boy that lived upstairs in his home.

Earlier that afternoon he had found me lounging in the hammock on the back porch, given me a disapproving look, and said, "What, nothing to do on this fine day?"

I shrugged.

"Well, come with me, then," he said, then bounded down the back steps to the driveway and the family car, a bulky old Plymouth Fury whose headlights stood out like eyeballs.

I followed my father down the stairs, asking along the way, "Could I drive, wherever we're heading?" He shrugged back to me. I got in the car and sat silently as he pulled the car out the long driveway, my face showing a faint sourness, the only form of rebellion I was allowed.

On the road my father drove at a leisurely pace through the village, careful to slow even further at the approach of pedestrians or bicyclists, which overran our small town that time of year. He nodded as Mr. Randall came out of Wooden Indian Sundries, and gave a short, cautionary beep on the car horn when he saw Joey York chasing Abigail Reece a little too aggressively up the bandstand stairs. In those days, Rehoboth was not much more than a six-street grid of homes, mostly summer properties with big front screened porches and a single street of shops, called "the avenue" for Rehoboth Avenue. The avenue ran perpendicular to the boardwalk, which was all of one mile in length, standing sentry to the large, sandy beach and Atlantic Ocean.

There was Lingo's Market, a sort of general store, and Carlton's haberdashery, along with the pharmacy run by Mr. Ventre, in which the gentlemen of the town would sit on the front benches and watch tourists wander by and grumble how crowded the village became this time of year. Mr. Howard had a boarding house at the far end of the avenue, where on the street level Miss Lane ran a little school for "dance, drama, and piano," which practically no one ever attended, so that her main source of income came from the selling of cakes and pies, something she learned during her previous life as a wanna be dancer in Washington.

From a great height, Rehoboth must have looked idyllic, and yet to me it was more like a prison, its squat buildings the prison walls, its yards and gardens strewn around me like fields of concertina wire.

My father felt nothing of the kind, of course. No man was ever more suited to small-town life than he was. Sometimes, for no reason whatever, he would set out from our house and walk down to the center of the village, chatted with whoever crossed his path, usually about the tourists, weather, or the progress of their garden, anything to keep the flow of words going, as if these inconsequential conversations were the lubricant of life.

That August afternoon my father seemed almost jaunty as he drove through the village.

"Do you remember that new teacher I mentioned?" he asked as we swept past Lingo's Market. "The one who's coming from Europe by way of New York City?"

I nodded dully, faintly recalling the brief mention of such a person at dinner one night.

"Well, he's arriving today, coming in on the Baltimore bus. I want you to give him a nice welcome. He took the train from Grand Central Station to Penn Station then the long bus ride, so he must be tired by now."

I did not reply, and my father drove farther up the road and over the wood boards of the canal bridge toward the white façade of Epworth Church. I considered his merry mood, and because of that knew something was up. For he always seemed in a good mood when doing some sort of a good deed.

We reached the bus stop a few minutes later. My father took up his place by the white fence near the column while I wandered over to the benches facing the canal, slumped on the end bench, and pulled the book I'd been reading from the back pocket of my shorts.

Looking down at the canal, I considered its uselessness in the modern world. This few miles-long canal led from Rehoboth Bay on the southwestern side of the town, north to the Lewes canal then connected with the Delaware Bay at the confluence of the Atlantic Ocean. Years before, fishermen would use a horse alongside the canal to haul the boats carrying the daily catch of fish and crustaceans from the village of Lewes here to be sold in Lingo's Market. Now they simply used the cold box trucks instead.

I was reading my book a half-hour later when the bus at last arrived. I remained in place, grudgingly aware that my father would have preferred that I rush over to greet this new teacher. Of course I was determined to do nothing of the kind.

And so I don't know how he reacted when my father first saw Mr. Baldwin emerge from the bus that afternoon, for I couldn't see his face. I do know how handsome Bradley Baldwin was, however, how immaculately pale his wrinkled cream linen suit was against his tan skin, the strong features of his face, with a square jaw, sharp eyes, and jet black hair cut in the style of the roaring 20s. I have always believed that as he stepped from the gray interior of that bus, his face suddenly captured in a bright summer light, his eyes settling upon my father with the mysterious richness I was to see in them as well, that at that moment in that silence, my own father caught his breath.

Chapter 2

Inevitably, when I recall that first meeting, the way Mr. Baldwin looked as he arrived in Rehoboth, so young and full of hope, I want to put up my hand and do what all our reading and experience tells us we can never do. I want to say, "Stop, please. Stop, time."

It's not that I want to freeze him there for all eternity, of course, a young man arriving in a quaint mid-Atlantic town, but that I wish to merely break the pace long enough to point out the simple truth that life teaches any man that lives into middle age: since our passions do not last forever, our only true task is to survive them. And one more thing perhaps: I want to remind him how thin it is, and weaving, the tightrope we walk through life—how the smallest misstep can become a fatal plunge.

Then I think, *No, things must be as they became.* And with that thought, time rolls onward again, and I see him take my father's hand, shake it briefly, then let go, his face turning slightly to the left so that he must have seen me as I finally roused myself from the wooden bench and headed toward him.

"This is my son, Robert," my father said when I reached them.

"Hi," I said, offering my hand. "Please call me Rob or even Robbie, as everyone around town does."

Mr. Baldwin took it. "Hello, *Robbie*," he said.

I can clearly recall how handsome he looked at that very first meeting, his jet black hair hanging just a bit over his forehead, his skin a perfect tan color, his features beautiful in a way certain antique portraits are beautiful, not so much feminine but more strength, masculine yet sensuous. More than anything, I recall his eyes, pale green and slightly oval, with a striking sense of alertness.

"Robert will be a sophomore this year," my father added. "He'll be one of your students."

Before Mr. Baldwin could respond to that statement, the bus driver came around the bus from the other side carrying two leather suitcases. He dropped them to the ground, then scurried back onto the bus.

My father nodded for me to pick up the two pieces of luggage. Which I did, then stood, feeling like a third wheel as he immediately returned the full force of his attention to Mr. Baldwin.

"You'll have an early dinner with us," Father told him. "After dinner we will take you to your new home." With that, he stepped back slightly, turned, and headed for the car, Mr. Baldwin walking beside him, I trudging behind, the suitcases hanging heavily from my hands.

We lived on Annapolis Street in those days, just down from Tidewater Academy, in a white cape-style home with wraparound front porch and small yard, like almost all the others in the town. As we drove toward it, passing through the town center on the way, my father pointed out the various shops and the stores where Mr. Baldwin would be able to buy his household provisions and supplies.

He seemed quite attentive to whatever my father told him, his attention drawn to this building or that one with an unmistakable appreciativeness, like someone touring a gallery or a museum, his eyes focused on the smallest things, the striped awning of the Wooden Indian, the large raised hexagon bandstand near the boardwalk, the large front lawn of the court house, a knot of young men who lounged in front of Affonco's Pizzeria smoking cigarettes and in whose indiscriminate habits and loose morals my father claimed to glimpse the grim approach of the coming age.

A flatland for a seaside town, with a low rise as it ascended to the coastal dunes. The old no-longer-in-service lighthouse stood at the far north end of it, its grounds used now as a park for children to play, with a few benches.

"That old lighthouse is no longer needed, so it now houses the office of Rehoboth Beach Patrol, the life guards, if you will," my father explained as he pointed to the structure.

I noticed Mr. Baldwin gazed at the lighthouse as we drifted by, deep in thought, it appeared. "It's good to have made a worthwhile purpose out of the old building," he replied to my father. He turned toward the back seat, his green eyes looking, almost searching, into my own gray eyes. "Don't you think so, Robbie?" I had no answer for him; surprised as I was that he'd bothered to ask, but then again my father appeared quite taken by Mr. Baldwin's observation.

"Yes, I think that's true," he said. "The town is starting to establish an historical society to maintain the architectural integrity of this beautiful seaside town."

Mr. Baldwin's eyes lingered on me an extra moment, a quiet smile offered silently before he turned away. Our home is situated at the end of Annapolis Street, near to the beach dunes, and on the way to it we passed Tidewater Academy. It was a large, weather-washed cedar shake building with white window trim and a concrete front porch and double doors. The first floor housed the classrooms, the second taken up by the dormitory, the dining hall, common room, and a large screened porch.

"That's where you'll be teaching," my father told him, slowing down a bit as we drove by. "We've made a special room for you, off one end of the building overlooking the interior courtyard to the rear."

Mr. Baldwin glanced over at the school, and from his reflection in the glass, I could see that his eyes were very still, like someone staring into a crystal ball, searching for his future there.

We pulled up to the front of our home a few minutes later. My father and Mr. Baldwin already out of the car and walking toward the front porch, where my mother waited to be introduced.

"Welcome to Rehoboth Beach," my mother said, offering her hand.

Mother was only a few years younger than my father but considerably less agile, and certainly less spirited, her face rather plain and round, with small, smart eyes. To the people of Rehoboth, she had been known simply as the "local music teacher" and more or less given up for a spinster. Then my father had arrived, twenty-eight years old but still a bachelor, eager to establish a household where he could entertain the teachers he'd already hired for the new school, as well as benefactors. My mother had met whatever criteria he had for a wife, and after a courtship of only nine weeks, he'd asked her to marry him.

Mother had accepted without hesitation, my father's proposal catching her so completely by surprise, as she loved to tell the women in her gossip circle, that at first she had taken it as a joke. As the wedding gift, my maternal grandparents, the Albertis, gave them the house we lived in, which had been in the family for many years.

On that afternoon nearly twenty years later, my mother no longer appeared capable of taking anything lightly. She'd grown wide in the hips by then, her figure large and matronly, her pace slowed by arthritis. She was so slow and ponderous that I often grew impatient with it and bolted ahead of her to wherever we were going, covering my embarrassment by acting as if I meant to get ahead to hold the door for her.

Later in life she sometimes had trouble making it to the top of the front stairs and would stay on the porch to catch her breath in pain and wait to regain it, one hand grasping the screen door frame, the other rubbing her hip through her dress, her head arched back as she sucked in a long, difficult breath. In old age her hair grew white and her eyes dimmed, as she often sat alone in the front room or lay curled in bed, no longer interested in reading or listening to the radio. Even so, something fiery remained deep inside her to the very end, fueled by a rage engendered by the happenings at Silver Lake, one that smoldered forever after that.

She died many years after the incident had run its frightful course, and by then much had changed in all our lives: The large house on Annapolis Street no more than a distant memory, sold and torn down for one of those modern ocean view homes, my father living on a modest pension at Beachfield, an assisted living facility, Tidewater Academy long closed, its doors locked, windows boarded, the playing fields gone to weed, its former reputation by then reduced to a dark and woeful legacy.

Mother had prepared a seaside meal of crab soup with bread and salad for us that afternoon, creamy and thick with claw meat, the sort typical for an autumn evening yet to come. We ate at the dining table. Carlo Romiti, a distant relative on my mother's side whom father had brought to live with us, helped Mother ladle the soup into the bowls. When father had learned that Carlo was orphaned in his home village of Lucca, Italy, he arranged for him to come to Tidewater Academy through a foreign exchange student program for the coming year. Carlo's enrollment was too late to provide him with room and board at the dormitory, and his grasp of the English language was weak at best; hence father decided that Carlo would live with us, in the room opposite mine upstairs, and would have to learn basic English before entering courses at the academy. Since Carlo's family had a bakery in Lucca, he was a godsend for mother in the kitchen and became her help when her pain flared up, such as today.

Sitting at the table Mr. Baldwin asked few questions as Father went through his usual remarks about Tidewater, what its philosophy was, how it had come to be, a lecture Mother and I had heard countless times yet clearly engaged Mr. Baldwin's interest.

"Why only boys?" he asked at one point.

"Because girls would change the atmosphere of the campus," my father answered."

"In what fashion?"

"The boys would, well, feel their presence," Father told him. "It would cause them to show off, to act foolishly."

"But is that the fault of the girls or the boys, Mr. Elliott?"

"It's the fault of the mixture, Mr. Baldwin," my father told him, obviously surprised by the boldness of his question. "It makes the atmosphere more…volatile."

Father had fully expected to bring the subject to a close with that statement. An expectation I shared so completely that when Mr. Baldwin suddenly spoke again—offering what amounted to a challenge—I felt something like a call to arms.

"And without the girls, what, pray tell, is the atmosphere? Mr. Baldwin lobbed.

"Studious and serious," Father answered. "More… disciplined."

"And that is the atmosphere you want at Tidewater Academy?"

My father's answer was firm. "Yes, it is."

Mr. Baldwin said nothing more on the subject, but sitting across from him at the table, I sensed there was more that he might have shared, thoughts that were in his head, bristling there.

At the end of the meal Father led Mr. Baldwin and my mother into the little front room for a glass of iced sweet tea. I lingered at the table, watched Carlo clear away the dishes. Though my father had closed the glass French doors that separated the front room from the dining room, it was still possible for me to see Mr. Baldwin as he sat there listening to my father.

"So what do you think of the new teacher, Carlo?" I asked as he gathered the last plates from the table. Carlo did not answer, so I glanced up at him. He was not looking at me, but toward the parlor, where Mr. Baldwin sat by the window, his legs crossed and intent on what my father was saying at the moment.

"A man of...*come direst tu*...how would you say...sophistication," Carlo said in an almost deferential tone. "The kind you read about in *libri*." I understood this to mean books from our previous discussion of our shared interest in reading while walking along the beach the day Carlo arrived at our home earlier this summer. Carlo had a weak grasp of the language, but we seemed to be able to convey thoughts respectably if I afforded him the time to think it through.

I looked back at Mr. Baldwin. He was taking a sip from his glass as my father went on, his green eyes peering just over the rim, sharp and evaluating, as if his mind ceaselessly sifted through the material that passed through it, allowing this, dismissing that, his sense of judgment oddly final.

I was in my room an hour or so later, perusing the supplies Mother had purchased for my coming semester at Tidewater Academy, when my father summoned me from the bottom of the stairs.

"It's time to take Mr. Baldwin home," he told me.

I followed him out the front door, then down the front steps to where Mr. Baldwin was standing by the car, looking toward the overhanging clouds above the ocean dunes.

"It's only a short drive," my father said to him as we all got into the car. "Perhaps we can get you there ahead of the rain."

But he could not, for as we drove south toward the cottage, the rain clouds suddenly disgorged their burden, thunderously and without much warning. Once outside the town center, my father turned onto Coastal Road, past the few great summer houses that rose along the ocean, then toward the outskirts, toward Silver Lake.

Given this torrent, the ride was slow, our old Plymouth wagon puttering along, battered from all directions by whipping gusts, the windshield wipers squeaking pathetically as they swept ineffectively across the glass.

My father kept his eyes on the road, of course, but I noticed that Mr. Baldwin's attention had turned toward the landscape along the road, its short, slight hills sparsely clothed in tangles of brush and scrub white pines, wind ripping through the sea grass that sprouted from the dunes.

"This region of Delaware is known as Cape Henlopen," Father explained, "from Lewes, the town north of Rehoboth Beach to the town below us, identified as Dewey Beach."

"The cape region is pretty, don't you think, Mr. Baldwin?" my only comment inserted into their adult conversation.

"It looks tormented," he said, staring out the window on the passenger side, his face suddenly quite somber, as if it came from some darker part of his mind.

His reply must have startled my father, who glanced toward him. "Tormented? What do you mean?"

"It reminds me of the islands of the Florida Keys," he answered, his eyes still on the barren landscape. "The name the Spaniards gave them."

"What name is that?" I probed.

"*Los Martires*," Mr. Baldwin answered. "The Keys were named that because they look to be tormented by the wind and the sea."

"Forgive my ignorance," my father said. "But what does 'Los Martires' mean?"

Mr. Baldwin continued to gaze out the window. "It means 'the martyrs,'" he said, his eyes narrowing somewhat, as if no longer looking at the dunes and the sea grass beyond his window, but at the ravaged landscape he must have experienced during a previous visit to the Florida Keys.

My father drew his attention back to the road. "Well, I've never thought of the cape as looking like that," he said. Then to my surprise, I saw his eyes lift toward the rearview mirror and fix on mine. "Have you ever thought of the cape like that, Robert?"

I glanced out the window to the east, toward a landscape that no longer seemed featureless and inert, but trampled and bedeviled, lashed by gusts of wind and surging storm waters. "Not until just now," I responded.

About a mile or so beyond town, we were on a stretch of the road bordered on all sides by dense pine trees and covered with a layer of fallen orange needles over the top of crushed oyster shells, which had become the roadway after the shells had been ground into a fine white powder. The woods encroached so much into the road that I could hear the vegetation slap and scrape against the side of the car as we bumped along.

"It's pretty deserted out this way," Father said. He added nothing else as we continued in silence until the road forked, my father taking the lane to the right, moving down it for perhaps an eighth of a mile until it suddenly came to an abrupt end before a small old gray cottage.

"There it is," Father said. "Robinson Cottage."

It was tiny compared to our home on Annapolis Street, so dwarfed by the surrounding pine trees that it appeared to crouch fearfully within a fist of green pine. Beyond the cottage was a large lake with a pier, the dark stretch of water sweeping out beyond it, still and lightless. At the end of the small pier was a gazebo.

"That's Silver Lake," Father said.

Mr. Baldwin leaned toward the front windshield, peering at the cottage very intently through the downpour, like a painter considering a composition, calculating the light, deciding where to put the easel. It was an expression I would see many times during the coming year, intense and curious, a face that seemed to draw everything into it by its own strange sense of gravity.

"It's a simple place," my father told him. "But quite nice. I hope you'll at least find it adequate."

"I'm sure I will," he said. "Who lived here?"

"It was never actually lived in year-round," Father answered. "It was built in the late 1920s as a summer cottage by the Robinson family, which has owned all of this land and lake since the turn of the century."

"But they never lived there?"

My father appeared reluctant to answer him but felt obligated to do so. "They were killed on the way to it that first summer," he said. "Their car got stuck in the train tracks in Ellendale on their way here from their home outside of Washington, D.C. The oncoming train couldn't stop in time."

Mr. Baldwin's face suddenly became strangely animated, as if he was imagining an alternative story in his mind—the coming of a family who never arrived, a summer that was never theirs. "Ah, yes, Ellendale. I passed through that little town on the bus. A sad place it appeared."

19

"It's not luxurious, of course," my father added quickly, looking back at the cottage, determined as he always was to avoid disagreeable things, "but it's certainly adequate. The landlord has chopped enough firewood to get you through the autumn, but then you'll need to continue to chop for the winter to come," then after a brief pause, "but a big strong young lad like you might enjoy that bit of exercise."

His eyes rested on Mr. Baldwin for a moment before he drew them away abruptly, and almost guiltily, so that for a brief instant he looked rather like a man who'd been caught reading a forbidden book. "Well, let's go inside," he said. With that, my father opened his door and stepped out into the rain.

"Quickly now, Robert." He motioned for me to get Mr. Baldwin's luggage and follow him into the cottage.

Father was already at the screened porch door, struggling with the key, his hair wet and stringy, by the time I reached him. Mr. Baldwin stood just behind him, waiting for him to open the door. As he worked the key, turning it left and right, he appeared somewhat embarrassed that it wouldn't turn, as if some element of his authority had been called into question.

"Please, perhaps I could try it," Mr. Baldwin offered.

"Everything rusts in this salt air," I heard Father murmur, "but why don't you give it a try?"

Mr. Baldwin did in fact give it a try, and as he jerked the key and pulled at the door, it gave, and the cottage porch door swung open. Luckily the interior front door to the house opened on the first try.

"There are sporadic outages of electricity out this way," Father explained as he stepped into the darkened cottage. "But the fireplace has been readied for winter, and there are plenty of kerosene lamps, so you'll have plenty of light." He walked to the window, parted the curtains, and looked out into the darkening rain. "Just as I explained in my letter." He released the curtain and turned back toward us. "I take it you're accustomed to things being a little...well, old and primitive, based on all your travels."

"Yes, I am," Mr. Baldwin replied.

"So before we go you should take a look around. I hope we didn't forget anything." Father walked over to one of the table lamps and lit it. A yellow-orange glow spread through the room, illuminating the knotty pine walls, the recently hung lace curtains, the plain wood floor that had been carefully swept, a stone fireplace cleared of previous ash. Although it had been cleaned, I could still detect a slight musty smell from the cottage having been closed up for some time, but knew that the odor would dissipate once the windows were opened and a breeze blew through off the lake and the ocean.

"The kitchen has been partially stocked already by my wife, Grace, and my cousin Carlo," Father told him. "So you've got plenty of milk and eggs, flour, sugar. Even some soap. All of your essentials." He nodded toward the bedroom. "And the linens are fresh, with a spare set in the wardrobe there. Mrs. Elliott, well, Grace, likes to use lavender from her garden in the wash water, so I hope you don't mind the smell."

"No, I rather favor it," Mr. Baldwin said. "It helps one to relax."

With that, Mr. Baldwin glanced toward the small bedroom, his gaze settling upon the old iron-framed single bed, the sheets stretched neatly over the thin mattress, a handmade quilt folded over at the foot of the bed, a single pillow at its head.

"I know things will take getting used to, Mr. Baldwin," my father said, "but I'm sure in time you will be happy here."

But as to the current contentment of Mr. Baldwin, I could not have said. I knew only that a strange energy surrounded him, a vibrancy that was almost physical, and that whatever happiness he would find living here he would have to answer to.

"I hope you like Rehoboth Beach as well," my father said after a moment. "It's really a charming little town."

"I'm sure I will," Mr. Baldwin told him, though even as he said it, he might well have been comparing it to Venice or London, the great cities he'd visited, the canals or spacious squares he'd strolled along, a wider world he'd long known but that I had only dreamed of.

"Well, we should be getting home. Your mother must be frantic with worry over us by now," my father said. He nodded toward the two leather cases resting on each side of me like large bookends. "Put those in the bedroom, Robert."

I did as I was told and joined Father as he stepped out on the screened porch.

"Well, good night, then, Mr. Baldwin," he said as he opened the door of the porch.

"Good night, Mr. Elliott," he said. "And I thank you for everything." Then, as if an afterthought, he stuck his head out the front door onto the porch as we were running through the rain to the car, "Please thank Mrs. Elliott for such a delightful meal."

Seconds later we were in the car again, backing up onto Coastal Road. Through the chords of rain that ran down the windshield, I could see Mr. Baldwin standing on the screened porch in front of a small window, the light from within the cottage silhouetting him as he waved good-bye. I have often chosen to recall him as he was that first night I met him, rather than as he appeared at our last meeting, his thinning hair disheveled, his skin lusterless, and the air around him thick with a dank and deathly smell.

Chapter 3

Today my father's portrait hangs on the wainscot wall of my office opposite my desk, where I look at it most days. He is dressed in a three-piece suit, the vest neatly buttoned, in a formal style of portraiture of that time. The portrait, done in oils, depicts my father gazing out a window toward a large body of water that took me years to realize was Silver Lake. These days, in the early summer of 2007, as I think back on the incident, my eyes are frequently drawn to the small signature of the artist in the bottom right corner: *Bradley S. Baldwin.*

The portrait was painted during the last weeks of the school year in 1967, my father standing by the window in his office peering out at the courtyard that was for some reason not painted on this canvas, while Mr. Baldwin sat stationed at his easel just a few yards away. By that point in late April Mr. Baldwin did not look as he had when he arrived the previous August. The blush of youth was gone, a haggardness in its place, and glimpsing him alone in his classroom during those last days or as he made his solitary walk along Coastal Road, I could see nothing of the vibrant young man who stood on the front porch of his cottage only months before, waving good-bye to my father and me as we left him for his first night in Rehoboth Beach.

I never knew what Mr. Baldwin did after we drove away from him that first evening, leaving him alone in that cottage. I have imagined that he opened his two heavy suitcases and began to unpack, making that cottage his new home.

From the look of the cottage when I saw it the next day, I know that he had found a nail already in place and hung a portrait of his own late father, one painted years ago in the courtyard of the Uffizi Gallery, the Florentine sun pouring over him. He was dressed stylishly, in cream trousers, a navy blue jacket, a straw bowler, and his fingers around the ivory head of a highly polished walking stick.

I could also tell that he had rearranged the modest furniture to face the lake-side windows and moved table lamps and kerosene lanterns from their positions the evening before, probably so they could cast the best light in the dark-walled cottage.

Mr. Baldwin had several cartons of personal belongings shipped ahead of his arrival, which the landlord had delivered to him at the cottage. The boxes lay discarded on his front porch, the contents removed and displayed in the tiny cottage, offering whatever semblance of a home for this man from a foreign land.

In later life, after college, when I returned to Rehoboth Beach and started my real estate brokerage, I had only to glance out my office window to see the man who had cross-examined Mr. Baldwin on that August afternoon in 1967. For after that case, which made his career as a prosecutor for Sussex County, Mr. Horton's private practice office was located just across the street from where I now have my office, and which his daughter,

Liz, still occupies as a lawyer who specializes in personal injury litigation and drunken driving disputes rather than the prosecution of criminal cases for which her father was renowned throughout the county.

Liz Horton's shingle is an antique one, as it was previously her father's, and hangs above the door to her office. I remember, in an ironic way, that the day Father and I picked up Mr. Baldwin from the bus stop, we passed this very office, and I saw the elder Horton standing along the street somewhere close to that squat building, looking at us as we drove past.

Certainly I would not have known just how often I would glance at the Horton shingle in the coming years, let alone conceive the notion that I myself would return to this seaside town to make my home and a modest living—and hear his voice thunder out of the past: *It was you, Mr. Baldwin, you and you alone who brought about all this death.*

In those days, when Mr. Horton held the position of county prosecutor, he was a large, intimidating man, over six feet, with rounded shoulders and a rim of white hair around his head, bald on the top. He wore tortoise shell-framed round glasses and often a black homburg, which he would doff to passersby as he walked from the courthouse to his offices a block away.

Later I would see Mr. Horton sitting on one of the benches in front of the bandstand, throwing broken pieces of french fries or bits of old bread to the seagulls gathered at his shoes, his eyes watching them but with a curious lack of focus. Then again before that, he had taken to long walks around the town center, apparently in deep thought. He spent the first year after retirement in the back room of his law office, working on a book of his accounts of the incident that occurred and the case that catapulted his fame in the county of Sussex. He was utterly convinced that he alone had unearthed the deepest of its secrets.

Down through the years I've often thought of him, the self-importance he carried in having discovered the malignancy of so much death, then the way he later strode the courtroom central aisle boldly, proudly, as if he alone was the exclusive guardian of the town's safety.

The day after Mr. Baldwin's arrival was a Saturday, hot and sunny, and I wanted to go play volleyball on the beach with some of my classmates who had just arrived in town on the final weekend before school was scheduled to begin, when I next saw him. My father had already left to go on a business errand to Georgetown, as mother told me that morning, and he had left instructions that I was to go to Robinson Cottage and see if Mr. Baldwin was making out alright and to assist him by running any errands he might require of me.

Robinson Cottage is almost two full miles south of the town center, so it took me quite some time to walk there. I arrived around ten in the morning, knocked on the screen door to the cottage, and waited for Mr. Baldwin to respond. When there was no answer, I entered the porch and knocked on the front door. Still there was no answer. I walked to the side of the screened porch nearest to the lake and saw Mr. Baldwin sitting on the pier with his head bent back facing the sun as if he was trying to capture the last of the summer rays of sun just as so many visitors to Rehoboth Beach were doing at this time, just past the pine trees and over the dunes on the vast stretch of sun-drenched beach. He looked like a piece of sculpture, with strong, wide shoulders and a long, lean body, clearly a man who prided himself in his physique.

Concerned I might be caught looking at him before I could gain his attention I yelled down to him, "Mr. Baldwin, it's me, Robbie Elliott. My father sent me to see if you were getting on alright or if you needed any errands run, to well, help you settle in, I guess."

He did not seem to hear me. As I left the screened porch, I let the door slam, intending to make certain that Mr. Baldwin would hear me now and not think I was eavesdropping or watching from afar, as I felt, in a guilty way, that I was.

I walked down the small slope of lawn to the pier. Well, not much of a lawn per se, since it was mostly soil covered in pine needles offering a sweet fragrance that wafted up to my nose as I stepped on them.

When I stepped onto the pier, Mr. Baldwin turned his head, not even startled by my arrival. "Hello, Robbie. It is a beautiful, warm day after that storm last night, isn't it?"

I continued to walk in his direction, noticing that he was dangling his long legs and feet into the water of the lake and wearing a swimsuit like none I had ever seen any of my friends wear; rather more like one from the big screen movies that he must have brought with him from Europe. It was small and square and barely covered his privates. I felt my face and neck blush as I approached him, concerned he might have noticed my discomfort in seeing him in so little clothing. Was it discomfort or another feeling?

"Father sent me. To see if you needed anything from town or perhaps help with the cottage," I said.

"Well, thank you for coming. I seem to be all unpacked. Not much to bring with me, as you recall. Again, thank you for handling the valises for me yesterday."

"Valises, sir?"

Mr. Baldwin chuckled. "Yes, that's an old-fashioned term my father used to describe the leather suitcases."

"Oh, I see. Well, it was no trouble at all; in fact, my father requested it of me."

"Yes, I recall. But I should have carried them myself."

"You looked, well…tired." I replied. "From that long trip… Um, that's not to say you're not strong enough to carry them yourself, I didn't mean it that way," blushing all over again, realizing I was stumbling over my words in front of my future instructor at the academy.

As he stood to face me and lifted his arms in a Herculean way, he said, "No, I was tired and appreciated your assistance. I just wasn't thoughtful enough to thank you last night as you left. So, as you can see, I am quite strong and capable of carrying my own bags, wouldn't you say?" he said while he kissed his right bicep and turned to me with a playful smile.

Flustered, I asked, "Is there anything you need?" I could not help but look at his teeth, so perfect and straight. He had dimples, did I see those before? I caught myself, realizing I was almost staring at him. "Anything I can do for you while I'm here now?"

"Follow me," he said as he led the way across the distance between the pier and the cottage. "There might be something you could do for me."

As I followed I watched his back, strong with muscles that bounced a bit on either side of his spinal cord as he walked. His legs looked strong as well; perhaps he had been an athlete in school or while at university.

"Well, I'm here to help, whatever you might need of me," I stated, a bit nervous as we entered the cottage.

"If you're heading to town, could you wait for me while I shower quickly? Then we could walk to town together and you can direct me to a few of the shops, since I'll need to stock up on a few things before classes start this Monday. Will you wait and show me the way?"

"I'll be glad to show you around Rehoboth," I said, and then sat on the rusting glider on the front porch.

After a while Mr. Baldwin presented himself on the porch, cleaned up and dressed to head to town. While he was in his cottage, I sat there wondering just what had caused me to blush and be embarrassed by his lack of dress on the pier when I arrived. There had been times when I was in the shared showers with other members of the Tidewater Academy lacrosse team after a game, yet never felt such a fluster. I was a bit plump compared to some of the stronger athletes on our team yet never felt the sort of discomfort realized when I approached Mr. Baldwin on his pier just minutes ago. So what was I experiencing? Perhaps I had never seem a grown man dress so...well, European?

Chapter 4

Mr. Baldwin had no trouble keeping pace with me as we walked the length of Coastal Road toward the town center and often asked me the names of certain foliage and vegetation that lined the road; many of which I did not recognize, let along know.

I explained, "I help my mother in her back yard garden and have heard the names of those plants, but none of these really look familiar to me. Sorry. They don't look all that meaningful to me…Just like scrubs or weeds, I'd guess."

"Its strange how certain plants seem to thrive in this sandy soil, like those over there—they look like rose hips to me. I grew up in a big city so I may be incorrect," he shared.

"Actually my mother has some of those plants with that bulb-looking thing on them, and I believe she called them wild beach roses. So you may be right."

In a matter of no time, we had made it to Rehoboth Avenue, and I was not tired of our time together or even surprised by the amount of time it took to reach this point.

As we walked the avenue and Mr. Baldwin looked into the shop windows, I suddenly felt I should maintain a conversation or he would find me boring and look for a way to get rid of me now that I had showed him the way to the town proper. Suddenly I found myself keen on keeping his attention.

So I asked, "What type of a teacher are you? Father may have told me, but sometimes I block him out in conversation. Sorry if I was expected to know this information already," I shared with the feeling of a blush coming on all over again.

"That's alright. I understand...You know I was once a healthy teenager myself not that long ago and didn't always listen to all the things my father felt the need to impart on me. Now that he's gone, I regret..." Then after what seemed like a long, uncomfortable pause, "I am an art teacher. I teach art."

"We've never had an art teacher at Tidewater before. Did you know that, Mr. Baldwin?"

"Well, as they say, there's always a first time," he stated as he looked into the front window of Affonco's Pizzeria. "This looks like a nice place to have a slice of pie. Would you join me or do you need to get back home?"

"Pie? I don't think they sell pies here; we'd have to go across and down the street to Miss Lane's shop. She makes pies from her own property way up near Lewes; you know apples, pears, and peaches this time of year," I said as I pointed across the avenue to the small dance school window she had her desserts displayed in.

"Back in New York, we call a slice of pizza a slice of pie." He laughed. "Do you get it? Pie, as in the shape, I gather...It must be a New York thing, because even in Italy they don't know what you mean if you say you want a 'piece of pie' either!"

"Well, a slice of 'pie' would be a lot better than one of my mother's salami sandwiches! Yes, please, I'd like one," I stated as Mr. Baldwin held the door to the pizzeria for me while all the local hoodlums sat there watching us enter.

After he ordered, Mr. Baldwin said, "Rehoboth Beach is a charming, classic American beach village, don't you think?"

I had never heard anyone say anything so odd, and I suppose it was at that moment that some sort of different feeling about this town, my town, entered my life.

After our slice of "pie," I walked Mr. Baldwin up to the boardwalk to show him the ocean waves breaking on the beach. At that point I saw the big boardwalk clock and realized I should be heading home now, or else my mother would have a dozen questions about where I had spent the majority of the day and whether I even showed up at Robinson Cottage to assist Mr. Baldwin as my father had requested.

There on the wooden boardwalk in front of Dolle's salt water taffy shop, I excused myself and left Mr. Baldwin and headed back home.

When I reached home, Mother said that Father had called and asked that I come to the academy as soon as I arrived so I could help the returning students with any luggage or boxes they might need help carrying. I immediately headed up Annapolis Street toward the campus, thinking about how I could be on the beach or anywhere else right now had my father not been the headmaster of the school, where I seemed to have to jump at his every whim.

Already many of my schoolmates were lugging their suitcases and boxes up the walkway to the front doors, then up the stairs in the large lobby to the dormitories, and putting their treasured items away in the trunks at the end of their beds.

Over time, many of the boys I attended Tidewater Academy with became a blur, yet there was one or two that I still remember quite fondly. Jon Reinhard was one of them, who later founded a very successful architectural firm outside of Washington, D.C. Another was Matt Mueller, a once pudgy kid who ended up running for some sort of political office out of college and later became a very handsome major politician in Hartford, Connecticut. Then there was my close friend Dick Renoff who went on to the Naval Academy and became a high-ranking officer. The funny thing was that Dick seemed the least likely of this group to make much of himself, yet he turned out to hold the most honorable and prestigious career of us all.

In general, my classmates were all from good families. Most of them were simply rude to their mothers or exhibited outlandish attitudes at their former schools, so they were sent to Tidewater to straighten up their behavior and grade point average, or the next step was a strict military school in the boondocks of Pennsylvania or Virginia. Later these young men who graduated from Tidewater Academy all seemed to conform properly, as they mostly ended up having acceptable professions, running their own businesses or those established by previous generations. In later life, they all seemed to do just as their parents had always hoped for—they succeeded in life, married, and had families of their own. I thought them uninspired and dull, while my father thought them all dutiful and fine young gentlemen.

Since no one particularly needed my assistance, and none of my closest friends, Matt, Jon, or Dick, had arrived, I snuck home to spend a little time on the porch in the hammock reading the book I was eager to finish. In a matter of two days, mere hours, it felt, I would be stuck spending all my time reading the required books and have no time for myself, so I felt this time was due to me.

I was engrossed in my book when Father stepped onto the back porch, apparently having left the Plymouth in the street or at the academy, since I did not hear or see it from where I was slouching in the hammock with my book held close to my face.

"Did you even take the time to go to Robinson Cottage and assist Mr. Baldwin as I instructed you this morning?" Father said as he startled me.

I shrugged in the affirmative.

"I never saw you on campus helping others as I instructed. Were you even there this afternoon?"

Again I shrugged in the affirmative.

"Well, were you of any help to Mr. Baldwin at all, may I ask?"

"I walked him into town, which was all he needed from me. There was nothing around his house that needed my attention, really," I stated as if I had been accused of not following his directions.

He thought for a moment then said, "Well, come on, get in the car and let's go make sure he didn't need help with anything."

Not a word was spoken between us as we drove the few miles to the cottage. I was unhappy with my father for doubting that I could have been helpful when expected. I think he still saw me as a simple child at times. The cottage looked deserted as we approached, and Father brought the car to a halt in front of it. The sun was not yet near setting, but there was a shadow looming over the small house from the large pine trees. No light was on in the windows and it appeared as though no one was there.

"Maybe he's still in town, getting items he realized he needed after all," I said as my father and I sat in the car looking at the quiet cottage.

"You might be right. We didn't pass him along Coastal Road either," Father said. He sat staring at the little cottage, probably deciding whether to knock on the door or simply leave, assuming he had done his duty of dropping by.

Just then the door to the cottage opened and Mr. Baldwin stepped through the screened porch and into the front yard. He was barefoot as he stepped on the carpet of pine needles, and as he walked toward us, I looked over to my father and saw his eyes drop to Mr. Baldwin's bare feet, then up his legs to his swim suit, then very quickly up to his face. Father looked lost in thought for a moment, and then he suddenly returned to himself, opened the car door, and stepped out.

"I only have a moment," he said stiffly and hurriedly, like someone with more important things to be attending to all of a sudden. "But I wanted to make certain, make sure, everything was in order," my father added in an almost harried tone. I could see that Mr. Baldwin's hair was wet and brushed back, as if he had just risen out of the lake from a deep dive.

"I didn't want to disturb you," Father continued.

Mr. Baldwin stopped no more than a mere four feet from where Father stood. "Thank you for sending Robbie to assist me this morning," he said. "There was really nothing he was needed for here at the cottage."

"Yes, that's what Robert said." Father paused for a moment then, looking at his jacket as if he did not recognize it, he patted his different pockets and pulled out a slip of paper from one. "Here's your schedule so you know when your classes are, scheduled breaks, and the time of your lunch. You may want to bring it with you to school on Monday. It will be orientation day, so you won't have classes, but you may want to take the time to set up your classroom."

Then, as I expected Father to retreat to the interior of the car, I saw him look to Mr. Baldwin's bare feet in the pine needles and ask an odd question. "Do you have a girlfriend back in New York, Mr. Baldwin?"

I could tell that Mr. Baldwin was confused by such a domestic question or the way of life that it suggested.

"No. No, sir, not at this time," he answered quietly. He looked at Father, puzzled, as I was, by his remark.

"Well, good night, Mr. Elliott. I'll see you at school bright and early on Monday morning. Thank you for stopping by," Mr. Baldwin stated as Father got back into the driver's seat and started the car, putting the gear shift in reverse rapidly.

When we returned to the house, Mother and Carlo were setting the table for dinner. Together they had made some sort of a roast with root vegetables, which seemed like another winter meal while it was still warm outside and other families were grilling burgers on their back lawns. As usual, Father sat at the head of the table, complimented the meal, and ate very quietly.

I had hoped to take Carlo over to the academy dormitory and check on my friends, introduce my newfound relative, and listen to some music. Jon might have even brought some cigarettes in his supply trunk and we could go out onto the big screened porch attached to the dormitory room and sneak a smoke together before the monitors sent everyone off to sleep. But my hopes were dashed when Father announced that he would be returning to his office at Tidewater for some "unfinished paperwork" and would not be spending the evening in his usual fashion with a book and glass of sweet tea in the front room, or the "parlor" as my parents had taken to calling it.

Neither Mother nor I questioned or doubted him. While Mother, Carlo, and I sat on the front porch, and each seemed lost in their own thoughts, I began to consider my father's reaction earlier today at seeing Mr. Baldwin in his bare feet and swimsuit. Had Father thought it inappropriate attire in which to approach the car of his headmaster? Did he consider the fact that the headmaster's son, one of his future pupils, was in the car, as he could probably see from the window or the door, and shouldn't he have pulled on more appropriate pants or even a shirt, given that we had not had time to even get out of the car yet? Or was there something else about how Father looked at him, appraisingly almost, from toe to head?

Chapter 5

Carlo was born and raised in Lucca, Italy, to a family who always baked bread. As simple as that, they baked bread. They baked bread each day for the village restaurants and a small food market. They did not own a proper bakery; rather, they lived in a small home where bread was made. Carlo's parents and my mother were distant cousins.

Unlike here, where you have cousins that live an hour's drive away who you see for holidays, weddings, and funerals and never seem to have words to share, stories of your daily adventures, or the like, just relatives you were expected to see on these shared occasions and occupy a space together so all of the elders could always say *"we went to family for Thanksgiving,"* these distant relatives in Italy sent a letter on occasion, but for no specific instance. They shared blood, yet were not compelled to be in the same house on the same day of the some holiday to feel any family connection.

This is how my mother tried to explain her relationship to me during our long ride up to Philadelphia to meet a train with a cousin or second cousin of mine. All this, because I decided to enter into the world of the adult conversation in the front seat and asked a simple question: "How come I never heard of this relative Carlo before now?"

I had already anticipated not wanting to know this cousin. After all, Mother said he barely spoke any English. Likewise, my mother can't speak Italian. Her family elders had chosen to begin speaking English the moment they set foot on Ellis Island, as they were now Americans and that is the language they chose to learn to speak. Good thing too, because here in Rehoboth Beach all these years later, no one spoke Italian, except perhaps in the kitchen at Affonco's Pizzeria, and that was probably a good thing.

I felt I had already gotten the best out of this deal, since Mother and Father finally agreed to allow me the opportunity to move across the hall from my cramped bedroom to the bigger room, with a double-sized bed and a desk.

This room, my new room, was always considered the guest room and therefore was off limits to me. Funny thing was that in my sixteen years on this earth and in this home it was used on so few occasions that I could actually count them on one hand. One hand, mind you, yet it always needed to be ready for whenever that next occasion would be. Cousin Carlo could have my old room, with the single bed up against the wall adjoining the bathroom and a small window that featured the beach dunes. At least in my new room there was a double window through which I could see the driveway, the garage, and Mother's flowers. Her flowers seemed to come and go with the seasons, so it would offer me new things to look out at as I pondered my dull life. No more looking at the same landscape of dunes with sea grasses that poked out like sprouts of hair on a bald scalp of sand.

As it turned out, Carlo was a great guy after all, and we hit it off immediately, as they say. The book I had brought for the long ride home lay untouched on the floor of the car as we traveled south and got to know one another, through fits and starts and a lot of "how do you say" or, in his case, he would turn to my mother, who certainly looked Italian, and would ask "*come direst tu*" expecting her to translate perfectly, to no avail. We just ended up throwing our hands in the air at these points, using the universal shrug for "I don't know" and started to laugh.

I thought that having Carlo around might lighten my parents' uptight personalities some, even make them more aware when I was in the room, the house, the car, or anywhere, now that Carlo was there as they could not help but notice him. After all, he was a large boy compared to me. Whereas I was of medium height with a bit of a husky frame, Carlo was tall and slender with features seemingly similar to the new art teacher at Tidewater. They shared that tall frame, long arms, and wide shoulders with well-developed biceps, similar hair color and, from afar, could easily be mistaken for the other. Carlo's legs stretched long in the back seat, even when he tried to pull them up to get into a fetal position to try to nap on the ride home between the fits of conversation or Father's need to point out every corn field as if they did not exist in Italy.

After Carlo appeared to fall asleep, my parents returned to talking as if I were not even in the car with them, shooting my hopes that we would be included in their lives. Or was I happy then that they did not include us, giving us our own space to grow and learn and experience together?

After the first few days of Carlo being with us, Mother and Father announced that it was just too unfair to Carlo to admit him to the academy for fall semester; rather, it would be better to let him get acclimated to America and get a foothold in English before he was thrown into the academics.

I never knew just how they broke this decision to him, with the language barrier like a massive wall made of bricks that neither could climb nor conquer to meet at the other side and share a conversation, but somehow they did. Carlo was such a happy young man, for someone the same age as I, especially considering what I learned he had been through in his home country before coming to live with us, and he was always at ease. More at ease than I—or any of my classmates at Tidewater Academy, as I saw it.

Somehow Father had discovered that Mr. Baldwin had lived for three years in different parts of Italy as a young man, when his father was working as a tour guide for Western Europeans and Americans and while working on writing his travel guide. Mr. Baldwin was schooled in English-speaking schools and therefore learned Italian superbly, probably even fluently.

The next morning at Sunday breakfast, using Mother's good dishes offering eggs and sausage, bacon and scrapple, I began to consider just what holiday was I forgetting when Father decided to share some news with us from his position at the end of the table. Without my knowledge it had quite simply been decided that Mr. Baldwin would now tutor Cousin Carlo in the English language, and for that I was to receive the best gift of all...Father had arranged for the purchase of a used VW bus to be mine!

I don't know whether Mr. Hazard had one on his lot of classic cars or, as was more likely, Father had arranged this purchase during his trip to Georgetown, but it was in our driveway, and as Father and I were the only two in this household that drove, I would chauffer Carlo to his tutoring at Robinson Cottage in the afternoons of Monday, Tuesday, and Thursday for the next many months, until he had enough of a grasp of the language to enter spring semester at Tidewater Academy.

Of course with this gift came a long set of guidelines, which I considered quite malleable once I heard most of them. No driving to the academy, since it was just a short distance to walk from home—no matter the weather or reason. No driving out onto the major highway west of Rehoboth Beach without one of my parents' permission and their knowledge of my intended whereabouts. No driving other students of the academy in this vehicle, even though I could easily imagine Jon and Dick, Matt and I going off for the first joy ride with the bus filled with cigarette smoke. And of course, Carlo would be welcomed along...

The guidelines established, I was informed that after the school day was complete, I would walk directly home, where I would find Carlo ready to go to his tutorials at Mr. Baldwin's cottage at Silver Lake. I would complete my homework assignments while I awaited the completion of the day's tutorial and drive Carlo back home, directly, in time to help Mother with dinner. Carlo would complete his given assignments during the day while I was attending my coursework at the academy. So this was, in fact, a gift, but with strings attached...Perhaps heavy ropes, I would later learn, and by which my parents intended to control me like a marionette.

Immediately I asked if Carlo and I could go for a ride in it, to show him the way around town, to which Mother stated, "Not until you've eaten up your breakfast, boys."

Father added, "I don't expect to have to tell you more than once the position this family holds in the town, and I expect that you will obey all laws while driving this vehicle, Robert."

"Oh, but of course, Father, of course," I added.

"Actually Mr. Baldwin is expecting the two of you this morning so he can spend a bit of time with Carlo and assess the curriculum he has taken on with this request. As his private tutor, Mr. Baldwin will not be compensated by the academy; rather, your mother and I will be paying Mr. Baldwin. I fully expect that you will not interrupt their lessons and that you will behave like a gentleman when at Mr. Baldwin's home during the tutorials. Am I understood clearly, Robert?"

"Yes, Father, I understand clearly. Thank you for the...well, what is it, a car or a bus?" I asked, puzzled.

"It's a used Volkswagen bus, as the dealer described it, very fashionable to younger drivers now, and while it might be called a bus, remember the guideline I've set of no more than you and Carlo in this automobile."

Chapter 6

On orientation day, that Monday, it was fairly warm inside the auditorium so they held the opening day gathering outside in the courtyard of Tidewater Academy, under the big expanse of ancient oak trees that provided a nice shade. Interspersed among the mighty oaks were tall, skinny scrub pines, which I noticed looked as uncomfortable and out of place as Mr. Baldwin did, standing behind Father amongst all the other staff and teachers. Perhaps Mr. Baldwin felt as though he should be sitting on the lawn with us students versus standing with all the older folk? After all, he did look out of place. Most of these teachers had been instructors for up to twenty years now, and some were considerably older than my father, let alone Mr. Baldwin.

Instead of attempting to blend in with the other teachers, Mr. Baldwin was dressed in a cream poplin suit and bow tie—bright orange, I recall—and he had on some funny-looking shoes I guessed were a throwback to the roaring 1920s or such. Most of our instructors, Captain West especially, were dressed in dark black suits like Father and looked uncomfortable in the sultry summer heat.

Mr. Baldwin looked fresh, like a bright flower in my mother's garden juxtaposed amongst dark foliage plants, as if he did not belong. The ladies wore sun dresses, but most of them were old enough to be my grandmother, so on them a sun dress looked more like a modified mu-mu with a scarf around the neck or a shiny piece of metal jewelry pinned to the chest as if part of a required uniform. No, none looked as relaxed or fun...Yes, that was it, fun, as Mr. Baldwin appeared. Perhaps he wanted to add a bit of whimsy to his first day at stuffy Tidewater Academy for the wayward boys.

After a lengthy speech by my father and then the lacrosse coach and physical education instructor, Mr. Jeffrey Robinson, which I could not recall mere minutes after they were completed, Father made the introduction finally. I knew all eyes had been on this one person who clearly stood out in the crowd, the teacher I thought others would come to like as I already had.

"And now I would like to introduce to you our first art teacher at Tidewater Academy. Mr. Baldwin has studied abroad and been to the most famous museums of the world and brings to us, to you, his talents to impart upon you," Father said to the sound of some groans in the crowd of students sitting on the lawn.

"Mr. Baldwin will be teaching you the skill of understanding art, not just creating art. These are good aspects of your character building for when you are grown men one day. You can appreciate the finer things in life so that you may take your future wife to a museum and show an interest in something other than which way the football has crossed the goal line. One day you will look back upon this aspect of your education and understand better. Now, with that, I give you Mr. Bradley Baldwin."

Mr. Baldwin looked reluctant to step up to where Father was standing, perhaps not certain if he was to speak to us or just take a bow. Then after a moment, and probably a cross look similar to those I frequently received from my father, he chose to step forward and say a few words.

"It is my honor to be here with you fine young gentlemen of Tidewater Academy today and throughout this coming school year. I shall make every effort to meet Mr. Elliott's goal, but also to be certain that we have fun learning. Art is about appreciation, yes, but also about feeling free to express yourself. Perhaps something you have been missing?" Mr. Baldwin said.

To that, a few students cheered and whistled, and for a moment I thought that the guys were going to break out in song or dance. This seemed to hit a chord with many of my classmates at this stiff and strict school. If that statement didn't make the new art teacher candidate number one for coolest teacher of the school, I don't know what would have. Seems he started off almost uncertain but got on the side of the students fairly quickly. I also recall the looks on the other teachers' faces, including that of my own father, as if Mr. Baldwin had told a secret that was only to be shared in the teachers' lounge, never to be spoken of in front of any student.

Quickly Father made sure our excitement diminished. He stepped forward and continued on to discuss new rules for the dormitory, the screened porch, curfew, etc. as I thought back to the dinner conversation where my father spoke of a school with discipline and how Mr. Baldwin's eyes seemed to latch onto a reflection he did not dare share with my parents, but one he felt for the students all the same.

With the final instructions of the day explained, we, the students, were free to return to the dorm and would be allowed a few hours of freedom after lunch, as long as we had completed a few tasks, such as check in with each teacher we would be studying under to verify our daily schedule; actually, it was an excuse to receive our first night's homework assignments, be sure that we had all the fittings for our school uniforms from the visiting tailor, and had cleared away all items we brought to the campus for the coming year. Since I was living at home and Mother had arranged for my uniforms, all I had to do was meet and greet with my instructors and then after lunch arrange a volleyball game on the beach with my buds. That was if I could keep out of my father's eyesight long enough that he would not assign me some chore that the other students would not be required to do since their father was not the headmaster of the prison I called Tidewater Academy.

I wandered to the farthest end of the school to avoid Father's office door and started my visit with Mrs. Crutchfield, who would be my English instructor again this year and with whom I associated the one significant word I had learned the previous year due to her drilling it into our brains as if it was the most important word in the entire language: redundant. Funny, I imagined this year's coursework would be redundant and therefore a class where I could dream and not worry about passing. Fortunately Mrs. Crutchfield had two students waiting and one in her room already, so I skipped that line and moved on to the next room I needed to visit, and it was Mr. Baldwin's art classroom.

As I entered, Mr. Baldwin and Chuck Pierce were just finishing up. I stepped back into the hallway and eavesdropped on their conversation. Chuck was all brawn and no brains and didn't care about anything except playing rugby. His parents sent him to Tidewater because his grades had slipped at some prestigious school in New Jersey and they wanted him in an environment where there was no rugby team, or so I overheard Father telling Mother on the porch one evening this summer, concerned that he would not be able to maintain the academic levels Father expected of each student. It sounded as if Chuck was trying to explain to Mr. Baldwin that he was just not fit for art classes, and if Mr. Baldwin could see to it that he was transferred into another class, Chuck would be grateful. The end of the conversation went something like this:

"I hear what you're saying Mr. Pierce...*Chuck,* but if I try to make special arrangements for you to skip this coursework, Headmaster Elliott will not approve. You see, this will be a required part of the curriculum this year," Mr. Baldwin said.

"But I don't need curriculum or art, I just need the basics so I can get out of here and go to a real school next year that has a rugby team, you see?" Chuck blurted out.

"Alright then, let me see if we can do something about finding you the basic, more remedial courses, okay?" Mr. Baldwin questioned. I could barely hold my laughter as I stood just outside his door and had to look away as big Chuck pushed past me headed down the hallway.

"Robert, you may enter now," said Mr. Baldwin, as if he could see through the wall into the hallway where I was standing. I entered, not certain if I was going to be in trouble for listening in on their conversation.

"I was just waiting to ask you about my assignment for this evening, sir," I said as I entered the room.

"Well, I saw you step in and out quickly, as if this room had the plague, and I figured it was you outside the door making those amused sounds as I was speaking with Mr. Pierce," he said with a broad smile on his face, as if he was about to burst into laughter.

"I don't need *no* curriculum, sir," I said as I mocked big Chuck. We both broke out in laughter.

This was the moment I realized that I was going to have a special connection with Mr. Baldwin. A friendship unlike most between teacher and student where there is no humor or shared stories. He was certainly different from the other teachers.

"Robbie, I'll need your help this afternoon, once I've finished meeting with the students, after their…your lunch period. Your father has asked that I begin tutoring your cousin Carlo to read, write, and speak the English language. Are you aware of this arrangement yet?" he asked.

"Yes, sir, Father bought me a VW bus so I could drive Carlo to your cottage in the afternoons, and I'll complete my homework assignments at the same time he's learning and then drive him back home for dinner," I shared with obvious glee in my voice.

"I see. Well, congratulations. I might ask then, in order to save us all a bit of time, if I could possibly get a ride to my cottage with you when you bring Carlo for his tutoring? The walk is long, and I haven't found a bicycle to purchase in town as of yet," he said.

"I don't know, Mr. Baldwin. I'd have to ask my father."

"Yes, of course you must ask your father. That might seem a bit strange, driving a teacher to his home after school," he replied.

"Oh, no, it isn't that, Mr. Baldwin. It's that I have strict instructions for when I can use the VW, whom I'm allow in it with me, and other 'guidelines,' as Father put it. I just need to ask his permission to let you ride with us."

"Well, then, let's wait until you've obtained approval from your father, of course. I'll see you and Carlo at my home at say four p.m.?"

"Yes, sir. Four o'clock sharp."

"Oh, and Robbie, your homework assignment. Let's not forget why you stopped by in the first place, right? Let me see, yes, you're in my second class tomorrow," he said as he looked at a black notebook on his desk. "I want you to come prepared to discuss your favorite piece of art, found anywhere in the world, famous or not. Just be prepared to share in the discussion with the others. Understand?"

"I think so, sir," I said as I left the classroom, though actually I really had no idea what I was going to discuss, but something would come to mind, I assumed.

My next stop was a visit to Father's office near the main lobby of the school to obtain permission to provide Mr. Baldwin a ride in the VW as he had asked. When I reached his door, I could see that his secretary and two teachers were standing in his doorway, and since I knew he would not approve of my being in the anteroom when such a conversation was taking place, I decided to move on down the hall to finish my meetings with my other instructors.

After my meetings were finished, I headed upstairs to meet with others to eat lunch in the dining room. Once I entered the dining room, I saw that Mr. Baldwin and Father were sitting at the headmaster's table along with several other teachers. I went directly to collect my lunch tray and was gathering my silverware when Mr. Baldwin got into the queue behind me.

"Robbie, I had the opportunity to mention to your father my idea of riding home with you and Carlo this afternoon. He seemed a bit surprised by my suggestion and said he would discuss it with you and your mother this evening at dinner. Mr. Robinson was kind enough to offer me a ride home with him this afternoon in time to be there for Carlo's four o'clock tutorial."

Chapter 7

Mr. Robinson had been teaching phys ed at the academy for a few years now after injuring himself in the professional minor league baseball leagues in Washington, D.C. As the distant and sole heir to the Robinson family, he was bequeathed the property around Silver Lake and had moved his family into a recently built home at the other end of the fork on Coastal Road from Robinson Cottage.

His home was grander than the cottage, with a large, covered porch that wrapped around the entire house like a hat and was a distressed shade of brown-gray. It sat between the lake and the ocean dunes. He and his young wife lived there, and from what I had overheard on our porch one evening, they were an odd couple. Apparently she did not want to live here in such an isolated place, and she was an author of some sort. She sent manuscripts to New York City on occasion through the postal desk at Lingo's Market. She kept to herself, rarely smiled, and had turned down two invitations for dinner at our home. That alone was enough to make Mother consider her obstinate if not rude. No one missed an invitation to one of Mother's suppers, let alone two invites.

After Mr. Robinson's injury, it was decided that they had to live here, where he could earn a living from teaching at a prominent school and collect rent from the lakeside cottage in order to maintain their respect amongst their own folk back home.

Mr. Robinson was a decent fellow in my book, knew I didn't really care much for the rigors of physical education, and perhaps thought that by being easy on me he might get in the graces of my father. I could imagine that he was always looking for ways to make up for Mrs. Robinson's odd behavior toward others. So I got to slack off when we had to run the mile under seven minutes and the like. Don't get me wrong, I loved a good game of volleyball in the sand, but I was not much for tennis, lacrosse, or even basketball.

I did not know much about Mrs. Robinson or the twin daughters they had living at the sprawling beach house. I do know now that she would often sit on their pier at the lake wrapped up in what looked like gauze over her head, writing in a big journal book as the girls would run on the pier screaming at the ducks, geese, and crabs on the pilings, as this was described later by one of the nosy townsfolk while on the witness stand during the trial.

Last spring I had ventured out on the part of the beach near the front of their home with a group of friends to have a bonfire and did not know that the Robinson family lived here. She came out onto their walkway through the dunes and told us that it was private, exclusive property and she would call the sheriff if we hoodlums did not evacuate immediately. We simply walked back up the beach several hundred yards toward town so we could be alone but far enough to be off her exclusive property.

Luckily Mr. Robinson had not been present, or he would have recognized all of us immediately and we would have been in inordinate trouble. My father would not have approved of this activity or my participation as the headmaster's son. Later, when this same event was described by my father at the dinner table, both he and my mother assumed it to be the young men that hung out in front of Affonco's Pizzeria, so I stayed silent as they discussed with dismay the future of such young people.

Like so many things that become more easily understood as we grow into middle age, I learned that Mrs. Robinson was not perhaps as peculiar as Mother and her gossip circle had made her out to be, since I learned during the trial and over later years that Mrs. Robinson was a well-respected author of several books on psychology. That she had been a practicing psychiatrist before they moved from Washington, D.C., and the shame of her husband's injury and subsequent downfall from the community of professional athletics. She once had a private practice in the district, often taking care of the elite politicians and academics that were their Georgetown neighbors.

After living in such a thriving place as Washington, D.C., then coming here to live in the boonies of sand dunes, I could see why she may have seemed a little different. To this day, I believe that had I known her, we probably could have shared a great deal with one another, and she could have been a savior to me when it came to being a friend with similar feelings toward this town and its memories.

When I finished a game of volleyball on the beach around three thirty that Monday afternoon, I crossed the dunes at the head of Annapolis Street to find Carlo sitting on the front steps of our house with books, paper, and pencils in his arms, ready to go for his first tutorial. The look on his face was clearly one of great excitement and anticipation of what was to come. He was going to learn the language of his new home and be entered into the academy with the rest of us, perhaps go on to a college of his choice and become an important man. Maybe he would become a doctor or lawyer, whatever his late mother and father had dreamed for him. I waved to him as I approached, and he was quick to meet me on the street.

"Ready now," he said with such stuttered excitement I felt like a parent about to send my child off to his first day of school. Wow, it was hard not to like this guy. Just to see his excitement in his face, his broad smile.

"Okay, I'm ready too. Let me tell Mother we're leaving and get the keys to the VW," I said to Carlo, realizing he probably had no idea what I just said, smiling at me nonetheless.

On our ride to Robinson Cottage, I realized that Carlo had never been through this part of town, at least not with me. He was looking around like a child on an adventure, the excitement and anticipation sparkling in his hazel eyes as he looked about in all directions. We played the music loud and had the windows open; it felt like freedom to me, even if the ride was only two miles. "California Dreamin" by The Mamas & The Papas was playing, and I was singing along. Carlo was laughing at my singing ability—or lack thereof. I could tell, without a word spoken. We already had that kind of communication between us.

As we approached the fork in the road near Mr. Baldwin's cottage, I saw a light blue Ford Falcon convertible in the roadway, with the passenger door open. When we got closer,

I realized that the leg and foot sticking out of the right side door belonged to Mr. Baldwin, who was wearing those antique-looking shoes. Wing tips was what they called them, but no one in Rehoboth Beach—and probably in all of Delaware—had been seen in a pair in the past forty years.

We slowed our approach, and when Mr. Baldwin got out of Mr. Robinson's car, he appeared to be laughing, as if some private joke had just been told. I waited for Mr. Robinson to finish his ride up the left side of the forked road and for Mr. Baldwin to approach my driver's window of the VW.

"So this is the new wheels you got. Cool, dude. Do you not love it?" Mr. Baldwin asked us as if we were his buddies not his students.

"I do like it, and it has four speakers, so we can play music in the rear too, unlike my father's Plymouth with only one speaker in the front," I replied, also feeling as though I was speaking with one of the academy classmates and not our instructor.

"Well, I guess your father wouldn't mind if I rode the distance from here to my house, would he?" he asked as he walked around the bus. He had the back door open and was already climbing onto the back seat before I could think of any response other than, "Well, I don't think Carlo will tell on us," as I looked back to Mr. Baldwin and his broad Cheshire cat-like smile.

While Mr. Baldwin and Carlo set to work at the small table near the window in his living room, I looked at his collection of art books on the side table and took a couple outside to review. I knew that I had to be prepared to discuss my favorite piece of art in class tomorrow and figured I better get up to speed, since my classmates were probably poring over the few books in the school library as I sat here. After all, I don't think there was one of us who knew anything about art. We would all be scrambling tonight.

There was one book that was bigger than the others, so I took it to one of the old wooden chairs near the pier, under a large pine tree. It was a book of Monet art. I had never heard of Monet, so at that moment, it could have been a place, a person's name, whatever...At that point in my life, I felt I was the one learning a foreign language.

I began by flipping through the book and saw many photos of beautiful works of art. Most were black and white, but several were in color, and those held my interest the most. There were paintings of fields of poppy flowers in the country, seaside scenes with people dressed from the late 1800s, sailboats gliding under stone bridges, and then there was one that really caught my eye. The title under the photo was "COLORPLATE 15."

This did not mean much to me, but one thing I did know was that most famous paintings had to have a name, so where was the name of this blasted painting? I stared closely at the painting. Something about it was familiar to me. Had I seen it before someplace? Was it famous? I did not believe so, but decided to read the following pages about it, referring back to the photo of the painting as I read. This would be my selection for class tomorrow. That settled, I put the book under the pile of my other books and moved on to my reading assignment for Mrs. Crutchfield. She was a stickler for detail, and it seemed that every time I rushed an assignment, she knew it immediately and eagerly used me as an example of the type of student that does not obey orders.

A few hours later, I heard laughter coming from the house and looked up from my reading to see Carlo and Mr. Baldwin standing at the window, pointing in my direction. Apparently I had fallen asleep, my head hanging over my left shoulder, and there was a large goose standing in front of me, staring me down. I must have looked ridiculous as I jumped up and the goose started to chase me in a big circle around my chair, squawking at me all the while. I had to admit to myself on the ride home a few minutes later that it must have been pretty funny to watch; more than to have participated in was all I could think of as I rubbed my thigh where the goose had bitten me.

The ride home was as high energy as the arrival trip, with the Beach Boys singing "Surfin' USA" at high volume, Carlos smiling from ear to ear, and me feeling good about completing most of my homework even if a goose had interrupted me and I was laughed at.

Once home, Father pointed Carlo in the direction of the kitchen, probably to assist my mother, while he told me to sit down opposite him on the porch. He looked tired and had an empty glass of sweet tea next to him with the newspaper on the floor by his feet.

"We need to talk," were the first words out of his mouth since we got out of the VW in the driveway and walked up and onto the front porch from the side steps. I sat down while he watched me with a stern look on his face. Had he somehow learned that I broke one of his guidelines on the very first day of driving Carlo? How could he have known that I allowed Mr. Baldwin into the VW already? Mr. Robinson...I bet it was him, and then Father interrupted my thoughts by saying, "Your mother and I have been talking and we would prefer that you not drive Mr. Baldwin home in the afternoons. The purpose of the VW is for you to carry Carlo to and from lessons. Perhaps later we'll lessen some of the guidelines, but this is one I cannot for reasons I would prefer not to explain at this time."

"How did you know?" I asked, feeling the guilt show on my face already.

"Mr. Baldwin mentioned at the lunch table that he made the suggestion to you when you stopped in his classroom for your assignment," Father said.

It was then I realized that my father had not learned that I allowed Mr. Baldwin to ride in the bus, even if for only the short distance of his driveway. I felt so relieved that Father was not going to take the keys away from me or take away my freedom to spend time with Carlo and even with Mr. Baldwin.

Then Father said, "Good, that's settled. Your mother said dinner will be a few minutes late, she's had a flare-up of her arthritis this afternoon and got behind in her preparation. Have you completed all of your home assignments for tomorrow?"

"Not all of it, sir. May I be excused so I can go up to my room and finish before dinner?" I asked. With a wave of his hand toward the front door to our house, he excused me.

Appreciative that Father hadn't questioned me about my failure to finish the assignments while at the cottage, I ran up the steps to the second floor and settled into my new desk in my new bedroom to complete my homework for my first day of classes tomorrow.

Chapter 8

Throughout my first class of the day, I kept thinking about how I would make my presentation in art class regarding my newly selected favorite piece of art. I barely paid any attention to the coursework for the history class I was currently in and was grateful that Mr. Latham did not call on me. Once the class ended, I started down the hall to the room that now housed the art classes. Previously it had been a science laboratory, but with the infusion of benefactor money last year, a new laboratory was added to the building, with three walls of windows. Father said it was to be set apart from the others because some of the teachers complained about the strong smell of formaldehyde and other chemicals. The windows were installed so the space could be aired out when needed.

Mr. Baldwin's classroom seemed ideal for art. We had shared tandem desks, with sinks in the corner, lab style. I sat next to David Whitman, and he started talking about his summer at home. By the time he had finished telling me of his adventures and a family trip, the room was filled and quiet with anticipation for the teacher to begin.

But there was no teacher. We sat there looking around at one another, seeing if anyone knew more than others as to his whereabouts. Finally Mr. Baldwin came into the room, apologized, and explained he was down at the auditorium between classes and lost his way finding his own classroom. After a collective laugh, Mr. Baldwin began his discussion of favorite pieces of art.

He told the story of how his father, the author of several travel books and articles in major magazines, traveled extensively. He brought his son along on many of the extended trips where he was then educated in the local English-speaking schools for children who had parents working in the Foreign Service and other government positions. During these years of travel, the senior Baldwin made certain that his son visited the museums and galleries with him, and a love for fine art began to formulate.

Mr. Baldwin further explained that at our age, we may not have had such an adventuresome life of travel, but that he expected that at some point our parents would have introduced us to art, whether in galleries or our own living rooms. With that statement, I felt the entire room grimace. Some of us did not come from worldly parents or, if we did, they seemed too busy to include us in such gallery visits.

Then, as a clever way of selecting the first student to give their discussion, Mr. Baldwin had written each student's name on a piece of paper and put them all into a large vase on his desk. He explained that this was to be the fairest way to select who goes in what order and that we had up to three minutes to explain the piece to the class. Those that did not get to give their discussion today would give it during the next class tomorrow.

David whispered to me that he hoped to be picked tomorrow because he had not prepared for this assignment. I was shocked by this statement, although I also hoped to be selected tomorrow so that I could bone up on my discussion after hearing how others presented their own today.

"And the first presenter will be...Chuck Pierce," he announced to the sound of several students making the drum roll sound on books and lab tables.

"I ain't got nothing to present," Chuck stammered.

"Why is that, Mr. Pierce? Each of you was given the same assignment and the same amount of time to consider the piece of art for your presentation," Mr. Baldwin said, more sternly than I thought he would.

"First, I don't like art stuff. Second, it's for fairies, not real guys like me," Chuck said with the sound of a challenge in his voice.

Mr. Baldwin very delicately explained that men of high levels of society held an appreciation of art, whether for paintings of bull fights or a sailboat similar to their own or even for a beautiful woman draped in minimal clothing. All of these types of art were worthy of appreciation, because that man, that *guy*, understood that something made him want to look at and enjoy that piece. He went on to further explain that sculptural art is more frequently admired by men than women. This lecture seemed to take most of the remainder of the class, and I could see by my watch that we were running out of time, and I realized that there would not be enough time for any other presentations after these two lengthy discussions of his background and the male appreciation of art.

"And art is not just for fairies, as you call them. You will learn more than you realize by attending this course, which is required by the academy in order for you to meet commencement at the end of your senior year," stated Mr. Baldwin as if he had thrown down the final gauntlet. "Tomorrow, you will present first, Mr. Pierce.

"We have just enough time for one of you to present, and it will be Rob Elliott," he read off the piece of paper and looked my way.

"Can I stay here or do I need to come to the front of the room, sir?" I asked, nervous to be the first.

"Please, come forward, and bring any materials you may have with you, Rob," he said.

I went forward, feeling my face and neck flush, unsure if it would be obvious that I had just selected a painting out of a book I took from Mr. Baldwin's house—and, I realized at that moment, that the book was in my hand and I never asked to borrow it. I stood where Mr. Baldwin had been holding his stance during his lecture and placed my paper and his book on the podium next to me.

"I have to admit that I never paid any attention to art before either. Like Mr. Baldwin said, we have art in our parents' homes, but I don't think I could describe any of it for you right now. Yesterday I had the opportunity to look at this book about art, by a famous painter named Claude Monet. As I looked through the book, I found a painting that I liked. I returned to this painting several times after looking at others. Oh, and in this book was art painted by other famous people too. The piece I have selected as my favorite piece at this point in my life is called 'Stormy Sea at Etretat' and it was painted by Mr. Monet in 1868.

"It reminds me of the dark afternoon before one of the storms that hit our beaches here in Rehoboth, just before a hurricane. I can't remember which hurricane it was, nor if there was much damage, but this painting shows people standing on the beach, looking at waves that are much higher and meaner looking than any before. And, well, that's why I liked it. That's my presentation." I said, looking toward Mr. Baldwin, eager to be back in the comfort of my shared desk with David.

"Very good, Rob. Thank you. I've seen that exact painting in the Louvre Museum in Paris. It's very large, much larger than you see in that book you have in your hands, something like five feet long. Good presentation. You may be seated," Mr. Baldwin said as the class bell rang. "The rest of you will present your assignment tomorrow. Follow Rob's lead. It isn't that hard, you see?" he said as he clapped his hands twice and everyone rose to leave.

"Rob, please stay a moment," he said to me.

Once the room was clear, he asked about the book, and I explained that I had placed it under my other books and forgot about it, that I was sorry I didn't ask for it, and he simply said, "Keep it. I'm pleased you've come to appreciate fine art on the first attempt. It's yours now, a gift."

"Thank you, sir," I said as I left the room. I felt as if I had been given a very special gift, perhaps something his father had bestowed on him once. I knew that I would cherish the book for that possible reason.

As I was leaving school at the end of the day, my father was standing just inside the front door and asked to speak with me. We stepped to the side of the grand staircase that other boys were climbing up to the dormitory. Many were probably planning to change into their swimsuits and head past our house to the beach and play volleyball or body surf until dinner. I knew by Father's look that I had something coming, a lecture or maybe he found out about Mr. Baldwin in the VW after all. Father interrupted my concerns and thoughts of punishment, as usual.

"I will need your help this afternoon, Robert."

"But how? I have to take Carlo to his lesson as you instructed me to do," I replied.

"Today you will drop Carlo off at Robinson Cottage and promptly return here to school. I need you to assist Mrs. Campbell in the auditorium. A shipment of books arrived late and they need to be taken out of the cartons and separated for the teachers, then delivered to their classrooms. Am I clear on what you will be doing today?" he said to me, but he was looking at two students up on the landing that looked as if they might begin to tussle.

"Yes, sir," was all I said. As I walked away I muttered under my breath, *yessa Massa Headmassa, sir.*

Driving Carlo to his lessons at Silver Lake did not seem like fun today but more like a chore piled up on other chores. Carlo was not deterred at all, smiling and happy, listening to the music.

As we approached the cottage, Mr. Robinson's Falcon was sitting in the driveway, right in front of the cottage, with the soft roof down this time. No one was in the car. By the time I had parked the VW next to it and Carlo and I got out, I could see that Mr. Robinson was coming out of the house onto the screened porch and was laughing. I guess the two men had a lot of jokes to tell one another.

I said good-bye to Mr. Robinson as we passed one another and went inside as he was pulling away, Carlo stepping ahead of me. We stood just inside the door of the cottage, but did not see Mr. Baldwin in the main room or the small kitchen to the right. Suddenly he stepped from what I knew to be his bedroom, pulling on a tee shirt over his naked chest.

"Boys, you're here already. Great! Well, it's hot today, so we'll sit on the porch and hope some air comes through these trees, alright?" Mr. Baldwin said as he walked into his small kitchen. "Some lemonade or water?" he asked.

"Um, Mr. Baldwin, my father asked that I return to school and help with a book distribution that arrived late, so I'll be going now. What time should I return to get Carlo?" I asked as I backed up toward the door.

"I see. Well, we can try something else today then. I'll bring Carlo by your parents' house when we're done. You see, I've agreed to meet someone for dinner in town. You won't have to come all the way down the road to get him." He turned to Carlo and said, "*Ti accompagnero a casa appena abbiamo finite, va bene?*" *I will walk home with you when we are finished, agreed?*

Carlo nodded.

Then, looking back to me, Mr. Baldwin said, "It's all settled. You'll not have to come get Carlo today. Good luck with the new books. I saw them; there are a lot."

"Okay and thank you. I have to be going so I can help Mrs. Campbell. She'll probably be unhappy no matter what time I get there or how hard I work. She's just like that. Have a good lesson then, bye," I said as I headed to the bus.

"*Ciao, grazie,*" *thank you,* said Carlo, smiling back to me as always.

Chapter 9

In the years following Mr. Baldwin's trial, I collected some newspaper clippings from the time, along with pictures that I had cherished back then, and saved them in a cigar box I had previously reserved for my baseball trading cards. It seemed the appropriate place as I had transitioned that year from a child collecting trading cards with bubble gum purchased at Lingo's Market to a young man, worldly and wise.

There was a photo of Carlo and Mother sitting on a wooden bench on the boardwalk near Dolle's taffy shop, a flock of seagulls flying over them like they wanted to cram into the picture as well. Carlo laughing just like he always did; Mother with a sincere smile of happiness, which seemed odd, as she was rarely as happy as that photo captured. Perhaps that day was one of little pain or little awareness of the black cloud that was looming over our lives.

Along with the cigar box, I kept Prosecutor Horton's memoir of the incident; a book I have read through completely several times, yet never felt had shared the entire story. Of course my parents could not tolerate the fact that it condemned Father for hiring this effete teacher from the big city with his worldly knowledge of art. I couldn't stand that either, but what I knew rang true was that Mr. Baldwin was a brilliant teacher, with an unusual manner of teaching, perhaps not as disciplined as the others at Tidewater Academy, but effective all the same. The memoir was one-sided and biased. It glorified Horton more than told the story in its entirety.

It was on another afternoon at Robinson Cottage that we were experiencing what we call Indian Summer with the temperatures reaching in the mid-90s compared to the mid-70s where they should have been. I never knew where the colloquialism "Indian Summer" came from back then, but now I know that it means a time between when the trees have dropped their leaves and snow has not yet fallen when there is a spike in the heat. Heck, with all the discussions of global warming in the past decade, I doubt there will be little time for Indian Summers in our future.

I was sitting on the screened porch at one end, while Carlo and Mr. Baldwin were on the other end, sitting at a large, sturdy table, the type ideal for picking and eating crabs. I had finished my work and decided to look through Mr. Baldwin's books, to see if there might be something of interest I could take to the old chair by the pier to read. Amongst the stack was one book written by Alexander Baldwin. I did not know whether this was the book of his father's travels, and I knew better than to interrupt their lessons, so I took it with me and sat in that old chair. It felt cooler down by the pier, since a breeze was kicking from over by the Robinsons' big house, across the lake, and heading through the growth of trees where I sat. I could smell salt and pine in the air. Carlo and Mr. Baldwin would not be able to feel this breeze up on the screened porch.

The book was titled *Just a Train Stop Away* and offered a photo of the author on the back sleeve of the cover. It was the snapshot of an elegant-looking man standing in front of an ancient fountain with a young boy at his side. I gathered that this was Mr. Baldwin as a child, standing in a pose next to his father, the travel writer. The elder Baldwin I recognized from the portrait hanging right here in Robinson Cottage.

I found the book to be enlightening and flipped through the different chapters titled by the countries they represented. Places I surely would travel to in my adulthood, unlike my parents, who seemed content to stay in this small, claustrophobic town where nothing exciting ever occurred.

I was engrossed in the book so I did not notice Mr. Baldwin standing barely two feet in front of me in his European swim trunks, holding a towel. Carlo was next to him in just his cut-off denim shorts, and he too had a towel in his hand. They looked like they could be brothers.

"Why don't you join us for a swim, or we could take a row in the boat Mr. Robinson seems to have left here by the pier? Just pull off your shirt and you'll dry sufficiently before you have to leave if we jump in now," Mr. Baldwin suggested. Carlo was already halfway down the pier, having dropped his towel to the deck.

"Well, I suppose we could, as long as Mother and Father don't find out. You think we'll have enough time for our shorts to dry before we head back home?" I asked, certain my parents would not approve.

"Of course! Come along," he replied.

While I was pulling my shirt over my head, I heard a loud splash and then looked to see Carlo's head break the surface of the lake as he came up from his dive.

"*E molto freddo, ma rinfrescante!*" *It's very cold, but refreshing,* Carlo told us.

"Last one in is a rotten egg," Mr. Baldwin yelled as he ran to the far end of the pier and dove into the lake.

We all swam in the cold lake for quite some time and enjoyed ourselves, splashing around and playing like children.

After a good swim, we climbed back onto the pier and sat there in the warm sun drying off as I explained to Mr. Baldwin that Silver Lake was a fresh water lake, even though it was so close to the Atlantic Ocean. I pointed out that this lake did not connect to the ocean, but was fed by a stream somewhere inland. As I was telling this, Mr. Baldwin was translating each sentence into Italian for Carlo, and by the look in his eyes, he comprehended it as if I was speaking to him directly.

We three lay there drying, faces to the sun, when all of a sudden Mr. Baldwin jumped up, said something quickly in Italian, and ran up to his house. I lay my head back down to rest in the sun, and after a few minutes Mr. Baldwin arrived with a pitcher of lemonade and three glasses for us.

A short while later, I could feel the movement of the boards on the pier and sensed that someone was walking out onto the pier toward us and looked up. It was Mr. Robinson, my physical education teacher. I immediately felt an internal panic, as if I had been caught doing something forbidden and he would surely tell my father.

Chapter 10

Recalling the boy I was in those days, I've sometimes considered myself one of the victims of the incident that shook Rehoboth Beach and Tidewater Academy, my life no less wounded by the crimes that rocked our town and that will always leave a palpable feeling about Silver Lake.

In middle age I've finally come to a time in life when I never expected to think of Bradley Baldwin again. When I thought of him at all, it was like thinking of a faded favorite book cover, a story once read and enjoyed, but not in the forefront of my current life.

Then, as if the book had a sequel, this life, this memory, came back to me by a route I would have never expected.

I was the first in my office that morning, as I usually was. I favored the quiet of the morning hours before the phones began to ring, before my associates presented me with problems to resolve in their ongoing real estate transactions, and the rest of the turmoil of a normal business day began. Just the smell of fresh coffee, the sound of seagulls outside my office window, and my thoughts, this is what I treasured about the pre-office hours.

As I sipped my coffee I looked out the window, and standing outside the office on the sidewalk was a vaguely familiar face, one I may have dreamt in a fog of scotch perhaps or after finishing a well-written novel and turned to dreaming. She was younger than me, perhaps in her early forties, and had the look of an athlete, toned legs, tall stature, and long, flowing brown hair. Clearly she was looking for someone or a place by the way she was looking about with concern. Then suddenly, as if she had made up her mind, she rang the bell by the office front door.

As my secretary was not yet in the office, I walked to the door and greeted her, asking if she was looking for this real estate firm. On occasion, the agents and secretaries shared stories of tourists in town who stopped by hoping to learn of the best café for dinner, where they could obtain coins to feed the parking meters, or asked to use our bathrooms. I was hoping this lady wanted none of these, but equally hoped that she was not here to complain about the performance of one of the sales associates who worked for me.

"Mr. Elliott?" she asked.

"I'm Robert Elliott. Please come in, and we can talk," I replied.

I led her to my office and offered her some coffee. She declined my offer, said she was only in town for a short while and that she had some real estate-related business she wished to complete if I would be interested in taking the case for her. I explained that I functioned as the company broker and therefore did not handle cases individually but could suggest one of my best agents to assist her in her needs.

With that, she began to explain her interest in my assistance.

"I am Laura Robinson-Cartwright. You may recall my family, the Robinsons, perhaps? My father, Jeff Robinson, once taught physical education at the Tidewater Academy of which I believe your father was headmaster?" she inquired.

"Yes, you're correct about my father, and as a matter of fact, I was a student of your father's back in…well, when his life ended."

"Yes, I seem to recall some of that. Well, after his passing and all of the other bad stuff, we moved away. Eventually I ended up in South Carolina where my husband is from, and I've returned to dispose of all the property now, since my sister is in need of the money for her long-term health care. I believe you know of the property surrounding the lake we knew as Silver Lake?"

"Oh, yes. I'm quite familiar with it. I used to spend some time at Robinson Cottage and knew of your family's home, the large one between the lake and the ocean. Over the years, the houses may have come to disrepair and might not fetch as much as you hope. But if I recall, there's a nice bit of land with these homes, isn't there?" I asked, even though I already knew there was substantial oceanfront acreage that had been sitting for many years, the nugget that many developers desired.

"I understand the market is not so good now, but I'm ready to just…well, get rid of it…and the memories. I hope this is something your firm could represent for me? To sell it, that is?" she asked.

"We'd be honored to represent you. I'll need to research the acreage along with the feasibility of developing it to provide you the most return possible. I'll select one of my finest Realtors and will oversee the transaction should you like," I replied. "You mentioned your twin sister, Maria, if I recall. May I ask about her health condition?"

"This isn't widely known, but Maria always had a tough life after we left Rehoboth Beach in 1967. She was plagued with psychiatric issues and on several occasions attempted to take her own life. In the process of her last attempt she failed, and in its wake she lost enough oxygen to damage her brain so that she is surviving in a hospital on life support. It's time to move her to a private facility, and the costs are astronomical. I had hoped to one day pass these properties on to my own children, but it looks as if their providence will be used to keep my sister on the breathing machine in a vegetative state until her natural death," she explained with little emotion.

After providing each other with the appropriate contact information, I walked Mrs. Robinson-Cartwright to the door. Before leaving my office, she turned and said, "Please refer to me as Cartwright. I don't use Robinson, but I made reference to it to provide you with my birth name."

I sat quietly in my office after she left poring over the memories of my time at Silver Lake, and how it had such a profound impact on so many lives. I could only gather that it had had the most lasting effect on dear Maria.

I called my best agent, Jean Tallman, into my office to explain the case that had just landed in our hands. Jean had been active in the real estate market of Rehoboth Beach since before many of the corn fields sprouted into cookie cutter neighborhoods of second homes for their wealthy inhabitants. Most home owners were weekenders from affluent areas such as Washington, Annapolis, and Philadelphia. The money these yuppies would spend for a home that they used only on weekends astounded me. Jean had been on the frontline of most of the development of these cornfields–to-McMansions and therefore would be the most appropriate agent to handle this property sale with experience, integrity, and discretion.

Jean assured me that she remembered all that had happened on the grounds of the property and how it held a stigma at one time, but perhaps no longer. She stated that there were over seventeen acres of oceanfront and lakefront property that could be developed, and using the right builders she was acquainted with, we could make the Robinson family a great deal of income.

"Jean, we have to keep the old stories to a minimum for the sake of the Robinsons and, well, for the sake of my family as well. You understand?" I asked with a sudden sense of dread.

"Of course. I think Roberts Brothers Home Builders will be very interested in the land, and they could tear down the two old homes, build many more, and in turn have our associates represent them in their sale. Maybe you and I can get out and see the properties that are going to fund our retirements later today?" Jean asked with a twinkle in her eye.

Leave it to her to always be the one to cheer you up and help you to evade the memories, if only for a short while. I agreed to meet her out at Robinson Cottage at four o'clock that afternoon.

A few minutes before four o'clock I found myself driving south on the old Coastal Road, now renamed King Charles Avenue to defer any association with the murders, which the local papers had dubbed as having "occurred off Coastal Road." The undergrowth had grown substantially over the past forty years and the scrub pines had soared to great heights, but it felt the same to me as that first day my father drove this same road, Mr. Baldwin in the front seat while I was in the back with his two large suitcases.

The fork in the road was hard to recognize after so many years with its heavy growth and vines. I instinctively turned to the right, fully expecting to see Mr. Robinson's convertible in front of the cottage, and I was a bit startled when I saw the large Mercedes sitting in front of the house. I had almost forgotten that I was to meet Jean Tallman here.

The cottage looked much smaller than it had the last time I had seen it. But that was not the only change that forty-plus years had wrought. The place was a shambles. The front porch had no screens, and the door leading to the porch was lying under a carpet of pine needles. The smell came to me immediately; that fond scent of pine and sea air combined. Plus more of a mold smell now that the place had been abandoned for so long, discarded from the family's memories.

"What a mess, isn't it, Jean?" I asked as I approached her standing at the far end of the former screened porch looking out at Silver Lake.

"Before all that tragedy, my then-boyfriend and I came out here and had a picnic on that old pier once and even swam in the lake. We were never caught. It was a fun time," Jean shared as I stood next to her, looking out over the lake with my own fond memories of a time on that pier.

"I doubt the pier would hold either of us; it looks like toothpicks sticking out of the water now, the gazebo long gone to the bottom of the lake, I suppose," was all I thought to reply. "The cottage is useless at present, but what a site, the view, the sound of the crashing waves, and it's not even on the dunes."

"The Roberts Brothers will probably snap this up once you and I can figure a fair market value. The concerns of your family name and that of the others I think will be easily overlooked by the media when they hear that the final large parcel of land has come available for development. What a treasure this will be," said Jean.

I turned and walked through the front door jamb, the door long missing from its connection to the frame. I felt as though I was invading someone's private mausoleum without being invited. Jean's chatter helped me to conclude my stream of sad thoughts.

Together we silently walked through the small cottage, leaving the memories to rest. It had felt so much larger when I was young.

"Mrs. Cartwright left me this bag of house keys, but apparently we don't need them here. Maybe they'll work for the bigger home on the beach," I suggested as we walked back to our cars. "Do you know the way, Jean?"

"Of course I do! You know there isn't an inch of Rehoboth Beach property I've missed after thirty-plus years of selling these grounds, and I know my way well. Do *you* want to follow me there?" she asked, perhaps as much as a joke to cheer me as a question of true interest.

I got into my car and waited as she pulled her car out of the driveway and was out of sight. I just stared at the cottage. The memories of those months a full lifetime ago were flooding back to me with great speed. The thoughts of the old wooden chair by the pier, that goose that chased and bit me, even the laughter of Carlo and Mr. Baldwin during their tutoring sessions, our swim in the cold lake water, and how happy Carlo was whenever we arrived here. Like quick movie clips in my brain, all of it coming to me, as if it was just yesterday.

As I pulled my car about and headed toward the larger of the Robinson homes, I actually said out loud what had haunted me for forty years. "Do you think anyone will ever know what really happened here at Silver Lake?"

Chapter 11

One day several weeks into that school year, Mr. Baldwin asked me to stay back at the end of class for a moment. When everyone else had cleared through his door into the hallway—throngs of young men eager to get on to the next class, with one more class finished for the day—Mr. Baldwin said, "I've noticed that your sketches are improving considerably."

"Thank you. I've come to enjoy sketching things from birds flying over the dunes to the shells in the sand after a storm. But I didn't consider any of it to be very good," I said in reply.

"I'd like to see these other sketches you mentioned. Can you bring them with you when you and Carlo come to my house later?" he asked.

At that moment, I noticed Mrs. Crutchfield standing in his doorway, and I had no idea for how long. She had a dour look on her face and it appeared as if she was looking straight through Mr. Baldwin.

In her curt voice she said, "Robert, you get on your way to your next class now, before the bell rings and you're late."

Just outside the door I stopped to hear the discussion between young Mr. Baldwin and old Mrs. Crutchfield, knowing full well that it was wrong to eavesdrop.

"Did I hear you invite a student to your home? I cannot believe you are breaching the line of relationships with students after school hours. I'll have to report this to Headmaster Elliott immediately!" she said, quite loudly.

"I encourage you to discuss this with the headmaster. Now, why did you interrupt my discussion with one of my students in the first place?" were the last words I heard exchanged between them as the bell rang and I realized I was now officially late for Captain West's class. Fortunately I could always say I had to stop by my father's office and he would accept that excuse as a fact. But I still had to run.

Later that afternoon when Carlo and I arrived at Robinson Cottage, Mr. Baldwin appeared to be in good spirits and immediately asked to look at my sketchbook. I was flattered that he remembered and was suddenly grateful I took the moment to run up to my room to gather the sketchbook when I picked up Carlo. Mr. Baldwin walked away from us toward the window nearest the lake and, using the light from the window, stood and looked through the pages of my work.

"This is very good, Rob, you've added something to these pieces most people don't capture. Depth is very important in sketches, as well as shading. We will work together on some shading techniques I acquired, but otherwise these are very impressive indeed." Mr. Baldwin was smiling like a proud parent as he handed the sketchbook back to me.

I could feel my cheeks warming, but also felt something inside I had never felt when discussing any of my abilities with my own parents, something I later in life could pinpoint to be pride.

Instead of completing my assignments as usual, I sat and watched Carlo and Mr. Baldwin working together at the small table under the window. I pulled out by sketchbook and a pencil and began to draw them. They held a certain gentleness between them, as if they shared a secret and enjoyed the fact that it was theirs alone. I enjoyed being able to invade this sense of secrecy while sketching them. Maybe I too was a part of this gentleness but had not yet realized?

Then while waiting on the porch for Carlo and Mr. Baldwin to finish their translation exercises, I noticed a fishing rod leaning against the screen. Beside it was an old tin bucket with fishing supplies in it. A while later, as they were finishing up and Carlo came out onto the porch, Mr. Baldwin stepped out behind him to tell me they had a great session today and that Carlo would be making a strong attempt to begin speaking English when at home from this point on, and that I should encourage him and not laugh when he made mistakes. He said Carlo felt a bit nervous about this prospect.

"Of course I'll encourage him. I look forward to all the discussions we can share. I feel like I've gained a brother," I stated.

"That's wonderful, and he's most excited about talking with you too," he replied.

Mr. Baldwin must have noticed Carlo looking at his fishing rod, because he said to him, "*Ti piacerebbe abdare a pescare, Carlo?*" *Do you like to go fishing, Carlo?*

"*Si, non-uno andato a pescare da quando ero ragazinno.*" *Yes, I haven't been fishing since I was a little boy*, Carlo replied.

"Mr. Robinson has been teaching me to surf fish at night. It's great fun, but the water is getting so much colder. Perhaps we could all go together, on a Saturday or Sunday after your lessons, before the sun goes down? Robbie, why don't you ask your parents' permission? I'm certain Mr. Robinson has more rods to lend you, or you can use the one he lent me," Mr. Baldwin suggested as we walked to the car.

While he was saying something very fast in Italian to Carlo, I thought about the idea, and when they were done, I said, "We would like that. I'll make certain to get permission. Mother loves fresh fish, and if she thinks we might bring some home, she'll help persuade father to let us go!" Carlo was standing on the passenger side of the VW nodding his head yes. Maybe he already understood more than I realized, in such a short time with Mr. Baldwin.

When we got home, I immediately went to Mother's bedroom where she was sitting in her favorite chair knitting. This was always a sign that she was not in sharp pain and that her mood would be light.

"Mr. Robinson and Mr. Baldwin would like to teach Carlo and me how to surf fish after one of his lessons this weekend. Could you persuade Father to let us go? We're both very excited about this," I asked in the same tone I had used as a young boy when I wanted to go play outside alone.

"That sounds like a good lesson for both of you. If you catch something, we can get it cleaned over at the market and have it for a dinner," Mother said, smiling.

"That's just what I thought! Wait until I tell Carlo."

"Let me speak with your father first," she replied, dampening my spirit immediately.

"Oh, that's right. I almost forgot," I stated as I walked out of her room, shoulders hung in prepared defeat.

Chapter 12

With Father's unexpected approval, we decided to try our surf fishing on the following Saturday. We drove to Robinson Cottage and, without exact permission, picked up Mr. Baldwin and headed to the larger Robinson house. Since it was a remarkably warm fall day, Mr. Robinson was waiting for us at his driveway, in a tight Tidewater Academy tee shirt and shorts. Carlo and I came in the corduroys Mother requested we wear. Mr. Robinson was ready with his supplies, and he started loading them into the VW.

"I thought we'd be fishing here, at your house, Mr. Robinson," I said, worried that I might get caught having them in the bus with Carlo and me.

"We have acres of beach here; let's go up the road a ways, where there will no prying eyes," he said with such certainty that I refused to question him further and got in behind the wheel.

We turned around and headed north along Coastal Road, and eventually Mr. Robinson said to stop and pull over.

"This is our favorite spot here, isn't it, Brad?" Mr. Robinson asked.

We unloaded our supplies and felt the cool breeze of the ocean as soon as we crossed the dunes to the deserted beach. For the first few minutes, Mr. Baldwin explained in Italian what

Mr. Robinson was doing as he prepared the fishing rods for each of us. I just sat in the warm sand watching Mr. Robinson. He looked the happiest I had ever seen him. It must have been difficult for him to have two feminine little girls when he was certainly a man's man, eager in his movements, but he appeared content to have us young novices with him.

"I'll set up Brad's rod first—I mean Mr. Baldwin—and then cast him out. Then Carlo and you last, Rob, okay?" he asked.

"Yes, sir, is there anything I can do to help?" I questioned.

"Thanks, but this is my lesson for the three of you, so sit back, relax, and pay attention. You'll enjoy this sport, based on the way Brad described your reaction to his suggestion."

"I really want to try casting for myself this time, alright?" asked Mr. Baldwin.

"Sure, come on over. Your rod is ready now," Mr. Robinson answered.

Carlo sat on the sand next to me, and we watched as Mr. Baldwin struggled to cast out over the breaking surf. After three attempts and having to start over, Mr. Robinson stood very close behind Mr. Baldwin and showed him how to do it by using both their arms together. It was almost an awkward, intimate moment that we should not have been watching, but then Mr. Robinson did the same with Carlo and me and it felt like it was normal.

We fished for hours before the first fish was brought in—a Spanish mackerel caught by Carlo. He jumped up and down so excitedly about his fish that it was fun to watch as he and Mr. Robinson took it off the heavy hook and put it into the big bucket. Shortly after that Mr. Baldwin caught two large flounder in a row.

"Now the competition is on, Robbie. Whoever gets the last fish has to go back to your van and get the beer in the cooler for us, okay?" Mr. Robinson challenged.

Having never drank beer with adults present; I was convinced that I had just turned the corner of maturity. Carlo was working on another fish, but it got away.

Then all of a sudden Mr. Robinson had something big on his line; his fishing rod was bending as if it would snap. He walked backward while reeling it in, and finally was standing on the dry sand, struggling to bring his catch in all the way. Minutes later, he pulled the flapping creature through the foamy waves and screamed for one of us to get the net, that it was a shark. Everyone's level of excitement escalated as we all ran for the net, even Carlo. Mr. Baldwin went into the water, ankle deep, trying to anticipate when he should step in and cover the shark with his net. He seemed to know, and together he and Mr. Robinson brought the three-foot shark onto the beach.

"She's a sand shark. We'll throw her back, but isn't she a beauty?" Mr. Robinson explained to us.

"Can you keep her long enough for me to go get my camera out of the bus and take a picture to show my parents?" I inquired, ready to run if Mr. Robinson agreed.

"Great idea, go get it now, and don't forget those beers, my friend," Mr. Robinson yelled to me as I ran through the sand toward the dunes.

The picture is one of the few cherished photos of that time I keep in that old cigar box today. It shows Mr. Robinson holding the shark, with its tail hanging down to the sand, and Mr. Baldwin and Carlo flanking him. This has always been one of my favorite memories of childhood.

We never had the opportunity to all go surf fishing again, but that day was memorable. Mr. Baldwin and Mr. Robinson donated their catch to the Elliott family dinner for that evening, and we all had a beer and sat and talked like guys of the same age. It was one special day.

Chapter 13

After a few minutes on the witness stand, I felt hot and flushed, as if I was coming down with some sort of a stomach bug all of a sudden.

"So from the beginning you were aware of their liaisons?" Mr. Horton asked me with his booming voice.

"Liaisons, sir? I don't understand," I replied nervously.

"Then let me make it more clear for you, my boy. From the beginning, you were aware of their meetings, their times together...alone?" he restated his question to me.

"Oh yes, sir. I was," I replied.

"And what were your impressions?"

"I didn't see anything wrong with it," I replied.

"And do you now?"

"Well, yes," I said.

I was not quite sure why this stinging memory came to me as I got out of my car in front of the Robinsons' oceanfront home, but I tried to shrug it off when I heard Jean Tallman yelling down to me from the dark porch that wrapped around the entire house.

"What a place this was in its day. Seems more like a home you'd find on Nantucket or Cape Cod than here. It's such a shame that most of the homes built here in Rehoboth Beach look like vinyl boxes with balconies poking out of them," Jean said as I climbed the steep, weakened stairs to the porch.

She went on, obviously excited about this business opportunity. "Look at that view, Silver Lake to the west and miles of ocean to the east. Maybe we could convince the brothers to build in this architectural style and bring back some charm to the town. What do you think, Rob?"

"I never went inside, but it was magnificent in its day, wasn't it?" I asked.

"Yes, charming. We'll do well with this location, and I'm going to urge the Roberts Brothers to follow this style. Can you try the key, Rob? I'd love to see the inside," Jean stated excitedly, oblivious to me staring at the top steps as if I could see the puddles of their blood mixed together there.

I opened the door on the west side of the house with little effort and was pleasantly surprised to see that the interior was in fairly good condition. The coating of salt on the windows provided a gray light, but the large main room ran from the lakeside porch all the way to the ocean-side porch; where four sets of french doors led onto the porch facing the dunes. All of these doors looked to be in decent condition.

"Wow, Rob. How long has it been since the family even used this place? I thought it was abandoned like the cottage and was going to be a mess inside. This looks nice, and the air will clear with a few open doors and windows." Jean pushed open a set of french doors. The rush of wind off the surf and the smell of sea salt pushed through the opening and took occupancy of this large, closed-up space.

"I really have no idea how long since they've been here. They could have continued to use it once they got past the stigma of this place," I replied, my eyes fixated on the view of the breaking waves and the empty beach, my lungs sucking in the salt air.

"I'd suggest you recommend to the Roberts Brothers to fix this place up and use it as a sales office model set-up. This view will make the sale every time," I shared with Jean as I looked around the great room with a dated but functional kitchen, a high ceiling of wooden beams that appeared undamaged, and furniture more in the style of the late 1950s and certainly not of the current century.

"Brilliant idea! What do they want to do with the furniture?" Jean asked.

"I gather the least amount of work on their part. Get a consignment shop in town to come and establish a value, and we can arrange for removal with all the funds directed to Mrs. Robinson-Cartwright." I looked at Jean. "Oh, did I tell you that we will now reference this property as the Cartwright property?"

"Yes, you made that quite clear. I'll get on this furniture first thing tomorrow," Jean replied.

We finished our look around the interior and found the remainder of the house in considerably favorable condition as well. I didn't want to stay in the master bedroom for long, but as usual, Jean looked it over as carefully as if she was picking a piece of fresh fruit.

As I locked the door, I suggested to Jean, "Why don't you go on? I want to stay here for a moment and watch the sun set over Spring Lake."

"Are you going to be alright, Rob?" she asked.

"Certainly. This is just flooding me with memories, some I'd like to recall alone."

"I'll see you in the office first thing tomorrow. Thanks for this opportunity. I hope it doesn't bring too many of the bad memories to mind. Call me this evening if you need me," she said as she stood at the bottom of the steps.

I watched as she got into her car, backed up, and drove back up the street toward town.

So much pain from such a beautiful spot of land; so much so that lives were destroyed, families ruined, and even the local town had to change the street name in hopes of washing the blood away.

Chapter 14

One of my memories I could not shake that evening after visiting the Silver Lake properties was of an afternoon when Carlo was sick and I had to drive all the way to Robinson Cottage to tell Mr. Baldwin that Carlo wasn't well enough to participate in his tutoring since there was no telephone at the cottage.

I recall how Mr. Baldwin then asked if I would like to take a walk around the lake. He said it was something he had taken to doing since the gusts of cold breeze had made it too harsh for walking along the ocean. We walked along the lake toward the bigger Robinson house. We were discussing something about art museums in America compared to Europe when we saw Mrs. Robinson standing on her steps facing the lake, and then she began yelling at us.

"You're ruining my family! Don't you see this? You are wicked. *Just wicked!* And you will pay, dearly. Are you listening to me?"

Mr. Baldwin suggested we not look up and that we should quickly turn and head back to his cottage. He looked very upset, even alarmed by her comments. I didn't know where that rant was leading, but I could sense Mr. Baldwin didn't wish to discuss it. But before we turned to go, I did look up at her. She reminded me of a witch on the top of a roof, shaking her finger at us, as if she was warning us of something terrible to come our way.

When we returned to the cottage, Mr. Baldwin suggested I head home right then and added that I should wish Carlo good health for him. I was more than eager to get in the VW and run away. I felt as if I had been assaulted; it was a very strange experience.

I never shared this with anyone when I got home and went up to my room immediately to complete my class assignments for the following day. Even when I was on the witness stand months after this day, I chose not to tell anyone. I wished someone had known to ask of it later, but no one knew except Mr. Baldwin and me.

Chapter 15

It was shortly after the final bell of the school day that I walked the hallway toward Mr. Baldwin's class room. The smell of autumn was flowing into the hallways with the main doors open. Leaves from the big trees in front of the building were dropping, colors of reds and oranges lying on the floor just inside the doors.

As I entered the classroom, I could tell that Mr. Baldwin appeared to be hurrying his cleanup for some reason.

"Oh, hey there, Robbie. Aren't you going to get on the bus and go to the big game against Georgetown Prep? I think you better hurry if so," he said.

"I have to stay here and help my father with some organizing and filing. Maybe he'll take me there when he goes," I replied.

"I'm going. Mr. Robinson will be meeting me in a few minutes, and then we're heading over to Georgetown. How long does it take to get there, do you know?" he asked.

Feeling left out and surprised that I felt any interest in attending this game, I simply said, "I don't know, sir."

As I turned to leave, Mr. Baldwin asked what was in my hand. I had totally forgotten that I had come to give him the sketch of him and Carlo working at the makeshift desk in his cottage.

"Here, I thought you might like this," I said as I laid it down on top of Mr. Baldwin's desk.

"Rob, this is amazing! You caught my likeness very well. And this is Carlo here?" he asked, clearly excited.

"Carlo was sitting at an angle that day, so I just caught his back. I guess it could be almost any man, eh?" I asked.

"No, no, no. We know it's Carlo, and that's what matters. You've captured an intimacy, which is very difficult for beginners. Now I have to run, but when you bring it back, we can discuss other methods too," he said.

"I thought it was done, actually. This is a gift for you, unless you don't think it good enough, Mr. Baldwin," I replied, feeling sort of embarrassed now that I had presented it to him.

"Thank you. Here, use my pencil and sign your name. You're the artist and you should sign it. I'll display it with great pride at the cottage." He beamed as I signed it.

By the time I made it to Father's office, I realized that I really did want to go to the game. I wanted to run past his office, out to the faculty lot, and get into the convertible with Mr. Robinson and Mr. Baldwin and get away from this school.

"Rob, your father is expecting you in his office," said Miss Scott, Father's secretary. "I'm leaving for the game. Maybe we'll see you there later?"

I entered the waiting area for the headmaster's office, where Miss Scott had her desk. When I approached Father's office door, I could hear him on the telephone and saw that his chair was turned and he was facing the massive mahogany bookcases that lined the wall behind his desk. He hadn't yet noticed me, so I sat in one of the two chairs facing his desk. These chairs were very uncomfortable, as I suppose they had to be, since the person most often seated in one was a student sent here because of some infraction their teacher felt the headmaster should handle. Uncomfortable and hard, unlike the two soft wing chairs and sofa across the room where Father entertained his benefactors and parents when visiting.

Since Father hadn't yet noticed me, I moved to one of the wing chairs and sat looking out the window. In all my years here, I had rarely sat on this side of his large office, rather always in the "troubled student" chairs. This wing chair was nice, nicer than our furniture at home.

I looked up at Father's diploma on the wall from the University of Pennsylvania. The diploma sat in the center of the wall, meant to draw your eye. Surrounding it were several photographs of Father and the mayor of Rehoboth Beach and another with my parents and the governor of Delaware outside the front doors of the school, amongst others. There were no pictures that included me, though. Perhaps Father didn't want to show that he was a family man, with a child of mediocre standing at his own academy.

Father finished his telephone call, instructed me on the papers to be filed on his credenza, told me he would be heading to the game, that he would meet me at home in time for dinner, and left. He gave no thought to my possible interest in attending the big game as well.

As I sit in my real estate office years later looking at the portrait of my father painted in that headmaster's office all those years back, I recall the day that I entered that same space, unannounced, when Father was introducing the district attorney, Mr. Horton, to Mr. Baldwin. It was several days after all the ugliness had occurred, in April of 1967.

I heard Father say, "Please, let's all sit down over here, where it will be more private," as he closed the door to his office. I turned from his door before he noticed me and went to sit in the anteroom near Miss Scott's desk.

"It's a shame, isn't it, Robert? All this pain and suffering associated with our little school. How is your father doing? I mean, well, I probably shouldn't ask this...well, never mind," Miss Scott said.

I just sat there looking at her, not certain what she meant and in too much of a fog myself to understand the consequences for Father's precious academy at such a time of my own deep personal pain.

"I'll return in a few minutes to see my father, I just need to, I'll be right back," was all I could say as I hurried to get away from what I thought must be happening to Mr. Baldwin. I ran down the hallway to get as far from the lobby and Father's office.

I already knew *my life* had changed drastically. No more going straight home from school to collect my books and Carlo for his tutoring at Robinson Cottage. No more drives with the music blasting and listening to Carlo trying to sing along while we laughed and made fun of one another. No more walking the beach with Carlo to share our stories in different languages, feeling it was one we alone could share. No more surf fishing with the rest of them, like four guys having fun together no matter the difference in ages. No more swimming in the lake, sunning on the pier, no more visits to Robinson Cottage alongside Silver Lake.

Chapter 16

In his declining years, after Mother had passed away and was buried at Epworth Church, Father took to daily visits to her grave. Several years ago I had a small concrete bench placed there so Father could stay as long as he desired, without regard to his own arthritic and failing body. His mind was still sharp as a tack, and all the memories were still in there, swirling around in his brain like dreams one cannot forget days after they are dreamt.

Often when I stopped by Mother's grave, it looked as though all the surrounding graves had been completely ignored, hers the only one kept free of leaves and always holding fresh flowers in the small brass urn. A passerby might assume Father was the caretaker of the graveyard who was simply taking a brief rest next to this grave, he was there so often. I no longer brought flowers since the ones Father had delivered always appeared full of life, which I still find strange in a place of so much death.

Once, I arrived as Father was sitting there in deep thought, and I said, "Mother certainly loved her flowers. These look as if you pulled them from her garden." I sat on the bench next to my father, who was so small and frail.

"Yes, she did love her flowers. Remember how you wanted to play beach ball or ride your bicycle, anything but assist her in tending to those gardens?" he asked. "That is, until it was time to join the sports programs at the school, then you were her 'second in command,' as you told me," he chuckled, as if at a funny story.

"I never was much for the sports programs at the academy. I liked the beach volleyball games though. Well, except when the beach patrol guards were on their break from watching the tourists in the water and they pushed their way into our games. They were always older, stronger, and aggressive. They took all the fun out of it."

"I'm sorry I didn't get to watch you play. Mother always said you came home with a light heart after those games. I guess you really did enjoy that one sport, didn't you, Robert?"

"I didn't realize Mother noticed. All I remember was being told to make certain I didn't bring sand into the house. In fact, one time I was wet and sandy, so I stripped down to my underwear right on the front porch, and as I stood up and walked toward the door, Mrs. McGuire was coming up the walk and saw me. She had a pie in her hands. I was surprised she didn't drop it."

Father laughed a wholehearted laugh as I had not heard from him in many years. Then he began to cough. After he settled, we looked at one another and began to laugh all over again, this time together. To this day, that is one of my favored memories of us, sharing a laugh while sitting next to my mother's grave.

Then out of nowhere came a question I had wanted to ask for so many years, as if my tongue had finally found the opportunity to present the query to my father independent of the rest of my body.

"Do you have any regrets, Father?"

Several painfully quiet minutes passed, and then he said, "Oh, yes, son…I have regrets too many to list."

Another long pause, and then he asked, "But I suppose what you're asking about now is Mr. Baldwin, isn't it?"

"Yes."

"I had such uncertain feelings about him that first day when I picked him up at the bus, when we picked him up. He just didn't look the part I had expected. Oh, I don't know, maybe I expected a worldly teacher who was going to be a strong influence on you boys, but he was a bit more effete than I could tell when we spoke on the phone during that summer."

He paused for a cough before continuing, perhaps gathering his thoughts. "You know I had planned for another teacher, had her hired and all set up to start the school year, then she found out she was pregnant and decided to decline the job. I had already told all of the investors and parents that this was the year we would implement art and art history into the curriculum at the academy. I needed to find a replacement, and the days were numbered. My interview with Mr. Baldwin was simple and smooth. He was available, and I had a position to fill."

"Mother never liked him, did she?" I asked, but I knew the answer.

"You're very perceptive, Robert. Mother never cared for Mr. Baldwin and told me so that first night after we returned from taking him to the cottage. She could not put her finger on it, but after…after it all happened, she said she knew it would have been him to cause so much pain and grief. Granted, this wasn't a statement she cherished making. Neither your mother nor I would have wanted such pain to besiege our home, our town, our school. Everything we had worked for, together, she and I. We sacrificed so much for that damn academy. Look where it got the three of us today?"

After he bowed his head, looked around us, and then again raised it, he continued, "Sitting in an old graveyard sharing the thoughts of my day with a corpse who may or may not even know I'm here, let alone understand what I'm saying, and you…You, who never wanted to end up here, watching over me as an old decrepit man. You were meant to find life away from here, perhaps in Washington or New York. I never expected to be sharing my old age with you in this town but visiting you in another place entirely, visits with grandchildren that never came. Trips to the south, to the warmer climes, Florida or Arizona, like my friends have done. But here we are. My regrets are in front of me as reflective as a mirror; each and every day there to remind me—of what? My failures."

After a long, quiet pause, I shared, "I too have similar regrets, Father. I regret I didn't show more compassion toward you when the trial began, when your school was falling apart. I guess I had reasons, some I still don't understand all these years later. I regret I didn't provide you and Mother with grandchildren. Maybe I assumed you would have been so engrossed in another project like the academy that I would have provided you with more of a burden to be a part of a family, like I was to you."

"*Burden?* What in the world are you talking about? We were a family, your mother, you, and me," he whispered.

"Compared to the other kids in our town, with their father home every night, I never felt that. Not with the students at the academy either, since they shared a dormitory and they had a bond. I was the only student that walked to school by way of the street, not by way of the staircase from the dorm and dining hall after they shared breakfast together. You had to work so hard to build that place, and Mother was always left to herself or in bed in pain. I now think her pain was used as a crutch to avoid spending time alone with me. Carlo was the closest thing to family for me at that time. And then he left me too."

I stood up and stretched my back before sitting down and continuing. "I felt as though I was a burden, that you would have been better off with no children except your students or, better yet, a son that was so happy to be a part of your program at Tidewater. Hell, I always wondered why I was even there, since I wasn't a problem student by choice in another school program where you and Mother decided to pull me out and place me in Tidewater Academy for corrective reasons. I was just the kid you had to put through school, and the academy was convenient. Most of the other boys resented me and said so behind my back. Mr. Baldwin was the first teacher to see me as someone other than the headmaster's son. He was the first adult to speak to me as if we were friends or perhaps comrades. Then of course Mr. Robinson changed and became very friendly to me once we spent so much time around one another. Do you remember the day he took Carlo and me surf fishing?"

"I remember all the fish you brought home. Also I remember how Carlo rambled on in Italian with such excitement and joy. Yes, I remember."

While I was sharing these long-seeded feelings with my father I hadn't noticed that it had begun to drizzle some, but now it was coming down harder.

"Dad, let's go. I'll drive you back to the home," I said as I helped him up from the bench. I thought he was falling, but he grabbed me into a strong hug and said, "I always wished you had called me 'Dad' and not 'Father,'" he said with a tear on his cheek as he looked softly into my eyes.

"I never knew," I said as I hugged him back. "Dad it will be from now on then. Now let's get you back before you catch a cold here."

"Can we go someplace to eat a real meal? The food at the home is no better than what we served you boys at Tidewater."

"Sure, Dad, sure. Wherever you'd like. Let's get you to the car and we can drive around town and decide." We walked arm in arm from my mother's grave to the small parking lot.

"Can we eat in Lewes or Dewey Beach, Robert? I have too many nightmares of my days here in Rehoboth Beach," my father said.

"Let's head up to Lewes. I read about a great new place in the *Gazette* last week."

Dinner was delightful. We shared a nice bottle of Cabernet from Australia, and our entire discussion was uplifting and pleasant, no further mention of regrets, the academy, or my mother. The dessert we shared was a plate of mini cakes, one from each of the larger slices you could order individually. When we had eaten a few, there were several still on the large plate, and I suggested we have them wrapped up and take them to the home, so Father could share with some of the others living there. At the very moment I finished suggesting this to my father, he said, "Take as much as you want, Robbie. There's plenty."

After returning Father to the home and getting him settled into his favorite chair with a book and a glass of brandy, I said my good-byes and headed home.

Chapter 17

As I was driving south on Route 1 to my home in Rehoboth Beach, a sentence Father had said at the restaurant stuck in my thoughts, like something stuck in one's craw. I just could not fathom the reason for this lingering thought... After all, he simply said, "Take as much as you want, Robbie. There's plenty."

It wasn't until a few hours later, as I stood at the kitchen sink washing out my wine glass that it finally occurred to me why this one simple statement was lingering around me like a lasting fog. Those exact words brought a shiver to the top of my spine as I dropped the glass and watched it shatter in the sink.

During one of our final visits to Robinson Cottage, while Mr. Baldwin and Carlo were working on their assignment, I was sitting near the fireplace working on math equations. On a table beside me was a plate of fragrant cookies. Mr. Baldwin must have seen me spying the plate because when we were preparing ourselves to head home, Mr. Baldwin lifted the plate and said, "Mrs. Crutchfield brought these to me today at the end of classes, maybe as a peace offering. We don't seem to see eye to eye sometimes." Then he held the plate closer to me and said, "Take as much as you want, Robbie. There's plenty."

Carlo and I ate our cookies on the ride home, singing along to a song by Sonny and Cher, which by that time had been around for a few years but was new to Carlo. "I've Got You Babe." To hear Carlo singing it made me laugh so hard... he messed up the words but was having great fun nonetheless.

It is curious how we relate certain events in our lives to music. This song, though rarely played even on the oldies stations today, brings me back to that very moment every time. But the statement uttered by my father at the restaurant had brought back a repressed memory as well.

I prepared for bed and then had a fitful night of sleep, thoughts of Carlo, Mr. Baldwin, and Mr. Robinson and even of Mrs. Robinson seemed to stick with me that night. Finally at four o'clock I could not stay in bed any longer, so I got up, showered, and shaved, and headed to my dark little kitchen for my first pot of strong coffee. Anything to clear my head of these thoughts and memories I had suppressed for so many years, resurfacing now after hearing one statement and recalling one memory and one song.

As the sun rose over the Atlantic just a few blocks away, I sat on the upper porch of my home, which I shared with two frisky Scottish terriers. I sat there because they were still asleep on the bed, and I knew that as soon as they roused for the day, they would wonder where I had gone, and if I wasn't found in adequate time, Spike would relieve himself, and I didn't want to find a cold puddle on the floorboards later. From here I could hear the pad of their feet on the hard floor and could go in to greet them.

Grunt, the older dog, could sleep for twenty hours a day, but Spike requires your attention every waking moment, whether to tug on his toys, of which there are plenty, or when he sits on the bench in the bow window watching for squirrels in my backyard, then turns toward me before running wildly through the house to his dog door on the back porch. At age six, he has yet to catch a squirrel, but I always tell him that when he does, I'll prepare it for his meal. Honestly, I hope he never takes me up on my offer.

Despite all the times I had been forced to recall those final days before the incident, such as when I was on the witness stand or when I read a story of those long ago days written by some up-and-coming reporter for the local *Cape Gazette* newspaper who decided to stir the old story up, thinking that no pain would come to anyone who read it some thirty to forty years later, I still had those occasional nights when sleep evaded me, and the only thing that came to mind was the event leading up to the incident.

I think of one evening months before the incident when Mother asked me to run over to the pharmacy to get her some pills for her migraine headache. I was rounding the corner of First Street and Rehoboth Avenue when I heard a familiar voice from the opposite corner. I glanced over and saw Mr. Robinson and Mr. Baldwin coming out of a local pub. They were hanging onto one another and looked as if they had drunk too much and were trying to support the other, to little avail. They stumbled as they walked in the opposite direction, laughing and slapping one another's back, obviously having fun. I wished at that moment that I was not a student at Tidewater Academy or the dutiful son collecting his mother's pills, but one of the two inebriated men struggling down the avenue while having so much fun.

I can only imagine the trouble this event started when the two men arrived home. Mrs. Robinson seemed a strict woman and seeing her husband that drunk and with Mr. Baldwin—well, I bet all of Mrs. Robinson's fury would have been let loose on one or both of those men.

Years later when visiting him, I asked Mr. Baldwin of the outcome of that night. He smiled a very sad smile and said, "It was just a misunderstanding. All of it was. But I imagine that's hard for you to believe now." Then he dropped his head to his emaciated chest and cried softly. I did not push any further.

Another time I frequently recall when all of this history floods back is of a time I was sitting near Miss Scott's desk waiting for Father to finish whatever meeting had caused him to close the door to his office when Miss Scott told me, "Your father is in a conference with Mr. Robinson and Mr. Baldwin and may be some time. Do you want to wait or should I tell him something for you?"

While I sat there contemplating my decision I overheard Mr. Robinson's voice at a booming level, "What relationship? This is ridiculous gossip from some of the old cronies teaching here!"

I thought for a moment and shared my decision to stay and wait for my father. I pulled out a history book I had to read that evening and acted as though I was reading, but in fact I was straining to hear the conversation just a room away.

I heard a bunch of muffled words and could sense the anger in their tone but had a hard time hearing anything clearly for some time. Then I heard my father yell for the first time in my entire life, "Well, this has to stop now. Do you both hear me? It stops right now!"

This was getting good, or so I thought until I caught Miss Scott looking my way, then ask what subject I was reading.

I looked at her confidently and said, "The battle of Gettysburg, from just over a hundred years ago and not all that far from here."

"It might be easier to read if it wasn't upside down, now wouldn't it?" she smirked.

I turned the history book upright and began to read without replying to Miss Scott's observation.

"Those two men do seem to be awfully chummy, don't you think, Robert?" she asked, looking over her glasses at me.

"Yes, they're very friendly; they do a lot of things together after school too. You know guy stuff. They fish, swim, and hang out together," I had shared before I even realized what I just let slip from my mouth.

"It seems a little strange of a relationship to me, an art teacher and a big, strong gym instructor who has a family to go home to. But what do I know; I go home to my apartment at Mr. Howard's building and I feed all the feral cats that hang out there…Some exciting life I lead here in Rehoboth, huh?" she said, almost more to herself than to me.

Fearing I had just opened a Pandora's Box or provided some juicy details for the teacher's lounge, I felt I had better get out of there before I caused irreparable harm to these men's reputations. Just as I was preparing to tell Miss Scott that I was going to leave, Father's door opened wide and the three men walked out. Father saw me and immediately told me to go home. His face looked red and angry. I got out of there as fast as I could, hoping I hadn't caused too much damage with my comments to Miss Scott.

So many years have passed, and yet I feel this tug of dread, of responsibility for this incident that shattered so many of our lives. Sometimes I cannot shake it off, I feel like I'm stuck in a snow drift, and the snow is piling up against my body, ready to take me under. Why would things like a simple statement bother me to this day? Was I regretful for things I hadn't done to stop all of the pain? Could I have stopped the pain?

Chapter 18

After a sales meeting with my associates, I retreated to my office, hoping to return any calls and leave early that day, feeling some sort of fog returning to my head. Usually when these fogs came, so did the memories of the incident, and my mood would subsequently darken. I was not pleasant to be around, so I took the messages the secretary had placed on my desk blotter and grabbed my coat and briefcase. I said good-bye, telling the staff I would be out for the remainder of the day.

When I reached my car, I had decided what I had to do in order to clear this cloud. I dropped my briefcase in the back seat of my car, threw the message slips in, letting them fall as they may, shut the door, and walked the few blocks to Epworth Church and my mother's grave.

The walk could sometimes clear my head, but not this time. By the time I reached the grave site, I was in a foul mood, and I was winded. I was not in good shape, never have been. Always regretted that I had not taken up exercise at the YMCA gym or run along the beach as so many in the town had turned to doing. I was living in a sort of paradise, at least for others, yet was trapped in my own neglect, for my body, my mind, my soul. If it wasn't for the evening walks with the dogs around the two blocks nearest my home, I would be a certified couch potato.

I sat for a long period just looking at Mother's stone. I had been here so many times, the dutiful son, but did I really think she could hear my thoughts?

Was this the place I could share the dread I carried like an oxbow on my shoulders and become relieved of the weight?

My thoughts returning to the days leading up to the incident, thoughts I usually pushed aside, but today felt I needed to let flow…Perhaps that was how I could get this weight off my shoulders.

It was two days after the shouting affair in Father's office. Mr. Baldwin had left a note on the tandem desk I shared with David Whitman. I happened to arrive ahead of David so I picked up the note, thinking it was from the previous class. As I walked it to the trash can at the back of the classroom I felt compelled to read it. I opened the folded paper to read:

Robbie,

Today's tutorial with your cousin Carlo must be canceled. I have urgent business I must attend to and will not return home in time to work with him. Please try to explain to him by showing him this note.

Carlo, Devo cancellare la tua lezione oggi. Ci rivedremo domain all'ura regolare. *I have to cancel your lesson today. I will see you at our regular time tomorrow.*

BSB"

I stuffed the note into my pocket and sat at my desk, curious as to why Mr. Baldwin had canceled Carlo's lesson. The thought dropped from my mind quickly as others entered the room and the noise level rose. Finally Mr. Baldwin came in and the lesson began.

That afternoon I ran home as usual, but without the lift in my step I got from knowing I was getting out of the house to be around Mr. Baldwin and Carlo. By the time I had made it to our front porch, I had decided not to show Carlo the note, but rather to act as if all was normal, and once we were away from the house, away from Mother, I would show the note to him. We could find something to do that day, as long as we stayed away from the academy campus or our house.

We drove out of town that day over the wooden bridge, past the church and Mr. Hazard's lot of shiny cars, and headed to Bertha's Ice Cream Parlor just before the highway. I knew I couldn't take the VW onto the highway. What if someone saw me and said so to my father or mother? What if I was involved in an automobile accident, how would I explain that to my parents and keep my driving privileges after I broke one of Father's rules? No, Bertha's would be safe.

This was a hangout for kids who went to the public Cape Henlopen High School. Some I knew as neighbors, but they would not have reason to tell my parents. When we went inside, I ordered two colossal sundaes for Carlo and me, and we sat in the big window overlooking the main drag into Rehoboth Beach. Carlo was like a kid as usual, big eyed and so excited with his treat. They had cool music playing and we ate slowly, watching the kids as they came and went, many stopping to talk to one another, but none stopped to talk with us. We were going to make it through this little adventure without scars.

When we finished, I suggested we walk over to Mr. Hazard's lot and admire the cars, since we could not go home yet without being questioned by Mother for returning too soon.

It was while I was standing admiring a blue 1953 Lincoln Capri convertible that I saw Mr. Robinson's car go by, heading into town. Mr. Baldwin was in the passenger seat, looking sad or unhappy. Why would he cancel his lesson to do something with Mr. Robinson and not tell us, let alone not invite us? I thought we were buds now, pals who did things with these two adults that no other students at Tidewater got to do. We were special friends; after all, we shared a beer together.

I looked over at Carlo who was looking into the window of a big boat of a car, a sparkling black 1960 Cadillac Fleetwood, just like the kind they showed Elvis driving on a news report we had watched recently. He had not seen the teachers drive by, and I was glad for that. I didn't want him to feel the same abandonment I was feeling.

By time we got back into the old VW, I realized there was not enough time to go to Robinson Cottage and talk to Mr. Baldwin then return home without consequences, so we drove through town and back to our house on Annapolis Street, avoiding the academy and Father's office windows, not to mention Miss Scott's eyes.

I was miserable that entire evening and decided to forgo completing my homework assignments. Besides, Father would have found it odd that I was at the cottage that afternoon and yet came home with work to do, so I justified my decision and went right up to my room, grabbed the book I was reading, and tried to concentrate on it. But I couldn't, I had to admit to myself. I just threw it to the other side of my room and lay on my back, looking at the sloped ceiling of my room and thinking. Now why would they go off for an adventure and not take us? What was his "urgent business" he could not tell me about?

We already had certain secrets that Mr. Baldwin had learned were safe with me.

I must have fallen asleep, because the next thing I recall was Mother's voice at the bottom of the stairs telling me dinner was ready and to wash my hands.

Sitting at Mother's grave, I noticed that the sun had begun to hide behind the western trees and realized I was sitting there chilled, so I got up and walked back through town toward my office and my car. I decided to stop at a new little seafood place on my way to the car, since my stomach was rumbling. I ordered some cream of crab soup and a beer and ate quietly, listening to families around me chatting, tourists asking their waiter where to go for seashell hunting, and another waiter telling the story of the abandoned light house. None of these conversations helped to shake my gloom. I paid my bill and left to walk down the street to my car.

When I returned home and walked into the quiet house I was eagerly greeted by two frisky and hungry dogs. In silence I prepared their meal and then poured myself a drink and went to my favorite chair in the front room, which I sit in while completing my Sunday crosswords. The silence was worse than having noise, void except for the sound of the dogs eating their kibble with hard bits falling to the floorboards. I had to shake this fog, but it was too early to go to bed.

I turned on the stereo and a tune from the early 1970s was playing and already halfway through. "It's a Heartache" by Bonnie Tyler. By the time it was finished playing I had it figured out and was pleased that no remembrances came to mind from that song. This was the plan—let the music lift my spirits. I settled into my chair with Spike in the chair next to me and Grunt lying between my outstretched legs on the ottoman. Leave it to two dogs and some soft oldies to lighten the spirit— or so I thought until another tune brought me right back to 1967!

It was the Four Tops singing "Standing in The Shadows of Love," one of the songs I heard Carlo humming as we washed the VW together in the driveway. That VW was as much his ticket to freedom as it was mine in those months, and we both took such pride in that bus. Never again did I care for it like that after Carlo was gone; it just didn't matter anymore.

We had been at the cottage for his usual lesson the day following our little ice cream adventure. I noticed that Mr. Baldwin was in a "mood" and was not as enthusiastic as usual when we arrived. Already upset that he chose to exclude us in their adventure the day before, I saw fit to just sit in the small chair near the fireplace and complete my assignments.

About an hour into the lesson period Mr. Robinson came to the door and rapped hard, as if he suspected no one was there. But the VW was just outside in the dusty driveway, so he had to know we were there. Mr. Baldwin met him at the door and then stepped out onto the porch with him. After a moment of them talking the door opened and they both came in. Mr. Robinson greeted us boys and took a seat in one of the other chairs in the room. Nothing more was said and Mr. Baldwin returned to his practice with Carlo.

I could not stand this strange silence and said a bit louder than I had wished, "What's going on here?"

All three of them turned and looked at me, no one certain what to say in response. I just looked back and forth at the two teachers, expecting one of them to answer me.

"Hey, I get the silent treatment really well at home. I don't expect it when I'm here though. Talk to me," I said, again in a higher volume than any of us usually used in this cottage.

"Its adult stuff, Rob," said Mr. Robinson. "Just some things Mr. Baldwin and I need to figure out, that's all. Nothing for you to be bothered with really. Okay?"

"Whatever," was all I could say. The tension after this brief but fruitless conversation was palpable to say the least. When their work was finished we left quickly.

On the ride home, I was steaming under my collar and just started talking out loud, unsure if Carlo would understand what I was saying, but I had to clear my head. "How dare they? Who do they think they are, not telling us what the hell is going on, when quite clearly something is going on! They didn't have to go out onto the damn porch to talk; they could have spoken right in front of us. Damn them!"

When we pulled into the driveway I saw Mrs. Crutchfield and Father standing beside her beat-up old Ford along the curb in front of our walkway, deep in some sort of conversation. I don't think they even noticed us pulling into the driveway. We ran up the back steps into the house, where Mother was in the kitchen, looking very happy, almost pleased with herself. Clearly something was up, as there was no dinner cooking on the stovetop, and Mother was clearing away glasses from the kitchen table as if they had just finished the meal without Carlo or me.

"Hi, boys, how was your lesson?" she chirped.

"*Ciao,*" said Carlo in her direction as he walked through to the dining room and up to his room.

I stood there next to Mother at the kitchen sink, confused but not certain what to say except, "Is dinner ready?"

"Oh my, I haven't even started. Dinner will be late, but it's leftovers from Sunday night, so I just need to heat them in the oven. Go clean up and set the table for me, please, will you, darling?" she replied.

As I pushed through the swing door that led into the dining room I thought to myself *"Darling?" When in the world has she ever called me that before? Are all adults just wacky today or what?*

Near the wrapping up of a very quiet dinner Father made one of his usual announcements from his end of the table, as if we were employees and this was a board meeting. The old man just couldn't shake the headmaster attitude even in his own home.

"Today Mr. Robinson informed me that he will be taking a new job at the Indian River School in Oceanview. He will begin next week, even though the school year is almost finished. They need him now. It will be an important opportunity for him there. He will head up the entire extracurricular athletic program for the students in ninth through twelfth grades," Father shared with a broad smile as he looked toward Mother at the other end of the table.

"But what about poor Mr. Baldwin?" I asked in this new, louder tone that seemed to possess my being.

For the first time in my recollection, Father raised his voice at the dinner table, saying, "What in Christ's name do you mean, child? *What about poor Mr. Baldwin?*"

"James! Please, not at my dinner table!" screamed Mother at him.

"Alright, alright, Grace. But I demand to know what he means by that statement," Father said through gritted teeth.

"Well, like, how will Mr. Baldwin get back and forth to school now?" I asked.

"What do I bloody care!" he replied.

"James," was all Mother had to say.

"He can get a bike for all I care," Father said in a hushed tone to me.

"But if he rides a bike, he won't be home in time for his lessons with Carlo," I responded, as if making a challenge.

"It will work out. That's all I can say on this matter. Is there any dessert, Grace?" With that statement, I was dismissed from the table and went to my room. Carlo started to pick up the plates and I heard father say, "No, no, Carlo. I will do that." And then to my mother, "Has he learned any English yet after all of this?"

I took the steps two at a time and slammed my door, but doubted the effect was noticed from the floor below.

Chapter 19

I simply had to rustle myself from these gloomy thoughts, and besides, it was time for the dogs' walk before bedtime, so Grunt told me by his deep growl while he stood by the hook that held their leads.

We started our walk headed toward the beach and the boardwalk. Spike was almost bouncing in his step because this usually meant a much longer walk. Somehow he just knew by the direction I turned from the front gate of my yard. So the long route we took.

It was a cool night, with winds off the ocean that alternated between strong gusts then light ones, but the boys couldn't walk fast enough. Spike particularly preferred it when we were on the boardwalk during the day and he could try to chase the seagulls. Grunt liked the idea of us stopping at Thrasher's French Fries and sharing a big tub, just the three of us. It is amazing how each has his own personality, how their excitement shows in their step.

I was beginning to feel as though I could shake off the gloom. We walked up the wooden steps leading to the boardwalk, and immediately I saw two men walking together, clearly chilled by the wind and hugging one another. Over the past decade or two, Rehoboth Beach seemed to have attracted many affluent homosexual couples.

It was a fascinating transition to watch, as these new neighbors were fixing up old buildings to maintain their historic integrity. They had a community center that offered all sorts of programs for them as well as the poor, seniors, and young kids struggling with their identities. Many of these couples were migrating from cities such as D.C. or Philadelphia initially as weekenders or summer shareholders in the big older homes, but then my sales agents were seeing more and more of them move here into permanent homes, leaving lucrative government jobs for a better way of life.

You couldn't walk a street in Rehoboth now without seeing shops and restaurants flying the ubiquitous rainbow flag on a holder by the door or a sticker in their window, indicating that gay and lesbian patrons were warmly received. Some of my finest quality sales agents were homosexual and treated everyone with great respect even when some did not deserve such kindness, let alone show politeness in return.

I see couples often happily walking hand in hand, arm in arm, but this particular couple struck me for some reason. It brought back another memory of the incident yet again.

"Did you ever see these two men walk arm in arm, Mr. Elliott?" Prosecutor Horton asked me as I sat on that witness stand.

"Well, sort of, yes," I said, and as I began to explain by saying, "They were once—" Mr. Horton interrupted me and turned to the judge and said, "That is all for this witness at this time. I reserve the right to have this fine young man return to the stand should I see fit."

With a wave of his hand, I was dismissed, similar to the way Father liked to do with me when he wanted me away from him.

I felt no better being dismissed by Prosecutor Horton than I did by my father.

The games played within the walls of the courtroom. I was about to explain that they were coming out of a pub and appeared to need each other's support after partaking of too much drink. But that will never be heard now in this courtroom. Had Prosecutor Horton already known this little fact but did not want it revealed? Did I just put a nail into Mr. Baldwin's coffin?

When I left the courtroom, Mother met me out in the hallway and gave me a five-dollar bill and suggested I go to the lunch counter at Lingo's Market on my way home, since I had already missed the meal at Tidewater Academy. She was planning to remain in the courtroom with Father.

As I walked away, money in hand, I thought of how much she was probably enjoying this charade and mentally collecting notes to share with her gossiping knitting circle, as she personally was in the know, having her husband, the illustrious headmaster and her lowly son witnesses for the prosecution of Mr. Baldwin.

I pocketed the five dollars and went home. As I was walking up the steps to the front porch I heard the thud of the newspaper landing by my feet. The bully who delivered our *Cape Gazette* twice a week was obviously intending to hit me with the thick paper but missed. I know this because he was also lousy and uncoordinated at volleyball the few times we allowed him in on a match.

The headline read **HEADMASTER AND SON TESTIFY FOR THE PROSECUTION**. I threw the paper deep into the hydrangea bushes. If my parents wanted to read it, they could dig in there for it themselves.

I was lying on my bed when Father came into the house and yelled up the stairs to me, "Mr. Horton will be calling you to the stand again tomorrow, so make certain you hang up your clothes properly. You won't be going to school for summer session again tomorrow. I'll get your assignments and bring them home. Your mother is working on dinner. Clean up and come set the table."

Last thing I wanted to do was to go to classes in the summer. The school building did not have air conditioning and I was tired of hearing the other students talk behind my back. If I hadn't taken off for those last few weeks of spring semester just after the incident, I wouldn't have been enrolled in the summer session.

I just stayed in my room until my mother called me for dinner. I thought about how much I loathed my parents more than I thought about anything else.

The table was set, and I did not get in trouble for failing to do it myself. Mother must have been in especially good spirits today. I think she would have driven a stake into Mr. Baldwin's heart had the Delaware court system of Sussex County permitted her to volunteer to do such a thing. She never knew Mr. Baldwin, but to see him convicted seemed to be her singular goal.

Grunt and Spike were beside themselves, since our walk included me letting them off their leads and allowing them to run around the little park at the base of the now ancient lighthouse. I had heard that CAMP Rehoboth Gay and Lesbian

Community Center was raising funds to restore the lighthouse and then provide tours when completed. They certainly had good intentions, that growing group.

As I was sitting on the bench and the boys were running with a shared piece of driftwood in their mouths, growling at one another in fun, I saw an elderly couple come over the dune rise with their fishing rods and tackle in hand.

"Good fishing tonight?" I asked, trying to sound more joyful than I felt.

"No, nothing coming in through that rough surf on this fine evening. But the fresh air keeps us young," the man replied as the lady next to him said, "Speak for yourself, you old geezer!" and flashed me a smile as she passed by.

And just like that, my mind wandered back to 1967. Mr. Baldwin did in fact get a bike to ride to school, one of the Robinsons' bikes, I believe. We resumed Carlo's sessions at Robinson Cottage as I dwelled over my homework, but the mood never seemed the same. The lightheartedness seemed to have vanished with the change in Mr. Robinson's career path. Carlo still loved his lessons and was getting more fluent by the day, and I could see that he and Mr. Baldwin maintained their bond. I just lost my sense of being with them, as if I had known in advance how my coming years would feel, and my heart was in a hurry to feel that way before the rest of me was ready for or aware of the coming future.

There was a gloomy pall in the cottage, as if the lights had been dimmed and could not get bright again. Mr. Baldwin certainly made us feel welcome, but some days I could tell he wanted to run from this town as much as I always had. He could have, whereas I couldn't. After all, he was a world traveler, he had the experience of airports and train stations and how to get around foreign cities and communicate with strangers. I would be lost once I crossed the bridge over Rehoboth canal and would run home, tail between my legs, before I had even gotten far.

Chapter 20

All of a sudden everything bad became good again. It was like the calm brightness of sunshine after a terrible hurricane had cleared out the town. Rides in the VW, Carlo and I were singing to the tunes on the radio, windows down, salty breezes blowing our hair to the side, and smiling. We were smiling.

Somehow Mr. Baldwin's spirit had lifted, and with it so had ours. I couldn't really pinpoint just what hour it happened, but it was as if life was suddenly returned to normal again. This must have been what Dorothy felt when she awoke in her bed to find Auntie Em and the others gathered around her—and Toto too.

The weather was warming and I could see sprouts of Mother's flowers breaking the surface of the earth in her garden from my bedroom window. That afternoon when we arrived at Robinson Cottage for lesson time, Mr. Baldwin suggested we take a well-deserved break from work, just for a little while. There would be time for me to finish my assignments before we returned home so my parents would not be suspicious, but for now, he suggested we take a kite he had purchased at the Wooden Indian the previous day during his lunch hour out onto the beach and fly it.

After he explained this all again in very fast Italian, the smile on Carlo's face was as broad as I'd ever seen it. We walked up the road together and found the first beach dune crossing and took it. The beach was deserted, the sun was shining, and there was a moderate wind. Even if we couldn't get this kite to fly, we were doing something other than school lessons and homework, and we were having fun again finally. We ran like kids with that kite, taking turns with the string and the stick on the end, or holding the kite as the other ran away, trying valiantly to get it up in the sky.

It went up a few times, but eventually we realized none of us knew that the line needed to be let out as you ran, or the kite would just fizzle out and crash into the sand again. We laughed and ran and got sand in our shoes and finally sat on the dunes for a break and talked about how much better we would get at this new game.

Just then I saw someone running along the surf, coming our way from the south. As he drew closer, I realized it was Mr. Robinson in a wetsuit with a surf board under his arm, splashing in the shallow waves as he ran.

I pointed to him, and at that moment Carlo said, "Mr. Robinson!" in what I considered to be excellent English. Mr. Baldwin stood and waved to him. We were all excited to see him, and he us, by the big smile on his face as he ran our way. He looked even taller and stronger since I had last seen him weeks before, but that couldn't be the case; he was already a grown man.

We talked for a long time, Mr. Robinson telling us how he learned to surf on this same beach as a young man and that he eventually stopped because his injured knee gave him issues sometimes. He offered to show us how to surf and ran into the water, pushing his board over the breakers, and then climbed up on it and paddled his way out to the deeper water, well past the depth I ever went even in the summertime.

We three sat in the wet of the sand so we could be close to the surf when he'd ride in, and he would take a few minutes to talk between his rides. The waves were not that big, but we got to see Mr. Robinson stand up a few times and wave his arms in the air, making generally silly motions like an orangutan, which caused us all to laugh with him.

When he was sufficiently cold and tired, he came on shore, sat on the surfboard right on the sand, and we continued talking about the sport of surfing some more. Then the subject changed a bit.

"Do you plan to teach your two girls to surf when they're older?" Mr. Baldwin asked him.

I added excitedly, "I've heard that girls are starting to surf in Hawaii all the time now."

"No way. Their mother thinks of them as china dolls. I wish I had a son I could teach all sorts of sports to, but I was blessed with two girls and we'll never have more," he replied with a forlorn look on his face. Then he continued, "Mary, err, Mrs. Robinson holds a strong belief that the girls need a good education and should become career women like her. She is a sort of doctor, you know."

"I didn't know that! Does she work at the clinic or a hospital someplace?" I asked.

"Oh no, not at all. When we lived in Washington and I was playing minor league ball, she had a practice in an office where people with…well…problems would come and talk with her about them. She's not a doctor in the way you think. She doesn't give out medicine or anything like that, but she is very smart and helps people who get sad or depressed and other things like that," he explained.

"Maybe my mother should see her," I said too quickly.

"Maybe, but she's not practicing with patients now; she's working on a book about how some families pass on the same problems from one generation to the next, such as sadness. I'm not allowed to look at her work though," he said.

"Really? And why is that, if I can ask?" questioned Mr. Baldwin.

"She just sees me as a dumb jock, I guess. Likes the money that came with the Robinson family name, but won't let me touch her now...I mean," he looked away toward his house, then finished, "her work, that is."

"Oh, I see what you're saying," was all Mr. Baldwin said.

The conversation seemed terse, or tense, and then Carlo started to play with the kite again, and Mr. Robinson stood, said he was going to run back to his house for a minute, and then left with his surfboard.

Mr. Baldwin and I walked over to where Carlo was struggling with the kite and helped him, this time getting the kite higher than before, and we all were watching it up in the sky over the dunes when we eventually heard Mr. Robinson's voice as he was approaching us with his two daughters each holding one of his hands. They all had an excited look on their faces.

He let their hands go free and they began to run in the sand toward Carlo and the kite. Without exchanging a word, Carlo showed them what he was doing then handed the stick with the string around it to one of the twins to hold onto. It must have been too strong of a pull for her little hand because she let go and the piece of driftwood and the balled string started bouncing along the sand as the kite pulled it away from us. Everyone ran toward it, Mr. Robinson being the first to reach it, and saved the kite from leaving us. We all laughed together. It was great fun.

Mr. Robinson introduced his daughters to us, and I noticed that they had his long legs and would eventually be tall women. One had a pensive look on her face, and the other was full of sparkle. With soft alabaster skin and the eyes of a tiger, almost golden with brown sparks, they must have had their mother's eyes, since they did not look like their father. They seemed socially awkward to me, but I did not socialize with kids of their age, so this may have been normal. They warmed up some as we all played with the kite, even if most of their attention and comments were directed at their father, tentatively ignoring the remaining three of us.

Time seemed lost as we were having so much fun. At some point we heard someone coming up the beach yelling, but no one could make out what she was saying. She looked angry and since she was coming from the direction of the Robinsons' beach house I assumed it was Mrs. Robinson, but her large, floppy hat gave no indication of her face. Quickly Mr. Baldwin turned to Carlo and me. "We need to get back to the cottage and start your assignments, Robbie. Let's get going, *now*."

Mr. Robinson waved good-bye as he and his daughters started to walk in the direction of the screaming woman while one of them, the one with that special sparkle, was looking back at the kite we were reeling in.

Not one of the three of us said a word about the kite, the surfing, the sweet and sour girls, or the angry woman as we walked back to the cottage. Each had his own set of thoughts. I was wondering why she didn't want her girls to play sports or even fly a kite with us, but I had no idea what either Carlo or Mr. Baldwin were considering.

Upon our return to the cottage, we resumed our positions in the main room of the cottage and began our tasks. I had trouble concentrating and thought about the few women I knew and how they all seemed to be unhappy people, from my mother to Mrs. Lingo at the market to Mrs. Robinson.

Outwardly they all appeared to have good lives, decent husbands and children, and yet none of these women smiled or sparkled like the young Robinson girl. Come to think of it, even old Mrs. Crutchfield never smiled, but I figured she had to be an authoritative figure when she had four classes a day with a couple dozen rowdy teenage boys in each. Would I find a woman to marry one day and then all of a sudden she become morose too? Was Mother so sad when Father met her, and if so, why did he marry her?

Chapter 21

That next day when I had to return to the witness stand I noticed that it looked as if Mr. Baldwin had aged ten years overnight. He sat behind a table with an attorney from somewhere up north called Magnolia, Delaware. His attorney did not look competent to argue with Mr. Horton, but I heard Mother tell someone on the telephone that no one in town would touch the case, so Father helped Mr. Baldwin, against her wishes, to find a lawyer that the art teacher could afford and trust, to save his life.

The attorney looked as though he had slept in his suit; it was all wrinkled and dirty looking. His tie was drab, and he looked defeated. Mr. Baldwin's clothing clearly did not represent his mood, as he was dressed in a blue seersucker suit that looked crisp on this hot summer day, a bow tie that I could only describe as between a dark pink and a purple and looked like something plucked out of Mother's flower bed. From the neck down he looked perky; ready for a late summer afternoon soiree under some big gazebo, but his face defied that appearance. His eyes and mouth looked as though he had lost this case already or knew he was doomed.

I smiled to him as I approached the step to the elevated witness chair, and he returned a sliver of a smile. Then I noticed Mother looking at me with her own brand of the look of disappointment. I took the seat and prepared myself to behave like a young man, more mature than my years, sitting in this chair, in this arena of so many adults with their attention focused on me and me alone. I could hear a pin drop.

After the formalities were completed, Mr. Horton stood and slowly walked in my direction, then turned with his back to me, facing the jury and the people in the courtroom. I noticed when the sun shone through the tall windows and struck his hair that he was losing it on the top and almost laughed, but realized I had to be responsible, even if my hands were shaking. I sat on them to get them to stop shaking, but even that did not work, not yet anyway.

After a long, pregnant pause for some sort of dramatic effect, Mr. Horton turned to me and began his litany of questions.

Horton: "So, young Mr. Elliott, is it true that you are in summer session at the Tidewater Academy as we speak?"

Me: "Well, not as we speak, I'm sitting here in the courtroom."

The roll of laughter must have started at the two legal tables and continued to the back of the courtroom as if it was a wave. Even people upstairs in the balcony hanging over the rear half of the courtroom were chuckling and looking at one another. I did not intend to be funny.

Horton: "Yes, well. Could you explain why you are attending summer session when you are *not* here in the courtroom, please?"

Me: "I missed the final couple of weeks from spring semester because of a death in my family, and I was sad. Mother and…I mean, my parents made this decision for me, and Dr. Prather agreed with them that it was best for me to remain away from the campus, even for the extra activities, the graduation of friends, etc."

Horton: "Do you know *specifically* why they recommended you stay away?"

Me: "Yes, sir. There were a few reasons, first, because I was sad over this...death, and second because there were rumors floating around the school that my parents did not want me hearing. Um, that's what I overheard my father telling my mother."

Horton: "So you are taking what is called a summer session along with other students who attended Tidewater Academy during the spring semester as well?"

Me: "Yes, sir, I am. I know everyone else in summer session."

Horton: "Since you are currently in classes with the same students that were in class during the weeks you missed, have you heard any of these so-called rumors?"

Me: "Um, yes."

Horton: "Please share with us some of these rumors, will you, young man?"

Me: "Okay. They were saying that Mr. Baldwin, the art teacher, and Mr. Robinson, the gym teacher, were, well, were boyfriends."

After much commotion in the courtroom and a moment of calming down, he continued. The judge had not attempted to stop the noise.

Horton: "Anything else, Mr. Elliott?"

Me: "Someone said that Mr. Baldwin killed Mrs. Robinson."

Horton: "Would this Mrs. Robinson be any relation to Mr. Robinson, the gym teacher you just spoke of?"

Me: "Yes, his wife."

Horton: "Did they say why he supposedly killed Mrs. Robinson?"

Me: "That Mr. Baldwin was mad at her about what had happened to Mr. Robinson...I think."

Horton: "Why is it that you think this is what was said, did you hear the rumor or not?"

Me: "No, sir, I mean, yes, I heard the rumor, but that isn't what happened at all."

Mr. Horton asked the judge to strike the comment and looked at me with rage in his eyes. The judge said, "The last statement by young Mr. Elliott will be stricken from the record. Go on, please, Prosecutor, move on now."

Horton: "Back to the rumors. Did you hear that Mr. Baldwin killed Mrs. Robinson at the Tidewater Academy or not?"

Me: "Yes, that's what I heard."

Horton: "Thank you. Now is it true that you were at the scene of the crime?"

Me: "Yes, I was right there, on the steps."

Horton: "Please explain to me what you saw and heard, starting precisely when Mr. Baldwin, who was also at the scene of this horrific crime, told you 'Get out of here, Robbie. Go now'?" He was reading notes off of a clipboard in his hands.

Me: "Ah, well, let me think. Mr. Baldwin told me to leave and to go home or to go to his cottage, and then I saw him go around the corner of the porch of the Robinsons' house, but I couldn't see him after that."

Horton: "Please continue. What happened next?"

Me: "Um, well, um, I heard, I heard a gunshot. A muffled shot like it was—"

But Mr. Horton interrupted me and said, "Thank you, that's enough of the story for the moment. Now let's move on. Where did you go after you heard this gunshot?"

Me: "I-I ran. I got into my car, and I guess I drove directly home."

Horton: "What you mean, 'you guess'?"

Me: "I don't recall exactly. I just remember being scared that I too was going to be shot and that I had to get away and get help for the others...To find someone who could, you know, to stop this mess."

Horton: "Where did you go to get help?"

Me: "Home."

Horton: "You didn't stop at the police station or the fire department on Rehoboth Avenue, but drove past them to go to your family's home on Annapolis Street, correct?"

Me: "Yes, sir. I mean, no, I didn't stop that I can remember...I went straight home."

Horton: "Yes, you must have been terrified, witnessing what you had. So please tell us what happened when you got home, starting with when you got out of your car."

Me: "It's kind of a blur. I remember my mother was in the garden alongside the driveway, back near the garage. She had a strange look on her face when I got out of the car. She screamed something and I remember hugging her, and then my father came out of nowhere and was standing over the two of us...and, well, I fell and think I passed out."

Horton: "Do you know why your mother was screaming at you when you got out of the car?"

Me: "I thought then that it was because of my driving, but later I learned she was scared when she saw my shirt was all bloodied. She thought I was hurt."

Horton: "And were you hurt?"

Me: "No, it was their blood, not mine."

Horton, directing his statement to no one in particular, but to all in the courtroom: "That is all for this witness."

Then there was some commotion and noise in the courtroom, and people began talking amongst themselves until the judge turned to me but directed the announcement to the entire courtroom: "And now the attorney for the defense will come over and ask you some questions, and after that this will all be over for you. Do you need a few minutes to go to the bathroom or get a cold glass of water, young man?"

"No, sir, I'm fine. Thank you for asking though," I replied.

Then the attorney for Mr. Baldwin came up and introduced himself to me and seemed to be embarrassed or even shy. He didn't look me in the eye when he spoke to me. Father always said you cannot trust a man who does not look you in the eye or offer a firm handshake. This only added to my worries for Mr. Baldwin.

"Mr. Elliott, I am Mr. Benson. I am the lawyer representing Mr. Baldwin in this murder trial, and I would like to ask you a few questions. Will that be alright?"

I thought *Alright? Why am I even sitting here with half of Sussex County watching me when I should be in school? Dufus.* But instead I replied, "Yes, sir, I understand. You may call me Robbie like everyone else does." This caused another chuckle in the courtroom.

Benson: "Very well then, Robbie. Yesterday you were explaining to us how Mr. Baldwin was tutoring your relative Carlo to speak and write in English, and that you were there during most of the lessons. Now, can you tell us if Mr. Baldwin ever raised his voice at either of you boys during the many months you were with him?"

Me: "No, never. I mean, Mr. Baldwin never yelled at either one of us."

Benson: "Did you ever see Mr. Baldwin mad?"

Me: "No."

Benson: "Lose his temper?"

Me: "No, sir, never."

Benson: "Yesterday you also spoke of a time when you saw Mr. Baldwin and Mr. Robinson walking arm in arm in town, is that right?"

Me: "Yes." Thinking, *Finally I get to explain this to everyone so it doesn't come out wrong again like yesterday.*

Benson: "Okay, so do you recall ever seeing Mr. Robinson walking arm in arm with anyone else?"

Me: "No, sir."

Benson: "Mr. Baldwin walk arm in arm with anyone else?"

Me: "No, sir." My irritation with his inability to ask the right questions was showing, I think.

Benson: "When at school, did you ever have the opportunity to see other teachers speak harshly to Mr. Baldwin or to Mr. Robinson?"

Me: "Well, yes. Mrs. Crutchfield seemed to dislike Mr. Baldwin."

Benson: "And did you ever see this Mrs. Crutchfield say anything harsh to Mr. Robinson, specifically?"

Me: "Not to him directly, but I heard her saying bad things about him to my father's secretary one time while I was waiting to see him. I think they forgot I was there while they were talking."

Benson: "Can you please tell me what Mrs. Crutchfield said about Mr. Robinson?"

Me: "She said that she always disliked his kind, the two-faced type. Something about being different at work than at home and thinking he could pull the wool over everyone's eyes."

Benson: "That doesn't sound very harsh. Was there more?"

Me: "Sort of…Miss Scott then told Mrs. Crutchfield that until the sissy art teacher came along she was the apple of his eye, and Mrs. Crutchfield said 'I would kill him if he ever laid a hand on a pristine young lady like you, God save me!'"

Benson: "And who is this Miss Scott?"

Me: "Oh, she's my father's secretary. I suppose she's the secretary for all of the teachers, but I think of her as Father's. I can't go into his office without her permission."

Benson: "Back to Mrs. Crutchfield. Did you see her face or look at her when she made this statement about Mr. Robinson and Miss Scott?"

Me: "I did look, but she didn't notice me. She looked very angry and had a funny face," as I squeezed my face up, "sort of like this." The crowd laughed at me again. I wasn't trying to be funny. This was important.

Mr. Benson then told the judge that he was finished with me. I wanted to scream out *I was there! I saw what happened! Ask me about who did what, dammit!*

Then as I was leaving the box, I heard Mr. Horton announce, "I would like to call Mr. Elliott as my next witness, James Elliott, the headmaster of Tidewater Academy."

Mother met me in the center aisle and pushed me out into the hallway as my father was coming in the door, and he winked at me. She whispered in my ear, "You did a fine job, Robert, now head on back to school, alright?"

"Yes, ma'am," was all I said. I wanted to say that she should have yelled objection like Perry Mason would have and helped Mr. Baldwin. That she should have told them who really did all of this. That none of this was fair. These people didn't know anything. But instead I said nothing and went on my way.

When I got outside, I sat on the courthouse stairs and looked at the seagulls flying all around. I looked up and down Rehoboth Avenue, seeing people walking along in their swim trunks with canvas rafts under their arms and a lady pushing a baby stroller, even a person driving by in one of the snazzy cars from Mr. Hazard's car lot. One lady walked by with mile-high yellow hair that looked like a cotton candy coif for the seagulls to eat, snapping her gum and making an annoying clicking sound with the straw sandals she wore on her feet, apparently happy she was away from home and here in perfect Rehoboth Beach for her family vacation…

How could life just go on like this? Didn't these people know that a man was fighting for his life inside this building and had a fool for a lawyer or that he was going to rot for who he was and not for something he did? Where was the justice in this town?

Chapter 22

I decided not to go back to school, but rather returned to this building of inequity and quietly snuck my way up the stairs to the gallery area. It seemed odd to me that they would call such an area a gallery, since there was no art here. I wondered what Mr. Baldwin would describe this space as if he were up here with me, instead of sitting all the way down there behind a table alongside a lawyer who looked as if he had already lost the case.

The townspeople that were sitting up here in the gallery all turned when they heard my footfall and the closing of the old, creaking door that separated the steep stairwell and the viewing stand. As if I was some sort of local celebrity, the owner of the gas station and another man made room for me to sit in between them down front along the railing. First I looked down into the congregation of people collected on the main level of the courtroom and located my mother's perfect head of hair and determined that she would not be able to see me if I stayed away from the railing and sat back.

As I was settling in, the smell of the gasoline and oil on the man's clothing next to me combined with the experience of having just testified was making my stomach rumble and roll. I was determined, however, to make certain that I stayed up here and heard every story told in court this day. No leaving to go back down those steep, narrow stairs to the restroom. I'd have to just sit there and deal with the stench.

Below on the witness stand sat my own father, and for once I could tell he was in a position of discomfort, as I had been when I first sat there with Mr. Horton standing over me. I didn't recall ever seeing my father look uncomfortable like this before. He was always the headmaster, the father at the end of the dinner table, the driver of the Elliott family car, the leader of the pack. I can't say that I enjoyed watching him in this state, but I was pleased that he was experiencing the same feeling I had just experienced under the tutelage of the judge and prosecutor, with hundreds of eyes focused on him.

By the time I was settled into the bench and had verified that Mother could not see me, Mr. Horton had already asked Father some of the initial and mundane questions similar to those he had asked me. I figured it was his duty to act like some sort of a parrot in a cage and repeat the same lines over and over at the beginning of questioning each so-called witness as some way of warming them up for the more difficult prodding he would hit them with. The term "witness" did not sit well with me, as I was the only witness to these crimes other than Mr. Baldwin, yet they used the term for each person who took that elevated seat and treated them as if they were a bystander to the murders. But there would come to be many terms used in the court system that I failed to comprehend—or justify—as my life went on.

Horton: "Could you explain to me the process of hiring the defendant to be the formidable first art instructor at your prestigious academy, if you would please, Headmaster Elliott?"

Father: "Well, yes, I can. We had decided in the fall of 1965 that the curriculum at Tidewater Academy was lacking in the arts department, so after meeting with the parents of the pupils and with the board, we determined that we would make an exhaustive recruiting plan to locate the most ideal teacher for the arts and art history program. We were building a new section onto the building for the sciences and had the former labs to fill, and we placed advertisements in many of the major metropolitan newspapers to acquire the best candidate."

Horton: "And how did you come about determining that Mr. Baldwin was the ideal candidate for this all boys' school?"

Father squirmed in his seat and then appeared relieved that he could get some of the blame for hiring Mr. Baldwin squarely off his shoulders as he replied, "We had begun the interviewing process and had acquired a highly qualified teacher from outside of Baltimore. She studied at the Maryland Institute of Art and had taught in the inner city of Baltimore for three years so far. She seemed the most likely candidate based on her criteria."

Mr. Horton looked irritated and turned toward the judge and then back to my father before bellowing, "That does not explain how you came to think of Mr. Baldwin as the most ideal candidate for this all boys' school, now does it?"

Father: "No, well I guess it does not."

Horton: "Then I repeat the question, Mr. Elliott."

Father: "Well, this candidate, the woman from Baltimore, had not informed me during the interview process that she had been trying to get pregnant. She learned several weeks after she accepted the job that she would have a child, and held off sharing this information with us—the academy, that is—until very late in the summer. She declined the job at the end of the summer. So I had to begin the process all over again and by that point all of the local qualified instructors that applied had been hired elsewhere. I placed calls to some colleagues of mine and learned of Mr. Baldwin through one of these inquiries. We spoke on the phone, we never met. He seemed most appropriate at the time, and did not...Well; let's just say he spoke well on the telephone. He was firm in his opinion of himself, confident in his abilities, and I was in need of an instructor as the school term was to begin in mere days. I hired him on the phone and made arrangements with Mr. Robinson for lodging at the cottage and a train and subsequent bus ticket so he could be in Rehoboth Beach in time to settle in and be on campus the day school began."

Horton: "And what was your first impression of this Mr. Baldwin when you met him?"

Father: "Young. I met him as he exited the Washington-Baltimore bus out by Epworth's bus stop. He was well dressed, well spoken, and seemed to take a shining to my son immediately."

Horton: "You exposed your son to this...this, *this man* at your first opportunity to meet him? Good heavens why?"

For the first time in my life I saw my father shudder and appear weak and small compared to the other men around him. He actually looked frightened. It took a moment before he replied, "Well, Robert was going to have to meet him at home when I returned from picking up Mr. Baldwin at the bus stop, as Mrs. Elliott and I had invited him for supper, and Robert was able to help with his luggage. I saw no harm in bringing my son along to meet Mr. Baldwin."

Horton: "I see, so you considered this hiring a feat complete and had no misgivings about hiring this man after first impressions?"

Father: "Not that I recall, no."

Horton: "Is it true that you had said to one of the instructors at your school, I mean academy, a Mrs. Crutchfield, that you thought this teacher was 'a bit too light in the loafers to be teaching a bunch of hormonal young men'?"

The entire place seemed to be abuzz with murmuring like a field of bees over clover for a few moments before the judge spoke up, "Okay, let's give the headmaster an opportunity to answer this question, people. Quiet, please."

Father: "I may have said something to that effect, but not then, when he arrived, rather later, at another time."

Horton: "So this leads me to the thought that you must have regretted the hiring of this man, this effeminate..." he looked to the judge as if for approval to use such language in his courtroom, "...teacher from the moment you laid eyes on him at the bus stop. Is this true, Mr. Elliott?"

Father: "Not immediately, no. I realize there are people who are worldlier; more cultured than many of us locals here in lower Delaware. But after all, Mr. Baldwin had been raised and educated in schools all over Europe. He came from New York City."

Horton: "Again, you are avoiding my question. I asked about his being, as you put it, light in his loafers. Not everyone from New York City is light in their loafers, now are they, Mr. Elliott? Please explain you're reasoning further then."

Again there was a lot of giggling and murmuring in the courtroom, but Father pressed on, "Okay, so I regretted hiring the man, but not until after I had seen him hanging around Mr. Robinson so much, taking walks on our small campus, riding in Mr. Robinson's car with him alone, and the rumors in the teacher's lounge…"

Horton jumped on this statement, and while not really interrupting my father, since he had paused for some dramatic effect, he lunged on the unfinished statement all the same. "So tell us about these so-called rumors that were circling around and around the teacher's lounge, will you, sir?"

Father: "Several stories were circulating about sightings some of the teachers had of these two men together, alone. One a married man with children and the other…not right for this town."

Horton: "Mr. Elliott, please. We need to hear these stories. Please continue."

At this point, I was ready to jump over the damn railing and go throttle the idiot lawyer representing Mr. Baldwin. He should have been on his feet requesting objections like any good TV lawyer. In my movement on the front bench of the gallery above, Father must have seen me, since he paused and looked in my direction for a few moments before he replied. "You hear stories of teachers having affairs and the like all the time in these lounge environments. I don't know if these sightings were anything more than two guys spending time—"

This time Horton did interrupt Father and treat him with some hostility. "You mean to tell me that when you hear of such goings-on between two of your instructors, whether it be the acceptable man and woman relationship or this bizarre man on man relationship, you do not investigate and clarify the relationship, Headmaster Elliott? What kinda school you running over there on Annapolis Street?" Then after what could be misconstrued as a bow to the crowd, he continued in just as loud a voice as before, "I have no further questions for this here witness, Your Honor."

Father sat there looking defeated. The judge spoke softly to him before he turned to Mr. Baldwin's attorney who looked as if he was just awoken by Mr. Horton's volume. "Do you wish to question this witness, Counselor?"

Finally Mr. Benson stood. "No, Your Honor, I have no questions for this witness at this time. Thank you."

I was never more embarrassed by my father than at that very moment. He could have, he should have, stood up for Mr. Baldwin, who was a fine gentleman and treated Carlo and me like gentlemen as well. If I could have, I would have run down the stairs and said something to my father like "you coward" or the like, but I could not move from my seat on that hot bench.

Then the judge said to the court, "We will take a short recess for ten minutes. Mr. Horton, who will be your next witness? Let's have them ready to finish this morning off before we break for lunch."

I was considering how I could get out of here unseen by the other Elliotts in the building when I changed my mind after hearing Prosecutor Horton announce, "My next witness will be Mrs. Crutchfield. She is here and eager to testify on behalf of the great state of Delaware, Your Honor!"

This I had to see, or hear, rather. What valid information could she contribute to this entire charade?

Chapter 23

It was a beautiful Saturday in spring, and we had permission from my parents to stay for a much longer session with Mr. Baldwin this day. Carlo was so excited because he knew that his lesson was to read the first chapter of a book Mr. Baldwin had given to him the previous Saturday and that on this particular day Carlo was going to read it out loud completely in English to Mr. Baldwin and me, as a test to see how well he could do. I too was excited, both for Carlo and for me since this was an opportunity to be with my favorite people for many hours and feel the freedom to do whatever I wanted, since I had completed all of my homework for Monday's classes yesterday.

Mother really wanted me to return home and work in her garden with her, but I was able to convey the importance of Carlo's assignment and that I was to be included in it. She gave me permission more easily than I had anticipated, and Father went along with this idea wholeheartedly.

Carlo and I had decided that we would treat ourselves to the large submarine sandwiches that Affonco's Pizzeria prepared and sold, and that we would bring two extra subs along for Mr. Baldwin and even Mr. Robinson, in case he showed up. It was decided that Carlo was to place the order only speaking English.

When we got to the pizza shop, he read the menu board and immediately asked for four Italian subs. The guy behind the counter at Affonco's happened to be one of my beach volleyball buddies, and he attended Cape Henlopen School. His name was Brent. He asked me, "Does your friend know what all goes in an Italian sub?" and I laughed, saying, "He ought to, he is from Italy!"

Just then Mr. Affonco himself stepped up to Carlo and spoke with him for a few minutes, but I could not hear what they were saying from where I was standing. Since Carlo had started his tutoring, he had quit the few hours he worked in the stockroom of the restaurant. I assumed Mr. Affonco was simply wishing him well.

When the subs were done and all wrapped up, I took them, thanked my friend, and headed to the check-out counter, where Mr. Affonco's sister was working the register. She was never one to smile much, but I had never heard her yell or raise her voice before this moment when she yelled across the shop to the deli counter, "Brent, what in the world are you doing making submarines with my long baguette bread? You should be making them with the submarine rolls!"

"Sorry, Miss A, I didn't realize, I just grabbed those. I won't do it again, promise," was how Brent replied, yelling back across the little pizzeria. I looked to the younger Miss Affonco, the owner's niece, stocking Italian spices on a shelf nearby as she smiled at me and rolled her eyes.

As she was putting the four oversized subs into a bag, the grumpy Miss Affonco mumbled to me, "All that boy-a thinks about is volleyball and girls. He ain't gonna get nowhere in life if that's all he thinks about, you understand me, Robert?"

"Yes, Miss A, and thank you. I know we'll enjoy these subs," was all I could reply and get out of the shop quickly enough before I starting laughing and running to the VW parked around the corner. Carlo ran alongside, laughing as well, as if he understood all that was just said.

In the bus I turned to Carlo and asked about the conversation with Mr. Affonco. He either did not understand me or did not want to talk about it based on his mute reaction, so I did not push the subject but rather turned up the radio and began our trek to Robinson Cottage.

It was only eleven in the morning, but I could tell by the sky and the temperature that we were going to experience one of those rare warmer-than-usual days in the mid-Atlantic area and hoped we could do something outdoors.

When we pulled up to the cottage, Mr. Robinson was just heading out, and I pulled up window to window with his car and said, "Hey, Mr. Robinson, are we gonna see you at all today?" to which he replied with a big smile on his face, "Yep. I'm going to get some supplies and I'll be back in a few hours."

"We stopped at Affonco's and got a sub for you too, so don't eat anything. Just wait until you see the size of these things!" I said. Sitting beside me, Carlo was all smiles.

"Okay then. Let me do my chores for Mrs. Robinson, get the supplies I need, and I'll be back to meet you in time to eat. See ya," he said before pulling away, and a cloud of oyster shell dust blew up toward my window like the wake of a big fishing boat when he increased his speed.

We got out of the VW, and Carlo carried the brown sack of submarines onto the porch as I stood outside. Over the many months of tutoring Carlo, Mr. Baldwin had made us both feel as if this was our home as well. Carlo must have clearly felt comfortable, since he took the food inside without asking or knocking on the frame of the open door.

Down toward the pier Mr. Baldwin was standing behind my favorite chair where he had set up two art easels side by side. On each was a canvas similar in size to the other with a table in between and a bunch of tubes of paint and what looked like an old rusted coffee can with brushes sticking out of it. Carlo must have realized that no one was inside, because he joined me with his book in hand as I watched Mr. Baldwin's silent movements.

"I have decided that today is going to be very special for all of us. Carlo will complete his assignment, and I have an artist's challenge for you, Robbie. Then afterwards Mr. Robinson will come over with his two canoes and we'll go explore the lake some. This weather is amazing, and we shouldn't waste the day inside, don't you agree?" Mr. Baldwin explained as we covered the small lawn of pine needles and reached him standing with the easels by the pier. We both nodded at the same time, leading me to believe that Carlo understood more than I thought.

"Robbie, you and I are going to paint the exact same scene, which we can both see easily from this location, with just a little bit of a different angle, or perspective, as it is described. Will you accept the challenge?"

"Hey, I'm up for anything!" I enthusiastically replied.

"Well then, you may want to go ahead and grab one of these pencils and begin your drawing, and then we'll work with the shared tubes of paint and each work on our different perspectives of the view. When we're done, we'll then show them, but we can't look at the other artist's work until the end," he explained.

"Sounds like fun."

"The view of the end of the pier and the lake will be our subject," he shared.

While I studied the view I was to draw and paint from this location, Mr. Baldwin spoke in rapid Italian to Carlo, and they shared a laugh. I was hoping that it was not at my expense.

It was at that very moment that I decided that I would take lessons in Italian from Mr. Baldwin, once Carlo was sufficiently educated, and that one day when Carlo and I traveled together we would share the two languages.

I had never painted in front of anyone like this before. I picked up a pencil and began to draw the pier that jutted out into Silver Lake. I decided that I especially wanted to capture the round gazebo at the end of the pier as I expected it once looked in better days. Now the cedar roof looked like the smile of a jack-o-lantern, missing shingles like teeth. The support posts were in good shape, but the weathering from the sea air had removed the layer of stark white paint that once graced them. I decided I was going to bring back the glory of what I could see with my artist's eye.

Carlo began to read out loud, in English, the first words of his book. He spoke very proudly with a beautiful Italian accent. The book they had selected was a classic, one I had to read in my literature class just last year, *The Catcher in the Rye* by J.D. Salinger.

"If you really want to hear about it, the first thing you'll probably want to know is where I was born, and what my lousy childhood was like, and how my parents were occupied and all before they had me,

and all of that David Copperfield kind of crap, but I don't feel like going into it, if you want to know the truth," Carlo read slowly, yet perfectly.

Both Mr. Baldwin and I clapped and beamed with pride at Carlo's ability to read English out loud without pausing too many times.

Just then there was a loud splash from the shallow end of the pier, and out of the corner of my eye I saw a massive fish thrashing about. We all looked at it in amazement, even ran over to the edge of the lake to get a better look.

"Guys, do you know what that is?" Mr. Baldwin said in an excited voice.

"Fish," said Carlo. "Big fish."

"Not just that, and you are absolutely correct, Carlo, but it's the one that Mr. Robinson has been trying to catch for a long time. He told me this story one day when we were running along the surf. This fish is a carp, the same as a small goldfish, and it was once the size of a child's finger, but now it's about two feet long and has never been caught since Mr. Robinson first tried to capture it. We have to tell him about it!" exclaimed Mr. Baldwin with great enthusiasm.

"He said he was coming back, but the fish may be gone soon. The fish looks like it's feeding on something out there now. Should we go fetch Mr. Robinson?" I asked.

"Yes, go. He'll be so disappointed if we don't help him. I better stay here; Mrs. Robinson is not very fond of me for some strange reason," Mr. Baldwin said to us as we turned to run, but then Carlo's right foot got caught in the leg of the easel Mr. Baldwin was painting on and when the canvas fell, it landed on his arm and stomach, leaving a large marking of splattered paint.

"Oh, gee whiz, we have to clean that up, quick, before my mother sees it!" I stated while rubbing a cloth on his shirt and smearing the paint even worse.

"Here, take my shirt, Carlo, put it on, and I'll have yours clean by the time you return with Mr. Robinson, okay?" Mr. Baldwin said as he pulled his shirt over his head and tossed it to Carlo.

Carlo pulled his shirt off and put Mr. Baldwin's shirt on and we all began to laugh. Mr. Baldwin and Carlo were very similar in size, build, and such, and Carlo looked exactly like Mr. Baldwin in his shirt. With little time to waste, Mr. Baldwin said "Go, *abrigati*, hurry!"

We took off, with Carlo a much faster runner than I, several feet ahead of me already and kicking up that oyster shell dust in my face. I was thinking about how he would try to explain the fish situation to Mr. Robinson if he reached him before I got there and smiled to myself thinking of this as I now trotted well behind him. By the time I had come close enough to the Robinsons' big house to see him Carlo was taking the steep front steps two or three at a time, like it was a race to the top.

I saw him knock on the door to the house and then turn to look back toward Silver Lake. He must have realized what a special view the Robinsons had of the lake from this big house with its wrap-around covered porches and rocking chairs. I thought about how Carlo probably never saw a house like this one back home and was probably impressed by its size and stature.

Just as I reached the area where the two cars were parked under the big pilings that held up the house, I heard an awful loud bang sound, which seemed to echo several times over the lake water. What was that?

As I reached the bottom of those tall steps, I looked up and saw Carlo lying on his side with what looked like red paint all over the front of the borrowed shirt he was wearing. This didn't seem right; he never got near the easel again after putting Mr. Baldwin's shirt on. The red tube of paint had remained unopened on the table back at the cottage.

I stood on the second to the bottom step of the staircase, staring at him when I noticed Mrs. Robinson stepping back into the doorway deep on the porch, and then Mr. Robinson came from the south side of the big porch and he screamed, "What have you done?" as he bent down and picked up Carlo to his chest. "This is just a child!" he screamed as if he himself was in pain. "Don't you see that you need help? You're crazy, woman!" he screamed in the direction of the door, which I noticed was slowly closing as I climbed the stairs.

"Wh-what just happened? We were coming to get you and Carlo was faster than me, and I heard this bang and...Oh my God. Look at Carlo; he has blood coming out of his mouth! Mr. Robinson, do something, he must be hurt! He must be hurt! He must be..." I was saying but was interrupted by the Robinsons' daughter standing over her father and Carlo shrieking very loudly. It was an ear-splitting sound.

When I made it to the top of the steps, which I don't even remember climbing but do remember feeling as if I was moving much too slowly, Mr. Robinson told me to remove my shirt and to help him put pressure on Carlo's stomach with the shirt and my hands. "We have to stop this bleeding, Rob! Quick, I need your shirt!" he yelled to me.

I struggled to take it off, moving in slow motion again, and as I was pushing the shirt into the big blood stain I saw so much blood that it was coming up through my fingers and there was a gurgling sound. The step below Carlo had a thick puddle of blood, and in it I could actually see the reflection of the clouds in the sky above. This did not seem right. I blinked and looked again, the liquid spreading out slowly toward the edge of that step to the one below it, the reflection of the clouds growing larger.

Mr. Robinson was pushing my hands down hard, and he told his daughter to go take care of her sister, to get away.

Suddenly the door opened and Mrs. Robinson was there with a small, lethal handgun gun in her hand just hanging from her side. Her hair was disheveled and she looked like some character out of an old horror film standing there over all of us. I looked up into her eyes and saw that golden color she shared with her daughters—and yet there was something more, something sinister about those eyes. A sight I doubt I will ever forget in my life.

"You did this! You brought this nightmare to our family. You!" she yelled in the direction of the three of us, from what I could tell. I looked down at Carlo's face for the first time and realized that his eyes were completely still, that they had this strange look to them, opaque in color with a stare far away over my shoulder, perhaps toward the actual clouds in the sky above.

"Making the girls and me leave the city, making us come to this God-forsaken hellhole so you could be big man on campus all over again! You couldn't even keep your pants on, could you? You are the one who is sick! I had patients like you, deviants and perverts. Now you bring this to *my* doorstep? You're never going to tarnish the lives of the girls, *never!*" She was ranting and I had no idea what she was talking about, but I was petrified because of that look in her eyes. My hands shook as I tried to apply the needed pressure.

"Mary, you don't even know what you're talking about! This is a child here, and you've killed him! Why? Why?" Mr. Robinson was sobbing now. I was absolutely shocked to hear him say "killed." I guess I thought Carlo was in deep pain and just being quiet. Was he really dead?

Mr. Robinson laid Carlo back down, his head on the second step, his legs up on the porch, that faraway look still there but now staring away from me. I reached down and pulled Carlo into my arms and held his head against my chest. I was mumbling something I still can't recall when it happened again, only this time it was much, much louder. I felt Mr. Robinson land against me, pushing Carlo and me down another two steps.

"What are you doing?" I screamed, but I couldn't hear my own voice. I realized that the door had closed yet again and I was lying under the heavy weight of Mr. Robinson, smelling the gunpowder burn my nose and unable to hear a thing.

I felt the shaking of the steps below me, and turned to look, seeing the bewildered expression on Mr. Baldwin's face as he climbed the stairs and was saying something to me that I couldn't hear or understand as he was forming the words. His lips were moving, but I couldn't hear anything. Was I dead too?

"Robbie. Are you okay? Look at me, Robbie," he said up close to my face, and I could begin to make out what he was saying. He slapped my face, and I looked at him with wonder in my eyes. "Here, let me get you from under them. Oh, you're covered in blood too. Stand up, Rob, stand up! I need to make sure you aren't hit too," he was saying, and I followed his command. I caught my balance against the stair railing and climbed up to the porch, not thinking about Mrs. Robinson nearby somewhere with a gun. That crazy woman had a gun!

"M-M-Mr. Baldwin," I was stuttering. "She has a gun. She shot Carlo and Mr. Robinson. I don't think she shot me," I said.

"Get out of here, Robbie. This is insane and we can't have her hurting you too. I'll be right behind you," he whispered as he pushed me back toward the stairs. "Go, now, quietly, but as fast as you can."

I made it to the bottom of the steps and then I turned back. Mr. Baldwin had just put his hand over the eyes of Mr. Robinson and whispered something I couldn't hear at all. When he moved his hand, I could see that Mr. Robinson's eyelids were closed and realized that he too was dead. My ears were ringing still, and I had trouble standing up. I thought I was going to bend over and throw up, but I refused to let that happen.

I stood there and watched as Mr. Baldwin looked over Carlo then got up and charged to the door. He banged on it with the bloody palms of both his hands but it must have been locked, because he couldn't get it to open. Suddenly he turned and ran the length of the porch and around the corner and disappeared.

I was struggling to understand...understand what had just happened, and why would she hurt Carlo, of all people? I was thinking how I could not leave Carlo here, not like this, not with that crazy woman still here with a gun.

Just then I heard another gunshot, not as loud as before, more of a muffled sound. Perhaps it was a car backfiring, but there were no cars near here except the ones sitting silently idle beneath this house, beside where I was standing.

I turned and ran toward the cottage. If she has shot Mr. Baldwin as well, I knew that she would have no mercy for me. I ran as fast as I could and got to the VW in a matter of minutes, out of breath and uncertain of what to do. There was no phone service at the cottage. I would have to drive the two miles north to town if I wanted to get help. What should I do now? I had left Carlo back on those steps, his head hanging down, blood on his chin and all over his shirt. *Mr. Baldwin's shirt!*

Chapter 24

Mother was in the side yard when I pulled into our driveway and ran over a rake she had left in the way. She was trying to get up, stabilizing herself as she made the effort. I jumped out of the VW, not sure if I put it in gear or even turned off the engine. Mother saw me, and I must have looked a fright. I could see it in her face, she was confused.

"Robert?" she screamed to me.

"Mother, I need help. Carlo, Carlo. You have to help me," was all I could say.

It took quite some time for Mother to calm me down, and then Father was pulling into the driveway from a golf outing with benefactors of the academy.

I somehow was able to convey to her what I had seen. When Father was standing over us, crouched together, I realized my mother had collapsed when I told her of Carlo. She was wailing and slapping my chest.

"What is going on, for heaven's sake, Robert? You have blood on your hands and you have no shirt! Where are you cut?" was all Father got out before I collapsed on the ground.

❖ ❖ ❖

When I woke in bed, immediately I realized that I felt funny. I felt as if my head was in a fog. Just then old Dr. Prather appeared at the foot of my bed and said, "Now, now, Robert. It's good you've had some rest. Your parents will be pleased to know you're awake." He handed me a glass of water. I took it and saw the red outline of my fingernails, as if I had dipped them in red paint and wiped it off but not all of it came away with the cloth.

"I don't feel right. Where are my mother and father?" I asked in a strained voice, as if I had laryngitis or a sore throat.

"They're downstairs, Robert. You just need some more rest. They're speaking with some officials, but I won't allow them to talk with you until I'm certain you're up to snuff. Do you remember what happened to you?" he asked, very calmly and very softly.

After a few moments, another sip of water, and a quick look at my hands, I replied "Oh no, it was real. Is Carlo alright, Dr. Prather? Did you get to him?"

He simply shook his head then told me that I had had a shot and would feel sleepy for some time. As if he willed me to fall back to the pillow and go to sleep, I quickly returned to a deep slumber.

Chapter 25

The ten-minute recess seemed much longer, and as all the adults began to take their seats around me and below in the courtroom proper, I could smell the distinct odor of the many cigarettes smoked during the recess. I could feel my stomach clench yet again; it felt as if all the fresh air of the room had just been swallowed up and replaced with this foul smell. I looked around and noticed some familiar faces, yet was pleased that none were my parents' friends. I also realized that the man from the gas station did not return but was replaced by a large woman with body odor. I wasn't sure which I preferred to have sitting next to me, but I knew I had to remain out of the sight of my parents if I wanted to hear what Mrs. Crutchfield had to say. When I turned to look for an available seat in the gallery, none were left.

After everyone sat back down from the arrival of the judge—another foolish tradition in my opinion—His Honor called the court back into session, and Prosecutor Horton was up and beaming as if he had just won a quick game of poker during the break. "We would like to call Mrs. Edith Crutchfield to the stand."

While she was getting sworn in and settled, I took a quick look over the gallery railing to find my parents, whom I quickly located by my mother's outfit and hair. They were deep in some silent conversation that I hoped did not include his potential sighting of a familiar young man in the gallery. I sat back and waited impatiently to hear the testimony.

Horton: "Thank you for taking time away from your busy summer session teaching to be with us today, Mrs. Crutchfield."

She nodded and looked around as if she was on stage. She was glowing with pride to share stories that could ruin other lives. What a nasty woman.

Horton: "Now we will try to get to the bottom of this unfortunate situation that has tarnished the town, your work environment, and the families associated with Tidewater Academy. How long have you been teaching at the school?"

Crutchfield: "I've been there for six years."

Horton: "Did you know Mr. Robinson, the late gym teacher?"

Crutchfield: "Oh, yes. While I know he is no longer with us, I have to say he was a bit below the standard of the faculty at Tidewater. He could not keep his hands off many of the younger single ladies on the campus. Then he had this fling with Mr. Baldwin, and well, the reputation of the school is now forever affected."

Benson: "Objection, conjecture!"

Judge: "Overruled! Continue please."

As I looked down to see Father's face cradled in his hands, Mr. Horton proceeded to push her further, "And did you have any impression or opinion of the new art teacher, now defendant, Mr. Baldwin?"

Crutchfield: "Opinion? Why yes! I even went to the headmaster's home to convey my disappointment in the hiring of this man. I could just tell he was trouble from the first time he walked the hallways of the academy with his arms full of art books and his, well, I guess you would call it his sway."

Horton: "Sway?"

Crutchfield: "He walked with fervor, like a model on a runway. More like a lady than a man."

Horton: "I see. Well, aside from his well-documented and obvious effeminate mannerisms, did you get the opportunity to speak with him or overhear his conversations with students, Mrs. Crutchfield?"

Crutchfield: "My, yes…I walked in on him speaking in an intimate fashion with the headmaster's own son, talking about their get together at his home later that day. I stopped it right then and there and sent Robert on his way before I told him it was highly inappropriate that he interact with the pupils off campus, especially in his own home and after dark."

Before I could jump up and call her a liar, as that was clearly not the conversation she had overheard, the lady next to me squirmed in her seat and pulled out some chewing gum from her bag on the floor and offered me a piece. I accepted and thanked her at a barely audible level and returned my attention to the proceedings. I had apparently missed Mr. Horton's last question, as she was now answering him, fully animated.

"…There was one evening that Mr. Crutchfield and I went for a nice stroll down along Rehoboth Avenue after dinner, and we were almost knocked over by two loud and boisterous men hanging onto one another and coming up behind us. I was mortified, thinking it might be some of the hoodlums that hang out at Affonco's, and as my dear husband pulled me aside just in time, I recognized Mr. Baldwin and Mr. Robinson walking arm in arm, hanging on each other and saying what was probably sweet nothings in each other's ear."

Benson: "Objection your Honor, this is conjecture and she is making an opinion she is not qualified to make here."

Horton: "Not qualified? She is a most decorated instructor at this prestigious academy, Your Honor!"

Judge: "The juror will overlook the last comment made by Mrs. Crutchfield. Move on Mr. Horton."

Horton: "Sorry for that interruption Mrs. Crutchfield, now please continue."

Crutchfield: "For God's sake, it was a school night, and these two were out cavorting like sailors in a foreign harbor. I can only imagine what they had in mind for the balance of that evening, honestly. If my husband had not been such a gentleman and kept me walking, I would have followed them just to see what they were doing out and about together, drunk as skunks on top of a hen house."

Horton: "And was this the only occasion you saw these two men together outside of the school?"

Crutchfield: "Lord, no. They had no shame. I saw them together when they arrived at the Georgetown Prep game off campus. I was only there to support our team, of course, but they arrived looking all disheveled and mischievous. I can only imagine what they had been up to…After all, they arrived ten minutes after the game had begun, unlike the rest of us who were there on time."

Horton: "Thank you, Mrs. Crutchfield; I know this is very difficult for you. I only have a few more questions for you, and we'll be done. Are you managing well or would you like a glass of water?"

Crutchfield: "It is my duty to share what I know about this man. How he came into town and messed up everything for that perfectly charming woman and her two daughters, now left orphaned. I plan to see that justice is served here in Sussex County. After all, this is *not* New York City! We behave properly and have a set of decorum here. Thank you, but I do not require any refreshment at this moment."

I was amazed that Benson was doing nothing to stop this ranting. He just sat there writing on a pad of paper, not even looking up at the witness. He acted like a defeated man. Mr. Baldwin sat there looking directly at Mrs. Crutchfield, witnessing her criminalize his reputation. Even Horton was letting her run with her stories and not cutting her off as he had done to me several times.

Horton made another of his twists like a ballerina almost, now facing the jury. "Mrs. Crutchfield, do you have an opinion on the murder of Mrs. Robinson that you wish to share with the rest of us today?"

Crutchfield: "I most certainly do. I believe that poor Mrs. Robinson was simply beside herself once she learned of her husband's infidelity with this poisonous so-called art teacher, and she confronted them. Mr. Baldwin should be hung for killing the mother of those two precious girls. I believe he then turned the gun on Mr. Robinson out of lover's rage, as they write about in *Reader's Digest* or maybe just to keep him quiet. The foreigner, well, I don't know why kill him since I know he didn't speak English, but there may have been some level of jealousy there amongst these lovers or he had to remove all witnesses. We're just lucky that dear Robert Elliott made it away safely before he turned his anger and his weapon on him too.

Perhaps he figured he could keep his job here, blame it all on Dr. Robinson, and even blackmail Robert. It's all a disgrace to our pristine town."

Horton: "Well, thank you, Mrs. Crutchfield. We appreciate your putting yourself through this to help us see the truth. I have no more questions, Your Honor."

Crutchfield: "Just as I told you at your office, I know this man is a bad apple and that I wanted to come here because I know he should be hung, not just sent to prison. People like him are sick and should never be allowed to teach our impressionable young people. And the Bible states that a man should not lie down with—" The judge banged his gavel and she sat there frozen faced, staring at him as if he had the nerve to interrupt her speech.

"That is quite enough, Mrs. Crutchfield. You are not to speak again unless asked a specific question. You do understand me, correct?" said the judge; almost as if he was afraid he would be reprimanded if caught for not cutting her off. This was all a joke.

Mr. Benson rose and walked toward Mrs. Crutchfield and looked at the pad of notes in his hand. The judge looked over his glasses back and forth from Mr. Benson to Mrs. Crutchfield until he lost his patience and said, "Do you have any questions for Mrs. Crutchfield?"

Benson: "Oh, yes, Your Honor. I was just giving Mrs. Crutchfield a moment to get over her emotional testimony. She looked quite upset there." He turned to her as I secretly cheered him on and asked his first question: "Mrs. Crutchfield. You say you saw these two men together on two specific occasions hanging on one another and acting inappropriately. Did you see where they were coming from on either occasion or if they had been with other people?"

Crutchfield: "No."

Benson paused—for effect perhaps—but it made him look stupid. Clearly even I could see she did not want to answer any questions that might help Mr. Baldwin win his case. I felt certain he would have a zinger for her, as Perry Mason always did. Something to make the entire courtroom sit up and take notice. Something that would prove Mr. Baldwin's innocence.

Benson: "And did you ever see Mr. Robinson talking with other instructors at the academy in hushed tones, or in corners, in private, perhaps in the lunch room near the stairwell?"

Crutchfield: "I assume I've seen him over his short time there, talking to others, but nothing that would get my goat up, nothing I found suspicious as with that homosexual teacher over there!" She pointed her long red fingernail in Mr. Baldwin's direction but did not look toward him.

Great Scott! Benson was not helping his client or himself. I could do better on my own. Then he came back quickly with another question: "Did you in fact have a heated conversation with Mr. Robinson during a school lunch break, and did Mr. Baldwin step in and recommend that you two take it outside or into the hallway so the students could not hear it?"

Crutchfield: "Yeah, so...It was wrong of me, but I had to say something to him about this inappropriate behavior I witnessed on campus."

Benson: "And what did Mr. Robinson say to you in turn regarding your accusations?"

Crutchfield: "Nothing. He was a very polite man when he wanted to be. He obviously knew I was right and just accepted that fact. That's all."

Benson: "So it is not true then that he called you a…Let me get this off my notes correctly please…" Then he paused and looked at his pad before continuing, "A nosy old gossip monger who wears too much perfume?"

The courtroom was aghast that such a comment was read out loud, but all hung on to the opportunity to hear more juicy gossip from the witness. You could hear a pin drop.

Crutchfield: "Well, I suppose it was something like that, yes. But he was always polite otherwise."

Benson: "No further questions for this gossip monger, Your Honor."

It was hard to hear the judge yelling over the noise of the gavel as he slammed it hard on the block of wood, but I gathered he was admonishing the lawyer and telling the jury to disregard the last comment. He let Mrs. Crutchfield know she was done, and she huffed and stormed her way down the center aisle of the courtroom with clear rage in her face.

Chapter 26

It wasn't until recently that Dad shared with me what had been happening on the main level of our home while I was upstairs sleeping that day. Mother was apparently beside herself with the news of Carlo, and Dr. Prather had given her something similar to what he shot into my arm but much stronger. My father was sitting at the dining room table with the chief of police for Rehoboth Beach, Mr. Yasik, our local funeral home director and a close friend of my parents, and the pastor from Epworth Church. They were on their third pot of coffee and were exhausted, not even sure what to say or do at that point.

Four policemen had been to the property and found the grizzly mess. Two had gone next door to Mr. Baldwin after following blood stains in the oyster shell road, and they entered the cottage to find him sitting in a chair with the two Robinson girls in his house, all apparently in shock and unwilling to talk to them at all.

The policemen back at the Robinsons' home found Carlo and Mr. Robinson slumped together as if they were rag dolls that a child had tired of playing with and discarded on the steps. Then they went into the house and found Mrs. Robinson on the floor of her bedroom with a gunshot wound to her head and the handgun across the room on the floor. There was a bed pillow lying next to her head with blood all over it. They assumed someone had tried to put it under her head after she was shot or used it over her face to quicken her death.

The pastor and Mr. Yasik took care of all the arrangements for the funeral of Carlo and had decided that it would be best for the townspeople, and mostly Mother, that it be a closed casket service. Mr. Yasik had a friend in Philadelphia who sang in a church choir and sang in Latin as well. Perhaps he could locate him for the service. All of this was decided and dealt with by the men while Mother and I both slept off the drugs Dr. Prather had given us.

Again I woke up, still feeling groggy with a sore throat. I went to the bathroom and was getting some water from the faucet to drink when I saw my clothes on the floor in there, and I turned to the toilet, lifting the lid just in time to be sick. Afterwards I felt so bad, all I could do was lie there on the floor and press my flushed face against the cold floor tiles. I did not dare move, lift my head, or look behind me where the clothing lay in a messy pile caked in dried blood.

To look at the bloody clothes again meant this was all real, but if I just closed my eyes, this nightmare would be over soon and I would awake to Carlo standing over me, pointing his finger at me while laughing. Yes, a little more rest and all would be fine again.

I realized why my throat was so sore; I think I had been screaming for anyone who would hear me the entire ride from Silver Lake back to town. I was surprised that I had any voice left. After a long time there on the floor, I got up and sat on the edge of the bathtub, trying desperately to remember what had happened. Why hadn't Father woken me so I could tell the police what I witnessed? I supposed he thought I was too immature to handle this after fainting in my mother's arms earlier. Wait, what day was this anyway? How long had I been drugged to sleep?

I cleaned up as best I could and went downstairs. It was eerily quiet in the front room, and my parents' bedroom door was closed. I walked through the dining room and pushed the swing door to the kitchen open to find several ladies in there, packing sandwiches in cling wrap and all looking very busy. I recognized Mrs. Hartman from down the street. She appeared to be in charge of whatever was happening. She wasn't the first to see me, but she came to me immediately and told me I should be resting and to go back up to bed. She would bring me something to eat and drink in a few minutes.

I walked back through my house, looking for my father and mother. I tried their bedroom door, then thought better of that and let it be and went to the front porch to sit and catch some fresh air from the ocean breeze.

The newspaper was on the chair my father favored, and I picked it up. Today was Monday already, and I read the headline: **ACADEMY ART TEACHER ACCUSED OF MULTIPLE MURDERS!**

I threw it down and screamed, "No! He didn't do it. No!" But no one heard me, not even the ladies in our house, no one.

Chapter 27

I needed fresh air, not the kind I could get here on the front porch, but from the ocean. I needed to go to the beach and clear my head. I had to be able to go to the police and tell them what happened. Why would they even think Mr. Baldwin had done any of this to Carlo or Mr. Robinson?

I realized I was barefoot when the washed-up sand stung the bottom of my feet as I walked on the sidewalk toward the dunes, but I didn't care. I wanted to be able to get my head wrapped around what had happened two days ago, two days ago!

The sand on the dune was softer and cooler than on the sidewalk. I sank into the sand and kept walking over the dune with no specific place in mind to go, but somewhere that I knew would be a quiet place to think.

I walked and ended up at the bench by the old lighthouse. The life guards would not report for duty here until Memorial Day, weeks away, and I could sit here alone. I had to get this fog out of my brain, which felt like a stranger following me down the street late at night.

I don't know how long I sat there, but eventually I started to think a bit more clearly. The paper said Mr. Baldwin was accused. Then did that mean he was alive? Did he survive a gunshot while the others did not? If I could just go to him, together we could clear this entire thing up. Was he there when Carlo fell? Or was it later, when Mr. Robinson was slumped on my back that he arrived? What did he remember? If only we could talk, then it could all be fixed.

Not fixed like my mother would prefer, of course. She never liked Mr. Baldwin, in my opinion. She would have wanted Carlo alive and Mr. Baldwin the one lying upside down on those stairs, eyes to the sky, dead.

I should have read the article and not just the headline. I should have gotten the facts before I came here to the bench. But I could not return now, not yet. I needed to continue to remember and I needed to clear my head, right here, right now. But how could they even be facts? The headline was wrong, and the so-called facts of the article would have to be wrong too.

Down by the surf two guys were throwing a Frisbee back and forth. The one to the north looked like my buddy Matt, but his hair was too dark. If that was Matt, he could fill me in on everything that had happened! I got up from the bench and started to walk, then run through the soft sand until I got to where the guys were playing. It was Matt!

"Matt! Hey, what's going on?" I yelled as I got close enough for him to hear me. He looked at me and then threw the Frisbee to the other guy, someone else from the academy who I did not know very well.

"Matt. Did you hear me?"

"Yeah, where the hell have you been, in the loony bin?" he asked in a serious tone.

"What? No, I've been in my bed. Dr. Prather drugged me up, and I've been sleeping. I just came out to think and figure this whole incident out."

"Incident? It has fucking blown the roof off the academy! Some incident, Rob! You know as well as I do that you knew what was happening all along." They continued to throw the Frisbee north and south to one another as if we were not having a serious discussion.

"What are you talking about, Matt? Can you stop and talk to me? I don't know what has happened these past few days. Tell me."

"Man, you need to talk with your father. I can't be seen talking to you right now," he said as he turned to the other guy and said to him, "Let's go get a slice at Affonco's before anyone sees us here."

I stood there dumbfounded. This was the guy I considered my closest friend, well, besides Carlo. Then it dawned on me, Carlo was gone.

When I returned home the sun was setting and the air was colder than I thought it should be this time of year. I had decided to grab the newspaper and take it up to my room so I could read the article. I had to figure out what was going on here. I had to get it straight for everyone, but mostly for Carlo.

The newspaper was missing. I looked all over the porch, under the cushions of all the furniture, and then in the front room of the house, on the seats of all the dining room chairs tucked under the large table, even the kitchen, now clear of the dutiful neighbors and church ladies. Someone had taken it away.

My parents' bedroom door was still shut, but this time I was determined to get my mother's attention. I entered the room and found her sitting at her makeup table, looking at her reflection in the oval mirror, just staring.

"Mother," I said as I too looked at her image, but she did not flinch or acknowledge my presence or my voice.

As I turned to leave, I heard her whisper to the mirror, "We must talk. You have to tell me how you could allow this to happen to such an innocent. Our poor Carlo, he wasn't capable of understanding what you'd gotten him into."

I ignored her, acting as if I didn't hear her while I pulled her door closed behind me. I headed up the stairs to my room, but went into Carlo's room instead. I lay down on his bed, my old bed, and I could actually smell him. I turned on my side with my back to the open door and began to cry harder than I had ever in my life.

Chapter 28

Father was shaking me and saying something, but I thought it was just a dream. Finally he roused me enough that I knew this was not a dream. I had been sleeping. "Come downstairs and eat something. One of the ladies from down the street has delivered a dinner for us to eat, and we should eat now while it's hot. So come," he said in that head-masterly authoritative voice he always used at the academy.

He and I sat at the table in the kitchen with what looked like a casserole comprising noodles and sauce. He poured me a glass of lemonade and sat down directly across from me, not at the end of the table the way he does in the dining room. We rarely ever ate dinners in the kitchen, just sometimes a breakfast. I looked around and saw that all of the counters were stacked with paper plates and food of all sorts—casseroles, roasts, pies, cakes, and other stuff all sitting under tin wrappers or glistening under the light on the plastic wrap. Mother had a lot of Tupperware in an ugly green color, but the colors of these containers were several, none green. Where did all this food come from, and why all of this food for us?

Father cleared his throat and asked, "Robert, how are you feeling?"

"Fine, I guess. For a long time I felt weird, like I had a lingering murkiness in my brain. I don't want to feel like that again," I replied.

"Well, Dr. Prather thought you were in shock and wanted to take you to his clinic in Lewes, but I thought it better that you wake up in your own bed, so he gave you a shot here at home to calm you. You slept well, so it seems I was right to keep you at home."

"How is Mother?" I asked, although I had my own opinion already.

"She's taking all of this very hard. She's very worried about you, and she needs more time to rest. Eat up; I want you to come with me to see Mr. Yasik after we eat."

"Why do I need to see Mr. Yasik? Oh, God! I can't, I won't, and I could never look at Carlo again, not after that, Father. Never," I said.

"Come on, you and I need to go over there to make certain all is ready, because tomorrow the wake begins, and then the funeral will be on Wednesday. Your mother is too out of it to make any decisions, and you knew Carlo better than I, so I need your help," he pleaded.

"Okay, but I can't look at him, Father."

"None of us will. That was already decided. Eat up; you must be starved after so much sleep."

"Actually I'm not even hungry," I replied, resisting his orders.

Mr. Yasik made the decisions very easy for us, and Father had arranged for a flag of Italy to be purchased to drape over Carlo's casket. The room his coffin was displayed in was not very large and there was a strange glow to the entire room, as if the bulbs or the glass lamps were all painted in red. Why red? All I could think was red is the color of blood. On the way home Father explained to me that the color was rose, like flowers, and was used to make it easier for the mourners to feel safe to cry in public, without harsh lights. I couldn't stop thinking of how it looked too much like blood.

Tuesday was one of the longest days of my life. Mother was a complete zombie and it took Mrs. Hartman and Mrs. Edel to get her dressed and standing up. The three walked into the dining room where Father and I had just finished a breakfast made from a hodgepodge of gifted foods he placed in front of me.

"Your mother is ready, so go get your tie and meet us out at the car," Father said as he dismissed me with the usual wave of his hand.

The funeral home was warm, and it seemed the entire town had turned out for this wake, as if it was some sort of a celebration. The room was too small, and I felt ill to my stomach, but Father told me I had to remain standing by the chair my mother was residing in, taking the hand of each old lady or man and thanking each of them for coming, over and over again. Other than a few faces, I did not recognize most of these people and thought I should go outside to see if there was a bus waiting to take them all back where they came from.

"Yes, he was our special boy," Mother said to someone, as if I was not even there, standing like a sentinel by her side. Didn't she think I would hear her?

I just wanted to run. I had to stand there and observe all of this morbid greeting and chitchat over someone these people did not know. Finally after a few hours, the event started winding down to just a few people, mostly staff from the academy. None would look me in the eye, and most never even acknowledged my presence as I stood there fulfilling my duty. The few that did were quick to move on after a brief "hello" or "I'm sorry for your loss."

As we were waiting for Mother to regain herself so we could go home, Mr. Yasik came up to me and said that I did a marvelous job, and that the next gathering this evening would probably be less crowded. I nodded. What was he talking about? Did I have to go through this damn charade by my mother's side again today? Father had said something about this wake thing, then a funeral tomorrow. Not multiple wakes. Were more people yet to come?

After we got back to the house, with Mother settled in a chair looking far away at nothing, Father came to me and said I would not have to go back to the funeral home for the second wake. I should stay home and rest, that tomorrow was due to be a harrowing day.

As I was pulling off my tie and heading up the stairs, all I could think about was how poor Carlo was lying in that box and hearing all the voices of strangers the last day he was above the ground. What a morbid ritual.

I was eager to shed these clothes, get into dungarees and a tee shirt and clean myself of the funereal smell I must have brought home with me.

That night I didn't sleep well and eventually moved into Carlo's bed. I knew that Mother had not cleaned the sheets since he died, since I could again smell him. I didn't realize that I could recognize the smell of Carlo, but somehow I could. After a long, fitful time, I fell into the slumber I needed for the coming day, the funeral.

Waking early to a quiet house was not unusual for me, but today the house was creepy quiet. I had gotten used to hearing Mother or Father trying to communicate with Carlo on what were once normal mornings. I walked through the entire house, poured myself a glass of milk from the Frigidaire, and took a tin of some neighbor's homemade cookies back upstairs with me. There would never be a normal morning again.

The shower water just couldn't get hot enough to clear my head, and I wondered if I was getting a headache. I pulled on what I wanted to wear and went back downstairs to find my father in the front room with a cup of coffee in his hand and a bible on his lap. He said Mother was trying to get it together and to go make myself something to eat for breakfast. I explained I had eaten earlier and that I was showered. I asked, "What time is the funeral?"

"Eleven o'clock this morning. We'll go to Epworth, then into the graveyard to bury him. After that, the ladies from the church and academy will be serving a late lunch here at the house. Make certain your bathroom is cleaned and pull the doors to both your bedrooms closed. I'll need you dressed and ready to go by ten thirty, alright?"

Before he could dismiss me, I turned and went up to clean my bathroom and prepare our bedrooms for those who would come up to use the bathroom but not know which door to open. No one but family ever climbed those stairs, yet today we must be expecting the same busload of old people from the funeral home to come here as well.

As was the new norm, Mother looked frail and more like a corpse than yesterday. I learned decades later that the stuff Dr. Prather was giving her to cope became her newest secret friend, but in pill form, always a bottle tucked in her bedside table with another in her clutch purse for the ready.

When we arrived at the church, the coffin was already in the front, with the Italian flag draped over it and loads of flowers surrounding the base of the stand that held Carlo in that wooden coffin. Father told me to go ahead to the front of the church and take my seat. He would stay back there at the vestibule with Mother, who would want to greet the mourners as they arrived. More likely she wanted them to see her, dressed entirely in black from head to toe, with that silly veil over her face, as if this was a Halloween wedding and the chosen color for this bride was black. Father and one of the Yasik ladies stood with Mother, each holding an elbow.

I stood for a very long time with my hand on the flag and felt the silk pressed against hard wood. I thought of how Carlo had once done this as well, when he lost his parents. I wondered what that had been like. I would never get the opportunity to learn of his experience or anything else from him.

I sat alone in the pew and thought about that day. How miraculous it was to listen to Carlo read. It was like a light switch; one day I didn't think he understood a word I was saying and the next he was reading J.D. Salinger. If only I had known; known that he would not be around, known that he and I could have spoken the night before, and known that we had so much we needed to share.

I looked back after a while and noticed the church was packed and people were starting to stand along the back and side walls. Had they all tiptoed in here without my knowing? It was so quiet and all of a sudden people were everywhere. Organ music began to play, and I watched as Mr. Yasik escorted my mother down the aisle toward me, with Father and the Yasik lady trailing behind. Mother looked dreadful, yet almost pleased with herself. This feeling regarding her performance did not sit well with me for a long time. They sat next to me, and we went through all of the rituals, the church filled beyond capacity, the smell of incense and the sounds of the voices talking up at the lectern, "Ave Maria" sung beautifully in Latin. We had been sitting there for over two hours.

Then the movement started; the escorted coffin was wheeled down the aisle toward the back of the church with Mother and Father in tow. I followed dutifully, but could not look at the fellow mourners; I just lowered my sight to the back of Mother's shoes and kept a respectable distance. It only seemed right, as it felt that this funeral was more about my mother than the distant cousin from a small village in Italy.

It was uncomfortably warm outside while we stood by the plots I just learned my parents had purchased for Carlo, themselves, and me. How morbid to be standing where I would eventually be buried and know of its existence from this point on to my final breath one day.

When all the pomp was finished, and Mother had been escorted away by several people now that she could barely stand alone, I took a few minutes to linger by Carlo's coffin. I guess I had something or other to say, but nothing came to mind. Now that Carlo was gone, he would speak my language and I his, so

I figured the only thing appropriate to say out loud was "Talk to ya later, dude." The grave diggers, two old black men from West Rehoboth, chuckled and one lifted his hat to me in an awkward salute.

Back home, I took up a spot on the side porch, which had not been noticed by the vast number of strange people wandering around my house. I thought of Carlo's bedroom as well as my own, wondering who was peeking their heads into the rooms to determine which room belonged to whom. I thought of our friend Mr. Baldwin and wondered where he was and if he even knew of the ceremony we had just experienced without him.

As soon as the last handful of people were saying their goodbyes to my parents, I approached Father and said I was going to change into comfortable clothes and head to the beach for a walk. While I was hanging up my suit, I had no idea I would be wearing it again so soon after that day as the uniform of the witness who helped to substantiate the rumors of Mr. Baldwin and the incident that wreaked havoc on my life.

I rolled up the legs of my dungarees and left my shoes and socks on the dunes at the dead end of Annapolis Street so I could walk along the surf with my feet in the ice cold water. I needed to feel something; I needed to know that I was really alive.

The most important people in my life, my entire life, I had known for less than one year, and they were all gone. Each one, in a matter of minutes, either taken from me by a bullet or was somewhere being punished for something he had not done.

I headed south, walked for what seemed like hours, very slowly so I could feel the chill of the Atlantic waters engulfing my toes, feet, ankles, and lower legs. Near the boardwalk someone had written in the wet sand with a stick or piece of driftwood, "Carpe Diem." I rubbed it out with my numb toes, knowing there was nothing for me to seize this particular day. Not the day that dear Carlo was laid to rest under dark soil and funeral wreaths.

Eventually I ended up close enough to the Robinson house to see its roofline. I stopped and just stood there for some time—how long I will never know. Could I manage to walk that much farther down the beach just to see the house? Should I be visiting this spot instead of where Carlo now lay, the place where I last looked into his eyes, where I saw the clouds in the reflection of a puddle of his blood?

I decided to go no farther in that direction, not then, not ever again. My life had been irrevocably changed and I would never again step foot inside Robinson Cottage or approach those wide, steep stairs that led to the Robinsons' oceanfront home. I would never again go near that hellhole called Silver Lake.

Chapter 29

I was not allowed to return to the courthouse after that day of testimony, and the case appeared finished before it even seemed to have begun. Mr. Benson did not put up much of a defense for Mr. Baldwin. In fact, he put up no defense. Mr. Baldwin did not testify on his own behalf. They did not recall me to share the truth. I assumed I would have to return to that elevated witness chair and get to finally tell what I did see happen, tell my part of the story, and show I was there for fairness and, above all, for justice. This had to be done for Carlo and for Mr. Baldwin.

I knew they couldn't finish this trial without me, since everyone else who was there at the mass murder was either a young child suffering shock over the loss of both of their parents or they were long dead. There was no one else that was a true witness. But I was never called back. I never got the opportunity to help Carlo or to help Mr. Baldwin in his defense.

My parents had stopped collecting the daily newspaper or they were hiding it from me, which meant I had not a clue of the outcome of the remaining days of this trial. Then one day when I came home from trying to enjoy a game of volleyball with a few of the life guards I smelled a delicious dinner, saw the table was set with the good stuff, and heard Mother on the telephone in the kitchen talking in an elevated and happy voice I had not heard in months.

When I entered the kitchen, she said a quick good-bye to whomever she was talking with, hung up the wall phone, and told me to go clean up, that we had guests arriving shortly for dinner. I was told to put on a shirt with a collar and wear a belt too. This was serious stuff if she was telling me to dress in such a way. I was feeling good for a short moment as I climbed the stairs but when I accidentally entered my old bedroom, now Carlo's old room, it suddenly hit me. There had to be a verdict and the news was good or Mother would not go to such trouble.

I decided I had to know the outcome immediately, so I ran back downstairs and as I opened the swing door to the kitchen, almost knocking my mother over with strawberry shortcake in her hands, I just blurted it out, "So the news is good from the trial, Mother?"

"Very good news, son. We'll celebrate a nice dinner with the chief of police and Mr. Horton as our guests. Now get cleaned up as I asked; they will be here any time now. I just need to make room for this dessert in the fridge and then put on a better dress. Go."

As I was looking for my brown belt, I realized that if the chief and that nasty Mr. Horton were our dinner guests for this so-called celebration, the news was in fact not good. At least not for Mr. Baldwin after all he had been through. I locked my bedroom door and sat at my desk just waiting for one of my parents to attempt to enter so I could lash out at them. I didn't care which one of them, as either would do at this point. Frankly I was disappointed in both of them.

Thirty minutes later I could hear them laughing and sharing cheers with cocktail glasses clinking over and over. I was surprised that Father had not come to the bottom of the stairs and made his customary yell for me to come down for dinner. I stayed in my room and pouted like a kid that didn't get the exact toy from Santa that he requested, and after pacing a path into my rug, I figured I would just head downstairs and blow their celebratory cocktails.

The first one to speak was Mr. Horton as I entered the front room. He stood and raised his glass in salute to my arrival. "There he is, the man of the hour. I can imagine you're happy to see this whole court case over with, now aren't you, son?"

"Yes, sir, I'm pleased it's finally over," I replied as I sat on the arm of the chair Mother was sitting in and looked at the table full of canapés and cut vegetables with a bowl of dip in the middle. I had never seen these displayed in our home before, not even for a special birthday celebration. Perhaps I was too harsh on my parents, and in fact the case was over, justice was served, and Mr. Baldwin would be arriving here to celebrate as well.

The chief then slapped old Horton on the back and said, "I thought they had you there for a few minutes, what with making Mrs. Crutchfield look bad and all, but the jury could see right through that in the end. Well done."

"Thank you. I believe a book about this little case that rocked our town is in order, or my memoirs will have a lengthy chapter on this one meaningful case," said Horton as he turned to Mother and added, "That dinner smells divine. When are we going to eat? After all, I've been sustaining myself late at night in the office on crackers and bourbon, you know!"

He had won the case. That meant that Mr. Baldwin had lost. We lost. It was not a fair hearing from the beginning to end, and now they were celebrating their victory in the face of Carlo and in my own home. Who were these people I called my parents? They had to believe me when I told them what happened at the Robinsons' house, what really happened.

"Robert, help me in the kitchen. Gentlemen, we'll meet you in the dining room with a feast to please your empty stomachs," Mother said as she rose and I followed. *More like for your empty souls* I was thinking.

Once we were alone in the kitchen, and while she was putting on her kitchen apron over her party dress, I finally had her undivided attention.

"Tell me now, please. I can't stand this talk of celebration and I don't even know what for." I was holding out some grain of hope, which dissipated the minute she turned and I saw her smile.

"That bad man will spend the rest of his miserable life in a prison far away for what he did to Carlo and you, my sweet boy. You have nothing to fear now," she said as if she believed I feared Mr. Baldwin.

"What? Don't you understand yet? I—he—this just isn't right, Mother! Mr. Baldwin did not kill all of them!"

"He was only convicted of killing Mrs. Robinson, but he will still be away for a long time. Poor woman was just protecting her family. I've forgiven her for the harm she caused our family. Carlo looked so much like Mr. Baldwin in that shirt; she just made a simple mistake is all."

"Am I the only one here to understand what happened? They put the wrong man in jail! Ask Father, I told him, I know I did!"

"It's all over now. Let's put this dinner on the table before it gets cold, and you are to be polite to the guests at our table. I don't want to hear another word of this foolishness ever, ever again."

"But he didn't kill—" was all I could get out before Father pushed his way into the kitchen to ask if there was any more scotch for Mr. Horton.

"Say nothing more, Robert! There's a new bottle on the stairwell to the basement, hon," were the last words discussed in our house about this murder case.

Chapter 30

Since Jean Tallman knew I was in the office early, she made a point of getting up early herself to come surprise me. She was known for her leisurely mornings over a pot of tea and toast, watching the wildlife and the flowers in her shaded back yard on Columbia Avenue. Her parents had purchased the home as a summer place decades before, and she and her two siblings, Liz and Charlie, grew up in this quaint cottage, running through the house with sandy feet, wet swimsuits, and friends. Later it became a year-round retirement home for Jean's widowed mother. After she moved on to an assisted living facility, the house was deeded to Jean and her brother Charlie. Jean moved into the house and Charlie took his share of the value and bought himself a little cabin by a fishing hole he was fond of near Hagerstown, Maryland. The third sibling, Liz, was well off and living in Nashville with her husband and family, having abandoned life along the Atlantic Ocean years before.

Jean is a smart lady, not just from the standpoint of real estate and how to protect her clients like a mother tiger, but she has always gotten the answer for any medical concerns, having been the daughter of a physician. After attending Duke University back in the 1950s she raised her three sons with a husband who was too busy at work to attend to normal family needs. I doubt her boys even noticed, since she was that good of a parent. Eventually her husband moved on and later passed. She still speaks fondly of him because she knew his faults but loved him nonetheless.

Now in her advanced years, men have been far and few between, but lately I have been hearing the name Richard pop up in her conversations near the coffeepot. She is one of my favorite people, aside from being one of my finest real estate agents. In my early years, she and another lady, Ruth Grimes, put my little firm on the map, selling more homes than some of the big box offices were doing, and they were always smiling.

So when I heard her yell her cheerful "Yoo-hoo" as she walked through the front office door after 8:15 a.m. I knew that something was up.

She bee-lined right for my office and rapped on the door frame when she saw that I was looking down at the morning paper. "Do you have a minute, Rob?"

"Always for you, Jean, come in. There's fresh coffee brewing that should be ready by now. Can I pour you some?" I asked.

"Oh, no, thank you. I had my tea at home. I wanted to tell you first thing that I spoke with the Roberts Brothers last evening…Actually ran into them at the Henlopen Oyster House, and we talked over a couple of crab cakes and beer. They are over the moon about the Cartwright property opportunity!"

"Is that right? Well, I'll be damned," I shared, grinning from ear to ear.

"I explained that we hadn't even established a price point to sell the entire parcel, and that it was, of course, raw land essentially. At the moment a price didn't seem to matter to them. Troy, the younger brother, said he was going to their banker first thing today, and as soon as we have established a price, to come to their offices before word got out. Isn't this great? I could hardly sleep last night, I was so excited!" shared Jean.

"Well, well…We had better get our thoughts together on a price…Have you any idea what you think yet, Jean?"

"Not exactly, so I thought we could work on this now, before the hubbub starts in the office today. Also, I had my friend Richard with me, and he got them to promise an exclusive listing of all the new homes with us and no less than a one-year cancelation clause…And they agreed with a toast of plastic beer cups!"

"I need to meet your friend Richard. I think he's brilliant. I would have never asked for a one-year cancel. That gives you the time to sell the entire project and retire the way you always threaten!" I smiled, and she laughed.

After we had completed the homework needed to recommend a price, I suggested we contact Mrs. Cartwright, who was in the area to spend time with her twin sister. I called her on her cellular phone to learn that she and her husband's brother, a retired real estate lawyer from New Jersey, would be in Rehoboth the following day and would review and sign the agreement to let us get the sale started.

I hung up the phone a bit deflated when I heard of this brother-in-law, since most lawyers want to change documents just to show that they've earned their ridiculous fee, even though lawyers prepared the boiler plate documents to begin with. That was one of the eyesores of the real estate business—lawyers.

"What's wrong? Did she change her mind about selling the land? You look forlorn now. Oh, don't tell me…" she faded off with the same look of defeat I was probably carrying on my face as well.

"No, she'll be here tomorrow some time and likes the value you've suggested. She's bringing a lawyer from within the family," I said as I dropped a pen on the desk, clearly frustrated.

"Hell, half the lawyers in Sussex County are afraid of me, I can handle this!" she laughed. Wow, what a good spirit.

The balance of my day was spent preparing the documents for Jean while she went to the Roberts Brothers Home Construction office in Lewes to tie this multi-million-dollar deal down. I wanted to have everything in perfect order so this lawyer would not find fault.

That evening I slept like a rock, with the dogs tucked behind my knees and my back, snoring as they lay with eight feet in the air. I woke refreshed and thought about how something that was so much a part of my history in Rehoboth Beach could possibly turn out to be a positive thing, even profitable.

I called my father and asked if he wanted a breakfast date at the home, and he sounded cheerful. He was impressed by the news, so much so that I think he was at a loss for words for once. He suggested we go tell Mother that afternoon when the business was concluded. I said that both she and Carlo would love to know this positive outcome and that it was a date.

When I made it back to the office and was parking my car, I realized that I had forgotten to turn my cellular phone back on after leaving the assisted living facility. I noticed a sleek Jaguar in our small office parking lot with New Jersey tags. *Oh please, don't be them here ahead of me!* Then I noticed Jean's large Mercedes next to the Jag and felt less panicked. The one day I arrive later than anyone else, wouldn't it be my luck.

I felt the energy in the air as soon as I opened the office door, with everyone buzzing around, dressed so professionally and all looking busy. I guess word had gotten around or maybe there was a rumor that Oprah was buying a home here yet again? I had never felt so proud of my staff. There were even fresh flowers on the conference room table and a silver coffee set that didn't belong there. I later learned that Jean had added these finishing touches. She is a classy dame.

My assistant, dressed as if she was heading to a soiree not the office, escorted me to my office, took my briefcase, and told me to sit down and get ready…The Roberts brothers and Mrs. Cartwright were all in Jean Tallman's office, having met in the conference room and agreed to all the terms over a cup of coffee. She said that Jean had asked that I meet them in her office as soon as I returned.

I went down the hall and knocked on her door, hearing several voices behind the door talking at once. When she said "Come in!" and I entered and found a festive atmosphere, with all sitting around Jean's and Ruth's desks as if it was a family gathering. I stepped in, closed the door behind me, and was amazed by the appearance of this lawyer who was in attendance—or whom I assumed to be the lawyer, having met all others in the room previously. He was jovial looking, smiling as if he had just won the lottery, and was the one in discussion over what type of home he wanted the brothers to build for him on the site.

I greeted each one, starting with Mrs. Cartwright, of course, and apologized for my tardiness. I quickly explained that my father needed a short visit on my way to the office.

"Oh, so that's why your cell went right to voicemail, Rob! I teased that you had taken the Cape May-Lewes Ferry first thing to go up to Atlantic City for a quick celebration!" said Troy Roberts. All chuckled; apparently he had not in fact said such a thing.

Mrs. Cartwright, looking both radiant and relaxed, stood and introduced me to her brother-in-law, Glenn Cartwright.

"Mr. Elliott, I'm honored to meet you. I've heard your name many times over the years and am pleased that you of all people could benefit from the Robinson property being sold," he said as he extended his hand. His touch was strong, his handshake firm. He appeared to be about my age, maybe a few years ahead of me, but clearly affluent and successful.

As I released his hand and took the remaining chair in the room, Jean gave me a little wink of her eye.

"Well, Rob, it appears we've all come to an agreement here. The Roberts will buy the land at the asking price and will settle, contingency free, within the next ninety days. Mrs. Cartwright is pleased with the terms and feels that the timing is ideal for getting her sister into an appropriate facility. I even mentioned the Beachfield Assisted Living facility where your father resides, since it's such a nice place. Perhaps you can give the Cartwrights a tour of it today, before they leave town," which she followed up with yet another discreet wink as she finished.

"Sounds great. I can call ahead and make arrangements. My father has been extremely happy there for several years now," I replied.

"The Roberts will bring in a one million dollar deposit by the end of the week. I thought you would find it acceptable that it takes a few days. They need to transfer funds," Jean finished the business conversation with this firm statement, more than a question for me. If only she was thirty years younger, I could retire and hand the firm over to her and finally get on with my dismal life.

"Perfect. That's pretty normal business practice." Then I turned to Mr. Cartwright before continuing, "That is, as long as you are comfortable with advising your sister-in-law of this delay of the deposit?" I asked, expecting the pleasantries to end and the typical lawyerly fighting to begin.

With a cheerful smile and sparkling eyes, he replied, "That's more than appropriate. I advised Laura to expect a few years for this sale to occur and that we would make arrangements for Maria with other funds in the meantime. This, as it turns out, will be ideal, swift and equitable. Don't you agree, Laura?" he asked her.

"Most certainly. I want to jump up and hug you, Mr. Elliott, I am so pleased," she beamed as she replied.

"Please call me Rob. Hugs are always welcome in this office. Let's plan on a good hug in ninety days or so," I shared optimistically. "With your business all concluded, may I congratulate you all, tell you that Jean will represent this transaction along with the new homes sales beautifully, but I'm here if you ever need me. Now, if I may be excused, I'll go and make the arrangements for you to see Beachfield. Jean, may I see you in my office for one moment please?"

Mr. Cartwright turned to Jean and said, "Can you look to see if that document has come through your fax machine for me yet? I can take care of that right now while you're meeting with your boss."

After she entered my office, I closed the door and gave her a big hug, knowing she had done well while she had a lot of work ahead of her. She sat and asked if she did alright, to which

I replied, "Better than I ever could have. So why all those winks in there, my friend?" I inquired.

"Oh, that…It seems that Mr. Cartwright spent a few minutes looking at that photo of you in the conference room, the one showing you offering the oversized check for the donation to CAMP. He was very impressed and asked who the man was. It appears he's not a typical lawyer jerk at all!"

"I see," was all I could think of to answer. It felt as if there was more to this thought, but I let it go.

"Glenn says he has always loved our town and just retired. He was planning to look at places to live in Lewes, but after Laura drove him by the old homestead early this morning he fell in love with the Silver Lake area. One lot could be sold already," Jean shared, clearly excited by her success in one morning, all of it completed well before noon.

I looked at her with a puzzled expression on my face. "What is this about a fax?"

"Oh, she'll be in South Carolina and he'll be nearby, so he offered to prepare a general power of attorney to address all of her affairs regarding this property, and his former partner is preparing it, sending it, and they are going to execute it here today. From this point on, I guess he'll be making all the decisions. But frankly, there shouldn't be many left, huh, buddy boy?" Jean shared with me as she walked out of my office.

"Go on back to your group and I'll make the call to the residence director at Beachfield now."

Chapter 31

As I sat on hold waiting for the resident director of the assisted living facility, I read through the hand-written messages from while I was away that morning. I could not believe that I had so many, and then one in particular struck me like a knife in my ribs. I had to read it three times and practice slow breathing before I believed it to be real and not a cruel joke.

The note said that Mr. Bradley Baldwin, an inmate at the Lewisburg Penitentiary in Pennsylvania, had asked for a return call. Then my secretary wrote "are we looking to hire inmates as agents?!?!" which obviously meant she had no idea who this inmate was and what horror his name was associated with. I tried desperately to accept her little joke, but couldn't.

I must have sat there for some time, realizing that at some point I had ceased to wait on hold for the resident director of Beachfield. I had apparently hung up while on hold. One of the best days in my professional career and this nightmare seemed to always find a way to crawl into my thoughts like a poisonous spider, ready to destroy any pleasure I held.

Jean was just outside my door with a look of concern on her face, and finally she said, "Rob, is it your father? What's wrong? You look as if you've seen a ghost!"

I handed her the note, she read it, and then crumbled it up in her manicured hand. "It has to be a joke. A sick joke."

"I haven't spoken to him in…what, forty some years? Why now?" I queried. "Why call me?"

Jean had the right idea when she suggested I shrug it off as a sick prank and get back on the phone, call Beachfield, and take the Cartwrights for a nice lunch at The Buttery restaurant while up that way. "It's a beautiful day and you can celebrate over a bottle of their finest wine. It can be my treat."

"That's a brilliant idea. Thank you, but I'll pay. Can you ask one of the girls up front to look up the number so I can make a reservation after I set up this tour for us?"

"Even better, I'll call personally and make the reservation. You've kept them waiting long enough, make that call, and let's get this show on the road, kiddo," was the last thing she said as she walked briskly out of my office.

In the office parking lot, Glenn Cartwright offered to drive so he could get a better feel of the area, and I opened the rear door, but Mrs. Cartwright refused to let me sit there, so I took the front seat after helping her into the back. The car was immaculate and smelled good—I guess the English leather and maple woodwork?

Our tour of the facility went exceptionally well, and there was an unlikely vacancy for the type of suite Mrs. Cartwright desired for her deteriorating twin and a private nurse. We had the opportunity to make a stop at Father's room to introduce Mr. Cartwright and re-introduce Mrs. Robinson-Cartwright. Father was still chipper, sitting at his desk playing solitaire while listing to Yo Yo Ma on the CD player I had given him one Christmas. The reunion was brief but pleasant.

When we were seated on the porch of the restaurant, right under the corner cupola, Laura Cartwright said that my father had been very kind to her and Maria after their parents died. He had made arrangements for them to stay with Miss Lane, who was very kind to them for the days that followed, until a relative could arrange to come and take them away. She then shared that she regretted not thanking my father when they just met. I suggested that the less we discussed those dreadful days, the better. And to that, she raised her water goblet and offered a cheer in agreement.

The lunch was simply ideal, delicious food and two bottles of excellent Chardonnay, and the chef for The Buttery stepped out to say hello. When I asked for the bill, I was informed that a Ms. Tallman had already arranged for it to be covered when she called in the reservation. She even specified this particular table for us.

What a gem she is, not just a good agent, but a dear friend, I thought. *I will have to remember to tell her this someday.*

We took a driving tour of Lewes before returning to the office. Glenn was satisfied with the prospect of buying in the future Silver Lake community versus Lewes. I had always desired the ship captain's charm of Lewes over Rehoboth, but I was a native, so what could I say.

Mrs. Cartwright and I exited the car, and Mr. Cartwright came from around the car as I was helping her into the front seat. He offered me his card with a cellular number hand-written on the back. He said that he would be in the area for a few days and would like to get together with me another time soon. I agreed and offered him my card in exchange. I said my good-byes and returned to the office, feeling as if a connection had just been made, but of what kind, I could not yet imagine.

With the pleasant events of the day I forgot about the Baldwin message—until I sat back at my desk and saw a second one from the warden of the Lewisburg Penitentiary this time. What in the world was this all about? Why today, of all days?

I let the message fall on the desk and left early. This would be a great day for the dogs and me to take a long walk together.

Chapter 32

I found Grunt and Spike fast asleep on the back porch when I pulled in the driveway. I was not sure if they were happy to see me or upset I interrupted their midday nap, but when I said "walkies," they moved as if their tails were motorized.

There was nothing better than a walk on the sand to awaken your spirit and clear your thoughts, or so I always assumed until we got to the beach and the boys were running free, barking at seagulls, and I started to consider the two telephone messages from Lewisburg.

Lewisburg Penitentiary was known as a mean place to end up; a high-security facility for inmates, it was located in a nowhere land of Pennsylvania some 175 miles west of Philadelphia. I remember looking up the information about it in the library after Mr. Baldwin was convicted of the first degree murder of Mrs. Robinson back in 1967. He was eventually not charged with the murders of Carlo and Mr. Robinson once it was established that Mrs. Robinson had committed those crimes.

He was sentenced to life without the chance of parole. Mr. Horton would never hear of the truth, nor would Mother. She had him pegged as a bad apple from the day she met him, but was she ever wrong. He was so good to Carlo, and unfortunately she never got to hear that from Carlo's own mouth. When I used to share my opinions, she would phase out and act as if I was a toddler rambling on, but I was seventeen when he was convicted, almost old enough to go off to war, so I should have been old enough to share my opinion with my mother and father. They never saw it that way. Father had softened over the years, but still we do not discuss this subject.

Mother went to her grave holding tight to her beliefs and opinions. Later I built the courage to defend Mr. Baldwin to Father after Mother was gone. He was more understanding, but I doubt he saw things quite the way I had. He lost his academy, his career, and he was personally devastated by the loss of Carlo and the rumors that trailed him for years. Which issue confounded him more, I still cannot establish.

During the entire trial period, Mother refused my requests to go see Mr. Baldwin, to talk with him about that day. I had no idea if he knew that my parents forbade me or if he felt I had abandoned his friendship singlehandedly.

Perhaps it was due time I speak with him now, although I had tried to put him out of my thoughts over the decades, probably to heal my own heart more than to dredge up my former fears of his condition in a maximum-security prison. Did I want to consider the way he had survived all these years, with no friends or companionship from the outside world or did I want to keep his memory locked up in that cigar box along with other painful mementoes of my childhood?

Watching Spike try to capture a flock of seagulls made me think of my life today. I had this decent life now, not what I had hoped for, but an okay existence. Would talking with Mr. Baldwin churn up all the bad memories and cause me to clam up all over again? At this point in my life, I had hoped to be more successful financially, to have traveled abroad annually, and have more of a family than what I had with the dogs. Now in my later fifties, with no children, no relationships to speak of, and no travel logged in my passport.

I tended to blame all of that on the safety of staying in this small town, the security of knowing the names of the other patrons in Lingo's Market, although now I tend to go to the big grocery stores out on the highway, shopping amongst tourists and strangers. The security of being able to have a small business that appeared strong and successful from the outside and going home to dogs, who could not tell me how wrong I was, nor complain that I did not take care of some plumbing problem left behind. Had I really wanted more but steered my heart away from it? From love?

My lingering thoughts of Mr. Baldwin after the trial evolved around pity, and I knew that going to visit him in Lewisburg would have been useless, as he would have seen right through to my pain and would have worried for me when he needed to be concerned for his own welfare. He always had my best interest at heart and was very much a friend. How come it had taken me so many damn years to come to this realization?

After Mother died I could have gone to visit him with impunity, and yet I didn't. Had the tables been turned, Mr. Baldwin would have been my loyal visitor, I believe this now.

By the time I returned to the house, I was determined to bathe the boys and then head back to the office to make those return calls.

Grunt fought getting into the tub at first, but then enjoyed the bath. I sometimes wonder how they think. Do they know that they rely on their human companions so much that they would probably starve if left alone? Do they even know how much pleasure and love we garner from their attentions returned?

Spike loves a bath and wanted it to last longer than I had planned. Both ran around the house shaking off the water, which I could never towel off completely. Then they each took turns rolling on their backs, rubbing their spines into the carpet and growling in happiness. If only my morning showers felt so invigorating.

Back at the office, I was luckily all alone. The smell of old coffee and the flowers from the front lobby and conference rooms blended nicely as I sat at my desk and looked at the message from the warden. Perhaps he would not be in at this time, and I could leave a message and head home to gather my thoughts before I went any further with these calls.

I was put through to the warden immediately and was greeted with a very pleasant voice. I had been expecting a gruff military-sounding voice and found myself put off guard to begin the conversation.

"Good evening, Warden Thompson, my name is Robert Elliott, returning your call from earlier today?"

"Well, thank you for your call. I wasn't certain you had recognized the name of one of my inmates who made a request to speak with you, a Mr. Bradley Baldwin? Does this name ring a bell, Mr. Elliott?" he asked politely.

Ring a bell? This name is associated with setting my entire life on its ear, was my thought, but instead I replied, "Yes, sir, I know of Mr. Baldwin, well, at least I did many years ago. How is he?"

"That's why he and I were calling you. He's not well. I don't know if he will share this information with you, but you are the first request for a telephone call in the forty-plus years he has been incarcerated here at Lewisburg. That's besides the usual lawyer calls, which ended months after he was brought to us. With that said, I feel his request needed top priority, and since he has been a model prisoner, and with his…" he paused momentarily before continuing, "…I just felt it imperative that you be reached if possible. You weren't hard to locate, still in his old town, I see, Rehoboth Beach, eh?"

"Yes, besides college, I've remained in this town," I replied.

"Baldwin thought you would be somewhere far and unreachable, so he'll be pleased to know you've returned his call."

"Actually, I returned your call, not his," I stated in a too quick matter-of-fact manner.

"I see. Does this mean you don't wish to speak with Mr. Baldwin? I will completely understand and will convey that to him this evening. But calling hours are over and he'll have to return your call tomorrow at this point in the day. What shall I tell him, Mr. Elliott?"

I did not know how to reply and let the silence linger over the phone. It seemed that this warden was a patient man, as he too let the silent pause take its time.

"Tell him to call. Let me offer you another number to use to reach me so we don't miss the connection this time, alright?" I offered him my number and he hung up. The handset of my desk phone felt very heavy in my hand, as if it had gained weight during the call.

I stared at the painting of my father on the wall and focused on the signature of Mr. Baldwin's in the bottom right-hand corner. Sick was he? How old would he be at this point, probably sixty-eight or nine by now? *Let's see, Father is eighty-seven, so that range would be about right.*

Forty years of his life had passed by just sitting in a cell with nothing to do but regret the mistakes he made and the mistakes of others that had affected his life. He was such a gentle person, and I think the system bowled right over him, sending him into the gutter of life as a criminal when I still felt in my heart that he never committed the crime he was so wrongly accused of...But why didn't I know enough then to stop the mess? Was I afraid of my mother and father?

I now think I should have stood up to them in those insane days after Carlo was killed. I loathed them, but why was I afraid?

Forty years, and he had made *no* telephone calls.

I left the office and went home quickly, eager to have a scotch or two and then try to figure out just what to say to this man I once cared so deeply for but then became a coward when he needed me the most. I know it was not his fault, well, unless he was actually having an affair with Mr. Robinson and I could not see it after all? To this day did I know what really went on between them?

Chapter 33

First thing after breakfast and a quick walk with the boys, I was planning to head into the office as usual. That is, until the cell phone in my pocket started to ring.

Looking at the small screen, I could see that the number was from the same area code as Lewisburg Penitentiary, and that this could be the call I had been anticipating for forty some years. I answered, "Good morning, this is Rob Elliott."

It was his voice, well, a hollow and sad version of it. Mr. Baldwin was on the phone and saying what a delight it was to hear my voice. Then he coughed for what seemed a longer than normal amount of time. He recovered, yet his voice sounded pained, as if his throat was suddenly raw. He simply asked one question, "Could you see it in your heart to make a visit up here to Lewisburg in the coming days, please?"

Dumbfounded and not at all prepared for this one question, I answered without a second thought, "Of course. I'll be there tomorrow."

"That will be nice," he replied. With that, he said "Thank you, and good-bye for now."

If the call was over one minute long, most of it was listening to the sound of him trying to muffle the sounds of his coughing and perhaps fifteen seconds of conversation. While a sad call, I felt excited that he had made it.

The balance of the day was used up with normal daily issues as well as organizing a dog sitter and travel arrangements so I could make the trip. I realized that it was only about five hours or more each way, but felt I should stay in a local motel just in case it was too emotional of a meeting and I would have to drive home in a preoccupied state.

The following morning, I set out for my trip to Lewisburg with a heavy heart and deep sense of guilt for letting so much time pass without making the effort to reach out to Mr. Baldwin. The ride felt longer than I had expected, and I realized that passages of time went by as I drove where I didn't think of anything but that day at Silver Lake.

The experience of visiting a prisoner in a maximum-security penitentiary was daunting. The inspection of my person and my clothing was strange and felt intrusive. As they were checking my pockets and patting me down, I considered life in a post nine-eleven world as well as how it must feel to be in a prison environment for the rest of one's life, with no sense of privacy.

I was led to a room with a solid wall of glass, more than an inch thick, with telephone receivers every six feet or so sitting on top of a counter. I was told to sit under the number "6" and wait for my inmate to arrive. While I waited I thought of the impersonal feeling this set-up had created for families to see their loved one like this, but also the safety of the thick glass and the feeling of imprisonment needed to separate the public from the prisoners.

After just a moment I watched a man come in with two enormous guards and thought he must be going to the lady just past me sitting under the number "8," when suddenly he was helped by the guards to sit across from me. This had to be some sort of mistake. The Mr. Baldwin I felt I knew once and remembered looked much taller, stronger, and healthier than this old man with a gray beard. His eyes did not show that green glint of sparkle but looked more like two milky balls with some darkened gray-green circle floating in the center. His hair was stringy and looked as if it was falling out. As I would later learn, Mr. Baldwin's face was ravaged from the side effects of AIDS medications; his skin was mottled and bumpy and, more telling, the sides of his face just below his cheekbones were deeply sunken in—almost emaciated, indented. At that moment, Mr. Baldwin seemed to me an embodiment of the fight against all the injustices and ills he had suffered in this prison.

We sat staring at one another for a few seconds, then I heard a guard behind me say, "Pick up your phone, you only have a few minutes to visit, sir."

I turned to look at the guard, and realized by the way he was looking in my direction that this was intended for me. As I turned and lifted the phone, so did Mr. Baldwin, or his ghost, I thought.

"I know I look like hell, but please don't look at me with such fear," he said as he tried to smile.

"Oh, I'm so sorry. I thought they made a mistake in bringing me another inmate, you know, someone else," I replied.

"Well, it is me, and I'm pleased you did come. Thank you. I've asked you here because I wanted to get some thoughts off my chest and I know of no one else I could share them with and feel as if I did the right…" then the coughing began, and after a few seconds, and him wiping his mouth with a damp napkin, he continued, "…thing by talking now," he finished before another coughing attack, which continued for such a long time the guard behind me tapped my shoulder and said that the inmate was near death and must return to his bed in the infirmary now, the visit was over.

As I watched them walk him away, hands under his armpits, their heads turned away as if he was contagious, I just sat there thinking how insane this idea was to come and see him. We had barely had a minute, and he didn't say but a sentence to me.

I asked to see the warden as I was being escorted away, and to my surprise was told that I could in fact see him.

The wait for a meeting with the warden was over an hour, but I was determined to find out as much as I could while I was here. He was very gracious and spent a long visit with me, explaining the life that Mr. Baldwin had experienced here at Lewisburg.

He explained that this prison was known for housing some of the nation's toughest criminals and many of the gang members often preyed upon the quieter, gentler inmates such as Mr. Baldwin. Over the years, he had been gang raped, probably during shower sessions, and never complained or reported the abuse until the physician diagnosed his illness too late. He was a stand-up inmate, taught languages to several inmates and an art course for many years. He seemed more like a volunteer there to help those incarcerated improve their lives rather than being an inmate himself. He even tutored a few men to help them earn advanced degrees. He never came to the warden to complain of his abuse, which he could have done easily since they spoke frequently about the progress of the inmates he was helping.

The warden went on to explain that while it was his job to oversee the prison and not to determine an inmate's guilt or innocence, he felt that Mr. Baldwin had been wronged in the courts, was indeed railroaded, and believed him when he told the story of what happened that horrible day decades ago.

During their conversations over the many years, it became apparent to the warden that there was an injustice here. Mr. Baldwin explained of a brief relationship that was misunderstood by the entire town, which was blown out of proportion based on his feminine mannerisms, and he explained how he could not convince the people who prosecuted him that while he may have been guilty of his innate mannerisms, he was not guilty of any murders.

At the end of our visit, Warden Thompson suggested that if I returned again the following day, he would personally escort me to the infirmary to see Mr. Baldwin. He further explained that for an inmate who had not entered the visitor's room in over thirty-nine years as well as the anticipation of my arrival together may have worked him up into a panic, based on the report from the guards. We decided that tomorrow's visit in the infirmary, unannounced, might make it easier on Mr. Baldwin.

I drove away from the prison regretting even more the fact that I had abandoned this friend. I found the first motel, checked in, and went directly to the small diner across the street and sat at the bar, then ordered a scotch that turned into four or five more. The meal was unmemorable and I walked across to the motel and crashed in a drunken slumber.

My appointment to return to the penitentiary was not until noon, so I slept in, took a long, hot shower, and decided to practice what I would say during this visit.

I arrived and experienced the same humiliating search before being escorted to the warden's office. The wait was just a matter of minutes, but I felt like a kid being sent to the principal's office. I almost laughed, because as a student, that meant my own father's office, and I never took his demeanor seriously.

The walk to the infirmary wing was long and quiet, as we had little to discuss. The warden finally broke the silence and said to expect that the surroundings of Mr. Baldwin's bed would be dismal. Having visited others in hospitals many times in my life, I was not fazed. Then we turned a corner and entered an area where surgical clothing and masks, gloves, etc., were laid out for the two of us. We had to dress in this protective gear from head to toe before we could enter this "wing."

The warden walked ahead of me and asked that I wait a moment, and he entered an area that had been curtained off from floor to ceiling. I looked around and noticed that the medical staff were also in the same get-up and that the other inmate patients each had one hand in a handcuff attached to the bed rail. How quickly I forgot that I was in a prison.

I was asked to come through the curtain as the warden and a male nurse were helping Mr. Baldwin sit up in the bed by propping more pillows behind his upper back. They removed the oxygen mask that was covering his mouth and nose, replacing it with a tube that was inserted into his two nostrils. He looked genuinely excited to see me, but still looked years beyond his age.

I sat and noticed that his arm had been removed from the handcuff, but that there was a mark there from its presence just moments ago. Then we were alone. Mr. Baldwin just smiled and looked at me.

After a long moment, I got up and went to hug him, but he put his hands up in fear of my touching him, saying, "For both our safety, please don't," with sadness in his milky eyes. "I'm not well, and you don't want to add to it, please understand," he said before another coughing fit.

"I don't understand. I can't catch what you have, Mr. Baldwin," I said.

"Please, after all these years, call me Brad."

"Brad, the warden filled me in on this insidious disease you have contracted, and how. I don't fear touching you at all."

"But I fear you. See, the pneumonia is taking my life, maybe days left. To add any other infection would be too much for my body to handle," he explained.

"Oh, I understand." I looked around at all the equipment sitting nearby and assumed it was all there at the ready for that inevitable moment.

"Please, let me share what I must first, then if I have the energy I would like to hear of your life, how your parents are getting on, and everything about Rehoboth Beach you wish to share," he said with relatively smooth transition between coughing. He laid his head back and closed his eyes. There was no sound out of him for a long time, and I feared he had passed, just like that.

He began to speak, very softly and slowly, "I was a different man than you ever knew. You see, when I first arrived at that Silver Lake cottage, I had a visit from Mr. and Mrs. Robinson. They were very kind and offered me the use of their canoe, a kayak, etc. They apologized for the condition of the old cottage, and I found them both to be charming, endearing, and possible future friends. *Coughing*. Within days of that visit, Mrs. Robinson would frequently walk along the shore-line of the lake and on occasion stop at the cottage. *Coughing.* These walks were always after the sun had set and her family was at rest. She explained that she did not sleep well and that Mr. Robinson could fall asleep in a hard chair. These walks became daily, and one evening I invited her up to sit on my porch, well, really her porch, *coughing uncontrollably,* and she made a pass at me one evening, and we kissed longingly and one thing led to another, and she asked that I take her to my bed. I was a virgin of sorts, and we fumbled, but it was a pleas-ant experience," he concluded, coughing again for several minutes.

I got up and poured him some water from the pitcher near his bed, which he accepted but then only drank a small sip through the bent straw, and with a shaking hand he gave it back to me, obviously eager to get on with this story he had held in his heart and head for so long. I was stunned by what I heard and was eager to hear the rest as well.

"She and I had a short affair, and then she cut it off. Within days of that break up, *coughing,* Mr. Robinson befriended me with the offer of rides to and from the academy and invited me to join him for runs on the beach, trips to the pub, or that little pizza place, you know." He looked at me with frustration on his face.

"Oh, yes, old Affonco's Pizzeria. It's now a seafood restau-rant with outside dining and is loaded nightly with tourists," I shared as he coughed some more. I was not certain why I contributed this much information about an old haunt, but somehow I believed it would keep him engaged as he was catching his breath from all the coughing.

"Yes, there. Thank you. Well, we had a few nights where we drank way too much and Mr. Robinson ended up staying over at my home. Since there was only one bed, he slept next to me, and I thought nothing of it. But Mrs. Robinson came into the house just before sunrise once and found us sleeping next to one another in my bed and screamed at us. It was awful." He laid his head back again, closed his eyes, and rested.

After two or three minutes of much-needed rest he resumed, "She became crazy, she was so mad, and she pointed her finger at him as she told him he had done it again, over and over. *Coughing.* I didn't understand at that time what she meant. Later, he confessed to me that during his days in the minor leagues his coach had walked in on him with another ballplayer in bed at a motel the team was staying in, and both players were dismissed from the team and the league. He never had the injury he spoke of to you and Carlo."

"So she didn't believe him when he explained that you two were in fact harmlessly sharing a bed?" I inquired.

"I would venture to guess not," he replied slowly, looking up at the ceiling, as if speaking to heaven now.

His coughing began to increase into a lengthy fit, and another nurse returned and asked me to step outside the curtain. I waited for many minutes, listening but unable to hear what was going on behind the curtain.

The nurse came out and said I could stay for a moment longer, no more. He was extremely weak and needed rest. I was impressed by the nurse's level of concern for this inmate, and how kindly she spoke of him.

Many minutes passed before the other nurse had left the curtain and I could return inside. I immediately grabbed his hand, without regard to disease issues. He looked at our hands and then raised his eyes to mine and a tear streamed down his cheek. I wiped it away and just said, "I am sorry. Sorry I never came to your side."

Mr. Baldwin, Brad, looked ever weaker than before. This visit was taking a toll on him, I could see it as each moment went by, wondering if I should leave for the day, when he turned his head to the wall away from me and said, "Please believe me, I didn't kill her. It wasn't me, but I couldn't let another life be ruined," and with that statement, his head hung down. His chin was now touching his shoulder. I noticed that his hand was still in mine, but it felt different somehow, like it had, he had, just died.

I called for the nurse, and three came into the curtained area. One asked that I step out and they huddled over him and spoke just over a whisper. "Finally he's at rest. What a shame."

I walked to the guard at the doors and asked to be let out. I removed the scrub clothing and walked the long corridor back to the exit with another guard, not a word exchanged between us.

Outside the gates, I walked to my car and got in and sat there shaking then started to cry as I had never before in my entire life. How could I have abandoned this dear person for so many years? Mother was long dead, and I could have made the arrangements to come see him so easily, but never did. Finally I couldn't cry anymore and just stopped, as if I could turn my tears on and off like a faucet. I looked at the clock and realized I had been sitting here in the car for more than two hours.

Chapter 34

As I walked back into the musty motel room, I dropped the room key on the small desk and pulled off my shoes and lay back on the bed, facing the ceiling. The overwhelming weight of this experience was too much to shake off. I wondered if I was feeling guilt, anger, disillusion, or just sadness. In all those years, I had never questioned that someone else could have been the one to kill Mrs. Robinson. I assumed that it was either Mr. Baldwin or that she had died by her own hand. This meant that it could only have been one of the girls. There was no one else in the house as far as I knew. But could it have been one of the twins?

The twins were young girls, and they appeared to have had so much love for their father, which was evident when he was with them. Could one of them have had enough disdain for their mother to have pulled the trigger mere minutes after she shot their precious father? When they were with their mother, they were silent and unanimated, but that was probably how people saw my family when we were in public. I had issues with my mother and my father, but never ever had I considered killing them. At such a young age, could one of the twins have been capable of murder? Could they maintain that secret all these years yet never share it with anyone?

I decided to walk across the street to the same diner I had eaten in last night and get a drink. As I sat there with my scotch, I tried to replay the conversation with Brad Baldwin. If I understood his last words, *"It wasn't me, but I could not let another life be ruined,"* correctly, then he was making reference to another person that had killed Mrs. Robinson; someone he had protected over all these many years. Another life ruined could mean so many different things, and I shouldn't take it out of context now.

If Mr. Baldwin had, in fact, been the innocent man I once believed in, then perhaps now in his honor it was my duty to figure this out, but how? Had I come here before now, he could have shared the story with further detail. By my third scotch, I had decided that he would not have shared more details with me any sooner, since he was a man with some odd sense of honor and allowed his own life to be stolen and destroyed in a disgusting environment rather than ruin the future of one of those girls. Why would he accept all that was said about him, the stories brought out during the trial, listen to all those painful accusations, and feel the heat of the angry eyes from the people in that courtroom to protect a child he barely even knew? Was his life with his own father so bad that he felt he was too far along in a painful world but that this child still could make something of her life?

The alcohol had taken its toll on my balance as I stood to leave, so I stayed and ordered a Coke and a pastrami sandwich to go. While I waited for my carry-out meal to be prepared, I decided that I could not expect to ever know the answer to these complicated questions.

Crossing the street with sandwich and soda in hand in my condition was a bit precarious, to say the least, but I made it safely across and entered the room alive. I flipped on the television for some distraction and watched their local version of a news report. I was surprised to see that the news of the day included the number of inmates that had "expired" at Lewisburg that day. With a small town that relied on employment from a penitentiary, I gather this was in fact news of the day.

My desired distraction was short lived as I began to think again of Mr. Baldwin and how arrangements were needed for his body. He had no family, or so the Warden shared and I believed, and I owed it to him to help out if I could. I made a mental note to call Warden Thompson first thing in the morning before I checked out of this place. I hoped a long, hot shower and a good sleep would clear my thoughts.

I slept deep and sound and woke with a dry mouth in the middle of the night. I took a drink of the heavily chlorinated tap water from the bathroom and returned to sleep until well after the sun had risen and was shining in my eyes through the dirty curtains.

I showered, checked out, and went across the street to eat something before the drive home to Delaware. Hoping my call to the warden would be brief and official; I decided to wait until I was on the highway before I called. Within a minute of the conversation, I regretted this decision and was looking for an exit to turn around and return to the prison, based on what Warden Thompson told me. I really wanted to shake myself from this miserable area as soon as possible, but I had one more thing yet to do.

I went through the entire visitor inspection and pat down process yet again, but this time the large female guard took her time going through my items in the small plastic basket before returning them to me, as if she might find a reason to keep me here long term in my wallet and car keys, watch, etc. I learned that my name was on a list provided by the warden himself and was to be escorted to his office as soon as I had arrived. I decided not to tell Mr. Thompson the attitude and treatment I'd received by this particular guard, as it was probably my imagination and she was only doing her job, although it had seemed a bit too gleeful to me.

I was seated across from the warden again and thinking of my academy days as he finished the call he was on when I entered his office. When he hung up the phone, he stood and came around to me and sat in the chair next to mine. It seemed odd until he put both his hands out to shake my one and told me he was very sorry for my loss of a dear friend. The warden was a really decent man, and it was evident he did care about his inmates, guilty or otherwise.

We spoke of the arrangements the prison system follows for bodies of deceased inmates without family and then I offered to pay to have Mr. Baldwin cremated and that I would take his ashes to an appropriate place. With that business concluded, all that was left was to address the reason I turned around and drove back here.

Warden Thompson rose from the chair and went to a file cabinet, pulled out a thick folder, and removed a small stack of envelopes held together by rubber band from the file before sitting behind his desk in an official capacity again.

"When Inmate Baldwin, err, I mean Brad Baldwin was told he was end stage with the disease, he asked if he could prepare a couple of letters that would be held until he passed away and then be sent to the recipients," Thompson said with a sad look on his face. "One of my staff volunteers after hours to try to help locate the recipients of such letters, and with all the letters Mr. Baldwin had prepared, we could only locate these few. All the others will be destroyed—unless you are able to provide us with addresses," he said as he handed me the stack.

I reviewed them and then laid a few letters back on the desk, retaining three. "Why would he write to people he had not spoken to in nearly forty years, not knowing whether they were even dead or alive?"

"Sometimes out of hope, I would guess. Baldwin never had visitors, so his connection to the outside world was essentially cut off, and he may have felt these letters were his way of explaining things to those people who meant something to his life."

"May I take these three?"

"Certainly you may. I see that you have one for someone named Mr. James Elliott and one for the Robinson twins. Do you know how to get these letters to the rightful recipients then?

"I do. One is my father, who is still alive and was Mr. Baldwin's employer at Tidewater Academy, and the other, well, I happen to be in communication with one of the twins and can get it to her quite easily," I answered.

With that, I stood, thanked the warden for contacting me on behalf of Mr. Baldwin and for being his friend during the final days. I turned and left with a heavy heart again.

As I walked out to the parking lot, I swore to the sky that I would never set foot on this ground ever again. It was simply too painful here.

Chapter 35

I had barely covered ten miles before the letter addressed to me was burning a hole into the front passenger seat of my car. I had decided to wait until I was at home before I opened and read the letter. Then I changed that decision to be until I stopped for lunch, and now, just miles farther, I was considering pulling off alongside the highway, I wanted to read it so badly.

Fortuitously I was saved by the ring of my cell phone. The screen showed Jean Tallman and I answered it.

"I've been thinking about you, buddy boy. So tell me, how the visit to Nowheresville, PA, has been so far?" she said with sincerity in her voice.

Relieved I had someone like Jean to talk with, I told her everything I had learned and what I had experienced. I didn't leave out a detail except that I drank myself to sleep each night. By the time I had finished telling her of these past days, with Jean patiently listening and not interrupting or questioning my feelings, I had come to realize that I had been driving for hours and was more than halfway home to Rehoboth Beach.

Jean then filled me in on what she had done with the Roberts Brothers and how the earnest money funds were deposited in the firm's account already, then added that she had a very pleasant conversation with Mr. Cartwright. She did not mention any discussions with Mrs. Robinson-Cartwright, but maybe she overlooked sharing this detail.

When we finished the call, I stopped to get some gasoline, stretch my back, and plugged my phone into the charger, but I did not touch the letter. It now could wait until I made it home before it was read.

For the balance of my drive, I considered all that Jean had filled me in on and how we should progress with the Robinson land sale, the marketing plans for the new community once it was in place, and the like. This mental diversion made for a pleasant return home from an otherwise emotionally draining trip. I even thought more about Glenn Cartwright and decided I would call him to get together and give him the letter to deliver to his sisters-in-law.

Finally close to home, as I was sitting at the light next to where Mr. Hazard once sold those shiny vintage cars, I recalled the man I had met that day so many years ago as he came off the bus. Mr. Baldwin was a different person back then, strong, tall, and virile looking. The man I had just left behind to be turned to ashes was but a shell of that man. Then I heard the honk of a horn, looked to my right, and saw none other than Jean sitting next to me in her big Mercedes, window down, a smile like Carol Channing's across her face and, as soon as I rolled my passenger window down, the sound of her voice.

"Yoo-hoo...Just stopped at the Lewes farmers market and got some beautiful veggies for dinner. Want to come over and be my date?" she yelled through the car windows.

"Thank you, Jean, but I think the boys would be disappointed if I get home and go right back out. I'll take a rain check, okay?"

Before I could get another word in, she was pulling forward and nodding yes. As I traveled on I thanked the heavens for providing me with such a dear friend.

I parked along "the avenue" and went to the Critter Beach pet boutique to pick up a couple of their special treats for the dogs and then headed home to a warm reception of wagging tails and jumping Scotties. I decided to sit and just enjoy this time with the dogs as they licked my face and then devoured their bones, and I realized just how happy I was to be alive and well.

While pouring my second cup of coffee the next morning it dawned on me that I had yet to open and read the letter addressed to me. I had been so overwrought about it when I first got it, but now…Maybe it was best to let my mind settle from the trip to Pennsylvania before I read it. The boys deserved a walk along the surf and I had plenty of work waiting for me in the office. I could read the letter later that evening.

We walked for a long time along the beach, and then I left the boys napping at opposite ends of the sofa, in the morning sun. I was in the office ahead of the others and was able to get my list of the day's tasks completed before I started in on my messages and mail.

There was a message from Glenn, several from other brokers, and one from my father. I found it curious that Father would leave me a message while he knew I was out of town, but after a brief conversation learned he was checking in on my mental welfare after the trip. I shared with him some of what

I had learned and that I had a letter addressed to him from Mr. Baldwin. To that, his reply was to ask that I simply destroy it as there was nothing that could change the history the two of them had shared. I thought it odd, but agreed to honor his request and destroy it. Just as we were finishing our conversation, Father said with that emphatic voice of his, "Please don't read it, Robert, just destroy it."

Before returning another call, I went into the computer workroom and put the sealed envelope into the shredder. To this day, my father could still get under my skin with his change of voice inflection. Will that ever change?

I was wrapping up a short conversation with a few of our newer associates when Jean entered the office and waved en route to her office. A few minutes later Ruth Grimes came to my door and asked if I could step into the office she shared with Jean when I was next available.

I entered their office to find the two of them deep in conversation. Ruth turned to me and welcomed me in and then said she and Jean thought I would probably want company when I opened the letter. I shared that I was fine, the letter was at home, and I would read it later. I thanked them for their concern and explained that while I had several changes of opinion while driving back from Lewisburg, I felt confident that the letter would not hold any shocking information and that I would be fine to read it alone.

We were interrupted by the receptionist coming to get me, to alert me that Mr. Cartwright was on hold for me in my office. Jean gave me her impish smile as I turned to go, and I wondered what she was up to behind the scenes.

"Rob Elliott, how may I help you?"

"Rob, its Glenn. How have you been?"

"Well, thanks. I returned late yesterday from a brief trip to Pennsylvania and am playing catch-up today. I understand that Jean has updated you regarding the progress of the deposit funds for your sister-in-law's transaction. It appears to be moving smoothly toward a clean closing."

"Yes, I tend to agree that this is all going smoothly. Actually, I was calling to see if you had time for lunch today. I'm in the area and thought we could get together perhaps?"

"How does one o'clock sound? There's a little place near the boardwalk called The Crab Claw that looks like a dive but offers the best seafood for lunch," I suggested.

Glenn confirmed the location and agreed to meet me there. I went about finishing up my return calls and was at the restaurant in a booth by the window ten minutes early.

He walked in, looking well rested, as if just returning from a Caribbean vacation, dressed in luxurious clothes with a newspaper under his arm. When I stood to shake his hand, he commented that this looked like the ideal place for cream of crab soup and an old-fashioned salad smothered in blue cheese dressing.

With that I replied, "So you've been here before, eh?"

"One of my favorite places, and somewhere I look forward to enjoying often once my home is built down by Silver Lake," he said with a wink as he sat across from me.

And just like that I had a twinge in my stomach, from hearing the mention of Silver Lake. I gathered it was only natural after these past few days and all of the dredged up memories.

Glenn told me how he and Jean had set up a meeting for him and an architect Roberts Brothers recommended, and how he was racking his brain to think how he could put his finger on the exact style of home to build prior to their meeting. I suggested we take a ride around Rehoboth and Lewes to see what architecture most suited his style and then shoot a few pictures of the houses for him to take to the meeting.

"It's a date. When can we go?" he asked.

"Tomorrow is good for me. How about you?" I replied.

"Newly retired, I have all the time in the world. So tomorrow it is. Now let's order, I'm famished from just thinking about this menu."

Halfway through the lunch Glenn told me that Jean had called him that morning and shared that I was back in town and that I had been visiting with Mr. Baldwin at the time of his passing. It took me a moment to consider whether I was upset with Jean for telling him this or relieved that I had an opening into the conversation about the letter for the Robinson twins.

Either way, it did make the conversation transition smoothly, and I explained how I had never been to Lewisburg in all these years and that I was surprised by my reaction to this old friend, the memories that were dredged up with the visit, and then his passing in such a sudden fashion, right in front of me. The conversation came easily, and Glenn was a good listener. He asked a few questions that eased me through my feelings of guilt and helped me to regain the understanding that I had not been a bad friend, but that I had followed my instincts to leave the friendship at the door of the courthouse as I had. We both decided that giving the letter to Laura at this time would be upsetting and unneeded, and that I should simply hold onto it for a later time.

As I was walking back to the office, I decided that I would in fact read my own letter that evening and get it off my thoughts. What more could come from this letter after all these years? I couldn't imagine there being any additional pain tucked away deep in my heart and forgotten somehow.

Chapter 36

Sitting in my favorite chair with Spike curled up between my leg and the armrest and Grunt resting his chin over my foot, scotch melting the ice in my glass and dinner cleaned up, I decided now was as good a time as any to open the letter. I grabbed the two letters and pulled them apart, opening the envelope with my letter opener completely before I realized I had opened the wrong letter. I wasn't thinking and I just opened it. If I hadn't looked at the outside of the envelope while pulling the letter out, I might have never acknowledged the mistake. Quickly, like a guilty child who had just opened someone else's diary, I stuffed the letter into the envelope and threw it on the coffee table as if it was possessed. What had I done now?

I decided to tell Glenn of the mistake and hand over the letter to him when we met tomorrow and hope he would believe me. I then opened my letter with shaking hands and set it in my lap, put on my reading glasses, and prepared myself for the unknown.

Dear Robbie,

This letter is reaching you after I have passed away and after so many years of no contact between us, but yet I feel that I owe you of all people an explanation of the deaths we experienced at Silver Lake together that fateful day in 1967.

First, I want you to know that I understand all the possible reasons you were not in communication with me after my arrest and later during my years of imprisonment. I know how influential your dear mother was in guiding your thoughts as a young man. I believe you will know me differently after you read this letter. I know she did not approve of me from the very first time I met her, but please realize, she did not know me. Your mother judged me based on my sense of style and mannerisms, which while more easily acceptable in Europe, I quickly learned when I returned to the States that the uninformed, like she, assumed I was homosexual first, before getting to know the real me, as only you and Carlo did. Please realize this as you are rewinding the memories we shared together.

When your father and you delivered me to Robinson Cottage that first day, I felt lost and isolated, but later was greeted warmly by both Jeff and Karen Robinson. I felt that there would be a budding friendship after their first visit. As it turned out, Mrs. Robinson, Karen, came by to see me on many occasions, after her family was settled in for the night, and rapidly a sexual affair began between us. As far as I knew, even after we broke it off, Jeff never knew of this affair, as he then became a close confidant and appeared completely unaware.

All the times we spent with you and Carlo were the times I have cherished over these many years of my isolation. We were simply four guys having fun, and none of you judged me for my feminine ways. For that I was and continue to be grateful.

Understanding the relationship between Karen, Jeff, and myself, you may now be better prepared to understand further what drove Karen over the final edge. While she of all people knew my sexual interests the best, she maintained some level of suspiciousness when her husband began to stay out late drinking with me and on occasions stayed over and slept next to me in my small bed. Once she came to my cottage before sunrise and found us asleep and assumed we were sexually involved. As God is my witness, I had no interest in Jeff sexually, nor had I any inclination to believe that he was bi-sexual. He never made any advances toward me and was always a masculine and athletic friend, nothing more.

Years later it dawned on me that Karen chose to kill Jeff or both him and me. That day we saw the fish and when Carlo ran to their home wearing a shirt which she knew to be mine must have triggered some reaction in her brain. I finally understand that she was unbalanced and probably resented the friendship building between him and me. I was nothing more than a pawn in her game to make her husband jealous, to prove she was desirable to other men, that I was convenient. She had to realize her mistake in shooting Carlo and even though she had an opportunity to stop the string of tragedies, she must have concluded that killing her own husband was the only way out of her pain. She had not been able to think it through, as a sane person would have called for an ambulance, and/or made up an excuse for the accident. She was not sane, and so the carnage escalated, quite rapidly.

As you might still recall, I ran around the side porch of their home after her...I tried to enter the house; I wanted to get the gun from her before you were shot as well. I feared for those two girls as well. I now know I had not even considered what she would have done when she saw me alive, but I had one thought and it was to get the gun away from her. Unfortunately when I made it to the window of the southern side bedroom, she was already lying on the floor, bleeding from her head. I just stood there looking through the window, perhaps in shock at what I saw...which was one of the girls standing over her, with the gun in her hand. She was staring down at her mother with a very strange look on her face.

The rest, as you remember, just seemed to happen in slow motion. I was arrested, accused, found guilty of a murder I never committed, and then sentenced to my lifetime of imprisonment. The girls know who did this. I never said a word, since I figured I had seen two of the most important people in my life destroyed that day, and the third, you, needed to be protected.

You see, I knew you cared for my well-being, and you would have done everything in your power to tell the truth and make certain I was found not responsible, but my life sort of died that day on the porch along with Carlo and Jeff. You had to go on, to become the fine man I am certain you have turned out to be.

Whatever became of the twins I have no knowledge, but I know now that while I was dead inside and my life and freedom were stripped from me, their lives were just beginning and they too had to go on, to heal and protect one another somehow. Those children deserved better than they were treated by their mother. She was a cold and menacing woman who showed little love for her family.

This was why I never spoke up during my trial, never told the truth, and because that was what I felt was the right thing to do at the time. I have had a long time to deal with the truth and to make certain I could face myself honestly.

What has caused my death is likely the most horrible disease I could have contracted, but as usual, I was living amongst people of a mindset established through their first impressions. In this prison community, I was seen as easy prey for the hardest of criminal minds and was frequently attacked, eventually infected. The only person I ever shared the pleasure of flesh with happened to be a mentally deranged woman who used me, so perhaps my life's lesson was to teach others in some fashion. I am still working toward understanding this myself as I write this letter to you.

As you are aware when reading this letter, the life of my body has finally ended, but my soul was taken on that dreadful day so many years ago in 1967. Hopefully you were able to place those horrific experiences deep in the reaches of your memory and were able to move on, have a career, a family, and found peace. Each year on the anniversary of the murders, I have prayed for nothing more.

You are the one friend who had such integrity as a young man, so I hope without doubt that your life now is happy and fulfilled. If not, let all of this pain wash away with my passing and find the life you so deserve, heal you, and make your peace. If you do not, I taught you nothing and my life was for naught.

Sincerest Thoughts,
Bradley Baldwin

After the third reading of the letter, with tears dripping from my chin onto my shirt, I was struck by the love and the care this gentle man held in his heart for me over those many years that I had abandoned him. Somehow he realized that I believed what I was told rather than stood by his side and learned the truth. I tried to consider how things might have been different had I visited him sometime in the 1970s or '80s, even later in the '90s…Would he have told me the truth about the twins and then would I have felt the pain and anguish I was feeling for him now? Would I have been half the man he was and worked to tell the truth to the world and make certain that justice was followed through for this good man?

I will never know. Instead I will have to let this settle in my gut with deep questioning. Questioning Mr. Baldwin and Mr. Robinson's relationship; questioning my own sexuality and long ago hidden desires to be with Mr. Baldwin; questioning my inability to move on with my own life, to actually be happy and settled; questioning how Mr. Baldwin seemed to know that I had never moved forward, even though he expressed his desires that I had done just that...

In honor of Carlo and Mr. Baldwin, I needed to get my shit together once and for all. I knew that I now held the key that answered the question of that dreadful day, but what would I do with it? Brad Baldwin was a man who had held some strange honor code within his own life, and he had maintained this code to his death. When he shared those last words with me, it was clear that he was sharing them for the first time, as if it was painful to let the words roll over his lips and be released finally.

That night was a fitful sleep for the dogs and for me. None of us found the right spot for a comfortable sleep, and once one got settled, another would roll or move. I slept little and knew I would regret it later in the day. But I was able to make one decision that night—perhaps the most important one of my entire life.

Chapter 37

Glenn met me at the real estate office five minutes early for our appointment. We decided it best that he drive and I shoot the pictures of the houses he most liked and pointed out. We ventured through the historic and classic communities of The Pines, Henlopen Acres, and the downtown district of Rehoboth before we ventured north to Lewes and travelled the length of Pilottown Road along the canal, as well as past the many charming homes spattered throughout the town's historic district. Glenn selected various styles of architecture and I began to think he was going to have a really hard time narrowing down to one specific style when he set out to meet the architect. It wasn't until we stopped at a waterside pub along the canal to have some beer and shrimp that I learned of his motives for that day.

After we left one another the previous day, and after I had suggested this driving photographic tour, he had decide that he wanted to hear my opinion of houses and styles of architecture best suited for his potential lakeside location. He explained that one of the business traits that had made him most successful as an attorney was to listen to what the other person said first, then determine from the conversation if the person he was with possessed a similar mindset as his own. He went on to explain that often he could make a judgment call regarding the person sitting across from him just by letting him or her talk.

Needless to say I felt odd that he was "working" me during a task that was to determine what type of home he wanted for himself—until he explained that I was a native to this cape region, that I had seen the architectural changes over many decades, and that I could advise him on what was appropriate and ideal for a high-quality home that would be a smart investment when sold, a home with the original character of the area, not like the unimaginative massive box-houses with minimal faux details and porches so often slapped in between smaller, more charming cottages. Wow, he was a bright guy with the right thoughts for how to create not only a home he would love, but one that would sell for high dollars in the future.

The time spent with Glenn flew by, and we had fun. I felt as though I had made a friend connection even though the time we spent together was generally brief and business oriented. We came to learn of our similar taste in music, in arts, in architecture, and when I mentioned in a nonchalant fashion that I needed to get home to feed my dogs, he immediately asked if we could go to my home together so he could meet them.

We left my car behind at the office and went directly home together. As soon as I opened the dog, Grunt and Spike were all over Glenn's ankles and lower legs, greeting him with an exuberance that surprised me. Often Grunt sits back and makes a deep, friendly growl to say hello, then after Spike has sniffed the new guest sufficiently, Grunt will come up to be petted, but not with Glenn. They were all over him as if they were old friends, and when he bent down to rub them, they were pushing their noses into his face, rolling on their backs for stomach rubs, and generally acting like old friends. I was stunned—and very pleased. The three of them played with a dirty old tug toy while I prepared the boys' dinner and opened a bottle of wine to breathe.

Once I placed their bowls on the floor, I had to beg them to leave Glenn's side to eat their dinner; something very incongruous to a regular day at Casa Scotties. I passed Glenn his glass of wine, and we sat in the study and talked about the dogs while they ate. Spike gobbled his dinner fast so he could get back to playtime; I was concerned he would gag up some dinner on Glenn's shoe or something. But it never happened. The love affair between the dogs and he was clearly cemented in place, and the three ignored my presence.

It was a good thing, because at that moment I started to realize that I had feelings for this man more than I had experienced since…well, since Mr. Baldwin was in my life, and I was a mere sixteen years old. Could it be, could I have feelings, was it possible I might be attracted to another man?

I pulled together a simple but quality dinner from leftovers and some veggies still fresh enough to use. While it was reheating in the oven I prepared from scratch a rich sauce to complement the meal. We all went out to the dining room and ate under candlelight, which Glenn had found and prepared while I was in the kitchen. Grunt lay with his chin over Glenn's foot, his eyes looking skyward for any falling bits of meat. Spike was next to me, sleeping after their rough ball and tug toy play. This felt so right, so normal, and so complete.

At the end of the evening, Glenn suggested we run back to the office to pick up my car, and I replied that I could walk to the office in the morning and, after this rich meal, should exercise better.

"You look fine. In fact, if I may say, you look great."

"Thank you. I don't work out, never was much of the athlete my parents had hoped for, and I get most of my exercise walking the dogs."

"So what are we waiting for then? Let's grab their leads and take a walk, for the good of all four of us. That meal was decadent and I think we could all use a little walk. How about it then, Spike and Grunt?" Glenn asked.

They started wiggling as soon as they heard the one word "walk" deep in his statement. Spike was at the door before I could agree.

As we walked, Glenn asked me to describe the diversity of the community of Rehoboth Beach to him. He said he had heard that over the past few decades, this village had changed from being known as "The Nation's Summer Capital" to more of a community of open-minded, highly educated folks who had accepted a large gay and lesbian community with open arms, invited many quality artists, and was much more blended than, say, Ocean City, Maryland, down the road, which was known as more of a blue-collar, hard-drinking, loud car-mufflered city of concrete towers and franchise restaurants.

"You've hit it on the nose. We do see a smattering of congressional politicos, right-wing up-tights sitting on the beach next to lesbian mothers with their children and getting along politely. The gay and lesbian community has done so much for this town. From the increased level of high-quality restaurants, the philanthropic endeavors, and the overall attractiveness," I replied.

"Overall attractiveness?"

"These folks came into town at a time when many of the old summer cottages were in serious need of repair and when the town could have started to remove these homes for newer, less appealing homes to attract the tourists to come and rent. But the gay and lesbian couples saw the charm in the town and came forward to renovate these old homes while maintaining the historic integrity, which costs about twice that of a teardown to build something new. Their gardens are the finest, and you wouldn't know the 'secret gardens' behind the fences if you just walked past the houses. The restaurant community used to be all crab houses and beer bars, but now those are harder to find; with all the more sophisticated palates in town came more martini bars, ethnic restaurants, and an exciting diversity."

I hadn't realized it while I was talking, but the boys were frolicking in the sand and a beagle puppy had joined them. The owners of the beagle, clients of one of my sales agents, came up holding hands and were deep in their own conversation. I said my greetings, embarrassed that I didn't know their names, but they introduced themselves as Rick and Joe, clients of Adam in my office.

I introduced Glenn and then the dogs and myself. The dogs took off running toward the surf, and Rick turned to me and asked if we had tried the new Spanish restaurant, Café Azafran, on Baltimore Avenue.

"Oh no, not yet. We ate at home this evening. I've been eager to try it. Was it good?" I asked.

"Better than good. Excellent wine selection, delicious tapas-style food, and incredible desserts. That's why we ran home to get Miss Daisy for a late night walk…to work off the meal. I would highly recommend it," Joe shared.

Rick added, "And when they found out that we were celebrating our twenty-ninth anniversary together, we were serenaded by a beautiful chanteuse that happened to be their bartender as well."

Glenn was quick to offer them congratulations in an admiring fashion.

The conversation went along smoothly, and we all parted after a half-hour or so feeling as if we had run into old friends. As soon as we were away from earshot, Glenn said something that shocked and pleased me at the same time.

"*We* ate dinner at home? Doesn't that sound as if you were referring to us as a couple back there?"

"Oh, my goodness. Please, please accept my apologies. I wasn't inferring anything of the sort," I stuttered, grateful he couldn't see me blushing in the darkness.

Glenn replied in a confident tone, "I have no problem with how you described it, in fact…" He paused, slipped his hand into mine, and continued, "I very much liked it. Rick and Joe assumed we are a couple, and the conversation felt normal and completely comfortable."

With that, we continued to walk through town toward my home with the dogs on either of our sides and our hands warmly clenched. In that moment, my life had changed—and for the better.

The following morning I was awakened by the smell of brewing coffee, alone in bed without my dogs. After taking a few minutes to gather my thoughts, I realized that they were in fact out of bed and were downstairs with Glenn in the kitchen. I pulled on my robe and quietly headed downstairs to overhear the stereo playing my *Tapestry* album by Carole King. An original vinyl record I rarely played nowadays, but cherished. Glenn had the boys at his feet as he was preparing a full English breakfast and they were as obedient as I have ever experienced. Even when the dogs saw me, they stayed in the kitchen at his feet, just looking my way.

And this was the beginning of my new life.

Later that morning, after a delicious breakfast, all four of us piled into Glenn's gleaming Jaguar and headed to my office. When Glenn dropped me off, he suggested I allow him to keep the boys for the day, and for me to get all of my work done as quickly as possible, since they would be out and about town preparing us a basket lunch for the beach. Grunt and Spike looked so happy in this nice car, with Glenn rubbing their heads, how could I deny them? I said I would meet them at the house at one p.m., but then Glenn said,

"No, we'll pick you up here at precisely one o'clock," and with that and a wink, I was told to go in to work.

The morning passed by so quickly, and as promised, there were guests in the lobby waiting for me as the clock struck one. The boys had apparently been to the groomers and had scarves on their collars, and Glenn was dressed as tastefully as usual, in expensive faded jeans and a blazer.

I had assumed that the beach lunch was to be over the sand dunes by the Atlantic. Glenn had other plans, and drove us to the location of the old cottage on the Robinsons' land at Silver Lake. We walked to the side of the lake, and we sat on a blanket as Glenn opened and removed all the lunch provisions. There was even a doggie pâté made for them by one of the gourmet shops, and we had a wonderful albeit abundant spread.

While Glenn was opening a bottle of champagne, he made another shocking yet insightful statement. "I realize that this property once held a strong meaning of security and comfort for you and that it was taken away from you suddenly. Jean told me she could read it on your face the day you two came back out here recently. So with what I hope will eventually be your approval, I felt it was most appropriate that we make that feeling of comfort and even security begin to return to your life. This is a very beautiful and very special location. The land and cottage have had their time of mourning those days, as have you, hopefully."

With that, he poured us each a flute of excellent champagne, and we toasted "to a renewed and a new love of Silver Lake!"

Chapter 38

Within days, my life had gone from a feeling of despair over the relationship with Mr. Baldwin to that of a complete and utter happiness I had never experienced before. Glenn and I decided to try living together, and very quickly it seemed as if we had been together for decades. He began to write a psychological thriller for fun and take over the primary care of the dogs, the house, and the garden. I was thrilled by these arrangements and found myself doing things such as going to the office about the time the secretaries arrived and leaving before they did. I would stop at old Lingo's Market and pick up freshly baked bread or pie and flowers and almost skip out the door. Glenn seemed to bring a cheerful and refreshing spirit to the house that had never felt like a home before.

Then one day as I returned home from another wonderful business day, he asked me to sit down, that we needed to talk. I felt the bottom of my stomach drop, and I had no idea why. Glenn had poured me a scotch and himself a Manhattan. We sat in the study, and he took my hand. I assumed this was a *Dear John* conversation I had not seen coming.

"I met with my brother and Laura for lunch today. They happened to be in town to pay a visit to Beachfield unannounced and told me that they were very pleased with the care and attention to detail the facility has provided Maria and her nurse.

"The conversation turned to our life together, and some-how I found myself telling them of the letter you hold in your possession for the twins. I fully expected Laura or my brother to tell us to destroy the letter, as your father did. With all the pain they endured, why stir it up now when all of your lives seem to be headed in the right direction? Laura was emphatic that she wanted to read the letter. She asked if they could come by your home this evening before returning south tomorrow morning. I said they could. I hope you're not cross with me. The conversation was so comfortable and fluid that I didn't realize I spoke of the letter until it was out of my mouth. Are you mad?"

"Actually not one bit. Not regarding the letter of course, but…" I let that statement hang in the air as I rose from my chair and went to a book on the shelf and returned.

"But what?" he asked, now the one with a fallen stomach.

"I would prefer it if you had simply stated that it was our house, not mine. You live here as well, and if it weren't for you, this house would not be the home it has become. Now I have something to share with you and ask that you not be cross with me either. Promise?"

"How could I be?" he chuckled as he sat back.

"On the day I finally decided to sit down and read my letter from Mr. Baldwin, I wasn't focusing closely and accidentally opened the letter addressed to your sisters-in-law, not my own."

"Well, you already know what it's going to say then."

"No, I didn't read it. Luckily I saw the name on the envelope as I was removing the letter and returned it to the envelope immediately. I just fear that you brother or Laura will think I had intentionally opened and read their letter."

"Don't worry about this, love. I know they'll believe you as well. I asked that they call to verify the time they're leaving their hotel room before coming. They should call anytime now. We can explain this situation to them when they arrive, agreed?"

With his statement, I felt secure and confident that the coming conversation would be handled properly. Glenn had a way of calming my nerves.

The Cartwrights arrived an hour later, and I had time to shower and relax, since all of my normal chores and dog duties had been met by Glenn through the day. Glenn had arranged a platter of appetizers and put on nice music, lit the candles, and had the place feeling very welcoming. We all sat together and enjoyed a martini before the conversation turned to our living arrangements or the letter.

Laura was first to say how delighted she was that we had found one another and shared her regret that she had not contacted me regarding the land years sooner. Had she, as she described, there might have been more time for the two of us to be together, and we could have been in a lovely home by the ocean at this point. Glenn was quick to point out that he would not have been ready to retire, that he would have recommended a local practicing attorney to advise them, and he may have never met me. We all laughed and talked a bit further about how timing is everything.

Just as suddenly, Laura frowned and said, "It can be a good thing or a very, very bad thing. Timing, that is. Wouldn't you agree, Rob?"

"If you're implying that we have had both good and bad timing in our shared lives, you are extremely correct. I doubt you gentlemen can understand how strange this moment has become for both Laura and me."

They both nodded in agreement. Obviously no further comment was needed. As I rose to retrieve the letter and Spike jumped into my chair, creating an ideal lighthearted diversion, Glenn refreshed the drinks.

When we settled back into the chairs and conversation, I began to apologize to Laura for the fact that I inadvertently opened the letter meant for her, when Glenn interrupted me to say that he was fully aware of this and knew that I felt awful about having opened it, but shared that I had never read it, nor shared it with him.

I handed the letter to her. She laid it in her lap for several quiet moments before saying what was clearly on her mind.

"I have always doubted the story of how my mother's death occurred, Rob. I just couldn't put my finger on the pulse of that day. I was only six at the time, so I give myself age as my primary excuse. And yet, yet I find that in the creases of my recollection, I should know what happened that day. And now, this letter here in my lap could explain all that happened one fateful day almost forty years ago.

"I'd prefer to rip it apart and never read it and equally want to devour each word, to know what has haunted me my entire life." She turned to her husband and desperately asked, "Darling, would you please read the letter aloud for all of us to hear together?"

I was profoundly impressed with the look in his eyes as he took the letter from her lap and kissed her forehead and whispered some sort of a sweet message for her alone to hear. Granted, Glenn was sitting mere feet from them on one side and I on the other, yet they were able to share this moment of intimacy that only a well-balanced, connected couple could share.

Glenn suggested a blessing of sorts. "We four know that the letter in my younger brother's hand may change all our lives irrevocably, and we know that we've spent many years wondering if the information we receive is going to make us think or feel differently. Let this document bring a final peace to all that hear it."

Laura said, "Amen. Thank you for those generous thoughts, Glenn. I'm so glad we're all friends, actually family of sorts."

We all sat in anticipation as he removed the letter from the envelope and unfolded it. The letter was not long, as it appeared to be only one sheet of paper. Slowly he began,

Dearest Ms. Laura and Ms. Maria,

Over the many years I have often thought of you both and wondered if you had children of your own now, along with careers, new surnames, and happiness in your lives. I have done a great deal of soul searching over this lifetime in Lewisburg Penitentiary regarding that fateful day at your family home along Silver Lake in Rehoboth Beach. I imagine that you also have had times of searching your souls.

To the moment I write this letter to you, I have kept a silent promise I made to the two of you when you were mere girls found in a tragic situation of losing both your father then your mother minutes apart. That promise was to be certain that I let the world believe I had been the one to take your mother's life, rather than one of you. I will only assume that with the end of my own life nearing, this promise will remain with me to my last day.

At the moment of your mother's death, I realized that a large part of my life had changed. My soul was suddenly and deeply pained by the deaths of Carlo, of your father, and even of your mother. I had different levels of feelings toward each of these precious people, and with their lives gone I didn't care to go on with my own.

I can only assume that you were both confounded with the way our lives changed that day, and how your future was oddly secured by my being prosecuted for your mother's death. Please understand that I wanted to come to you, explain what I was doing for you, and offer that you let it rest, to go on with your young lives. But that was never allowed. I heard that you were taken in by Miss Lane and hoped that she was able to comfort you in those following days. I had a few occasions to meet Miss Lane and thought it ideal that you be together. She was a fine woman.

I had hoped that as you grew to young women, you would have chosen to come to Pennsylvania to see me, to question me of my motives or to have written to me. Since this never occurred, much to my dismay, I realize that you may have found the visit difficult and may have been concerned with the complexity of such a conversation with me, let alone worry for your future had word gotten out that one of you was a murderess. This sad story will have died with me, and you may rest assured that your secret continues.

May your God bless each of your souls, and may you have found comfort to manage good lives. I have found my peace.

Sincerely,
Bradley Baldwin

The three of them sat there dumbfounded while I watched Laura over my drink, which I perched at my lips in order to disguise my ruse of watching her reaction. Either she was sincerely shocked by the letter's content or she was a brilliant actress. I suspected the former. No one said a word for several long minutes. Laura was the first to speak, in a voice I didn't recognize. It was almost as if she had turned into a child and asked this adult woman to recite her thoughts for her.

"I don't know what to say. I know several thoughts have haunted me all these years, thoughts I chose to hide deep, for fear of learning the truth had I brought them out into the open." Then she paused for a long moment. "This is not easy for me," she looked to her husband, who pulled her closer to him on the sofa and wrapped his arm around her shoulders to comfort her.

He said, loud enough for us all to hear, but barely over a whisper, "Sweetheart, you don't need to share these thoughts with any of us right now. This is a shock and you and I both know what you've questioned over the years. Now may not be the best time to disclose these thoughts, agreed?"

"Certainly not!" she replied quickly. "I've waited as long as Rob has to know the truth. I have to believe Bradley Baldwin would never write such an accusatory letter had it not been true. He had no reason to make such statements after his death if not. No, we need to think this through and understand it for what it is."

"What is it?" I asked, the words spoken before I censored them.

"My sister, Maria, was always a very strange person after the day of those deaths. As her twin, I thought I knew her, and I read extensively on the connective personalities of a set of twins. We're identical twins, as you know. When we were children, we could finish each other's sentences and thoughts. Sometimes just a look explained all sorts of actions.

"That day, when my mom slammed the door to the house, Maria and I had just entered from the french doors on the ocean side of the house, and we were both petrified, and I recall I was crying and having trouble breathing. Mom looked like a wild woman; even her hair was a mess. Years later when I read the stories of Medusa, I pictured my mother at that very moment.

"Mom pushed past Maria and me and went to the side bedroom on the main floor of the house, the one where she would read in bed all day when she wasn't feeling right, when we knew to leave her alone. I went to the door because someone was…I believe someone was knocking on that door."

I interrupted, "That was Mr. Baldwin, Laura. I was at the bottom of the steps and saw him beating on the door to get in. In his letter to me, he shared that he tried to get the gun away from your mother, to protect you, your sister, and me. He believed your mother wanted to kill him and your father. Carlo, killing him was a mistake." I paused, not certain she wanted my input at this time of her revelations. I was wrong.

"I see how that explains so much. When the noise at the door stopped, I heard a thunderous bang inside the room where Mom went. I turned and looked through the great room for Maria. Then I panicked and went into the dining area and hid under the tablecloth. If Mom had killed Maria, I would have been next. But there was no other sound for a long time. The house smelled funny, like rotten eggs or something. I remember I wet myself but stayed there under the tablecloth for what felt like hours. Finally Maria walked toward me with blood on her hands and chest, and I grabbed her and pulled her under the table. I tried to find where the blood was coming from and then realized she wasn't hurt, but there was that look in her eyes…

"She changed at the moment when she must have done it. She just kept mumbling and I couldn't make out one word of what she was saying, none of our special words we used to share between ourselves were said. The look in her eyes; I can only describe it as the same look as Mommy's eyes. We sat there and held one another until the sirens started coming to our house. In fact, I don't know how long we were there, but it was Mr. Baldwin's voice calling our names that brought me back to the reality of the moment. I think he was in the house, or maybe he was outside but yelling loud enough that I could hear him.

"I was so afraid of him after that day, afraid that he had done what everyone was saying. We stayed under the table so he couldn't find us, so he couldn't kill us. Then later I heard people talking about it when Miss Lane took us places and the people didn't know who we were. If Miss Lane didn't overhear them, I would just listen and believe what they said. When she did hear them, she would hustle us out of the store or wherever and tell us not to listen to what these people were saying about our mother and father.

"Rob, you were there as well. What do you remember?"

"Not what you remember. I was outside, and I too was scared for my life. I held Carlo in my arms as he died, or was dead, I don't recall now, and I remember Mr. Baldwin yelling for me to run away. I eventually did run to the cottage and got into the car and had to drive all the way back to town to get help. You may not know, but there was never phone service in the cottage. Once I got to my family's home, I collapsed in my mother's arms. The rest was a blur."

Using a tone that I suspect he maintained for clients, Glenn turned to Laura and asked, "So then the prevailing or obvious thought is that Maria shot your mother since you never entered the room where she was found dead, right?"

"Right. Yet until this very moment, I assumed Mr. Bradley killed her or that our mom shot herself and Maria saw it or tried to help her and that was how she got the blood all over herself. But she changed so much and she tried to commit suicide countless times afterwards, almost succeeding this last time. So if Maria did this, it would explain why she was so miserable for all these years and wanted to die from the guilt."

The dogs were looking anxious so I excused myself and stepped out into the yard with them, and I used the time to catch my own breath. I resolved in those few minutes outside that I believed Laura, and that it was obvious that Maria was the one who would have shown the signs of mental breakdown if she had killed her own mother and no one but she knew it. With this decision completed in my head, I decided that it was all water under the bridge now, and that Maria got what she was asking for by her own hand. She would never be tried for this murder if the four of us kept it to ourselves. Who else needed to relive this pain, and what would become of her if she was convicted in her current condition?

I returned to the study and sat down. There was a pregnant silence in the air until Glenn spoke up.

"Rob, the three of us were just discussing the ramifications of this information getting out at this point. The potential harm to the land sale, the fact that Maria has obviously taken her life as far as she could to the brink and isn't coming back to the former person she once was, and that this pain should be put to rest for all of you, finally. What do you think? Should we pursue this further or let it lie?"

"I would like to say let it end here tonight. I agree with you, Glenn. What good can come from stirring it all up again? Rehoboth Beach suffered years of controversy and stigma and is finally a lovely seaside village again. Your family was destroyed and my own family has suffered irrevocably."

With that, the Cartwrights stood to leave, and we all hugged. They stated that they were simply exhausted and declined our offer of a late supper. They were going back to their room and maybe order something if they felt any hunger. We watched them clutching one another as they walked to their car and then drove off after a few minutes in the car talking.

Glenn and I decided to make a sandwich and put on an old movie. He wanted *Sherlock Holmes,* but I asked for a more uplifting story. We fell asleep in front of the television sitting on the sofa, feet on the coffee table, and two dogs in between us lying on their backs, snoring. A complete viewing of Monty Python's *The Meaning of Life* would just have to wait for another time.

Chapter 39

Considering the topic of conversation and the number of cocktails after the Cartwrights had left, I woke up the following morning well rested. Glenn and the boys were downstairs, having just come in from a short walk. It appeared that after so many years of being an early riser, I was now able to sleep through the three of them leaving the bed and not wake until I smelled fresh-roasted coffee.

This day I needed to prepare for a series of meetings coming up in the following week, so I headed to the office with a bundle of thoughts in my head. Glenn and the boys were happy to see me go. They probably had hours of playing in their plans and needed me out of the way.

While sitting on hold waiting for another local broker to return to our conversation, I turned my head from the phone to the painting on my office wall. Since returning from the visit to Lewisburg, I had decided that I wanted to take the painting home to be enjoyed there. It was a very good likeness of my father during a period of my life that was once marked with many questions. Now with those questions answered, the painting deserved a place in my home.

Once the calls of the morning were completed, I decided to pay a surprise visit to my father at the Beachfield facility. If I left soon, I could get there in time to convince him to join me outside the complex for some lunch together. As I was preparing to leave, one of the agents came to tell me that my father was on the phone. Wow, great minds must think alike.

"Hello there, Headmaster. How are you today?"

"As well as can be expected for a man of my age and mental capacity. I lost at UNO twice this morning, so I need some excuse to get out of the game room. That's why I'm calling you. I had an idea, and if you're not too busy, perhaps you could—"

I interrupted my father by saying, "I was just heading in your direction, to kidnap you for a lunch outing. So what do you think, Dad?"

"Fantastic. Please stop at Lingo's on your way here and get one of those nice arrangements we put on your mother's gravestone. Oh, and one for Carlo too. When will you get here, so I can go back to the game room and gloat over our leaving for a while?"

"Give me about forty-five minutes, and Dad..."

"Yes, son?"

"Put on your cap. I have some news that's going to blow your hat off," I said in a jovial voice.

Our lunch out was very nice, and Father was in good spirits even after I explained all that I now knew about the Baldwin-Robinson murder case. He was not amused, nor disinterested, but he listened. We then went to Epworth Church and walked through the graveyard, stopping at Mother's and Carlo's graves. Dad laid the flowers at each of their stones and said to them that it was a special day, a day of understanding and love for the Elliott family to share.

As we walked slowly down the hallway to his room back at Beachfield, I asked him what caused him to want the gravesite flowers today of all days. As usual, his capacity to understand me more than I even believed as a child was displayed.

"Robert, I've been thinking about all you've been through in these past weeks, with the big land sale, the trip to Lewisburg, your budding friendship with this Mr. Cartwright, and then last night it came to me in a dream. The questions would be answered soon, and today I felt was going to be the day. And so it was."

"And so it was."

I saw my father to his room, where we said our good-byes. I walked out of Beachfield Assisted Living and walked direct-ly to my car. I noticed a large, dark car parked a few spaces before my own with a South Carolina license plate. By the time I reached my car, I thought it resembled the car out-side my home last evening and perhaps belonged to Laura Cartwright.

This one looked so similar to the one they were sitting in just before they left that I got into my car, found my cellular phone in my briefcase in the back seat, and dialed home.

"Hello, not buying today, but I will accept my winnings if you are offering," is how Glenn answered the house phone. What a goofball, I was thinking when I realized I had yet to say hello back.

"Hello?" he repeated.

"Glenn, hey, it's me. Sorry, was thrown off by the way you answered the phone for a moment there."

"So it does work, bravo! I've always wondered if it caught anyone's attention. What can I do for you, handsome?"

"I just returned my dad to Beachfield from a lunch out and a visit to my mother's grave. There's a car from South Carolina near mine in the parking lot and I was curious about what kind of car the Cartwrights owned. Do you know?"

"I do know. It's a dark gray Buick. My brother has always been a bit on the conservative side. I assume that will change with this pending land sale though. He deserves a fun car now. I suspect they're in the facility to see Maria. Why don't you go in and meet her, poor thing. She's unable to converse, but I believe Laura can introduce you to her, and another familiar face may do her some good."

"I think your idea is great. I'll go in and introduce myself if you think Laura and your brother are comfortable with it."

I headed to the front desk to inquire of Ms. Robinson's room. The ladies on duty looked oddly at me and stated that she did not receive guests because she was incapable of communication. After a long pause, they looked at one another, reviewed a chart, and told me the room number.

I located the room at the end of the long hallway. As I approached, I noticed that several of the rooms I passed were vacant. It seemed odd to me that Laura would want her sister's room so isolated, when she could have asked for one of the suites near the nurse station. Then I remembered that the Cartwrights had arranged for her private nurse to live here with her, and so perhaps these far away rooms were the only ones that could accommodate the two of them. Even still, it seemed like a long walk to get to the room. What if there was an emergency?

At the door, I paused hearing Laura having a conversation with someone. I decided to wait a minute or two to let them finish before I would knock. After all, I was a much unexpected guest.

To my surprise, Laura's voice escalated as she continued talking and began taking on that childish tone she had used the night before when the letter was read to us. She was now loud enough that I couldn't ignore her and so I just stood there in the empty hallway as quietly as I could.

"...It's all dangerously closer to us now. You must have known this would happen, you wretched bitch you! I told you not to tell anyone, or else I was going to have to take care of you just like I took care of Mommy. Then you had to survive this last attack. I'm lucky no one has figured it out yet. It looked like a failed suicide attempt and no one has ever accused me. Not me, the quiet and considerate sister who was forced to take care of you, albeit in a different fashion than I had ever antici- pated! Not until that man sent out those letters. Who knows what he wrote to others? He knew it was one of us! So now you have to finally let go and leave us. You can finally be yourself again, in hell or heaven or wherever your soul ends up. I've been too careful all of these years! So now, Laura dear, it's time for you to die...

"I was this close to being exposed last night, and that would have been unacceptable. You were always Daddy's favorite! You had his attention all of the time, while I had second best and was stuck dealing with Mommy and her crazy thoughts. The best part of all of this is that you were so traumatized and afraid of me that you never fought me on the identity change. Even my husband and kids think I'm you. I will always be the good child."

I could not decipher the noise I was hearing, but it was like a swooshing sound, followed by a loud clanking and the metallic sound of something heavy being thrown against the wall or floor.

Laura continued, "I will not let you exist one more day. You're exhausting all of my funds, and I alone should get what's due from the beach house. Just do me one favor when you see Mommy and Daddy—tell them I never regretted killing the bitch. She ruined all of our lives, she was an evil woman. Tell her that!"

At this point I realized I had to do something, so I rushed into the room, and what I saw was Laura standing over Maria's breathing tube with a pair of large scissors in her hands. Maria was gasping for breath, unable to move a muscle and clearly losing the battle to breathe.

Before I could move or say a word, there was a great deal of commotion outside in the hallway. I darted outside as people rushed toward me. They all looked frantic, but there were no audible signals or buzzers, no alarms going off. It was almost a dignified way of responding to a crisis without letting other residents know of the elevated state of emergency taking place. No one paid any attention to me, including a man dressed in a lab coat who clearly had a pistol holstered on his hip, only evident as he pushed past me and the bottom of the coat lifted in the breeze. It was surreal, seeing Laura standing over Maria and now this sophisticated and muted handling of what they knew was a crisis in the facility.

"What's going on?" I demanded, recognizing a nurse named Erin who visited Father occasionally.

"A silent alarm went off, and it means someone has removed the breathing tube of one of the residents without the proper precautions. This is highly unusual and in fact the only patient under those conditions is Maria Robinson. You'd better leave this area immediately."

I took her advice and left through a side door and walked to the car. I could hear the sound of the police sirens as they approached the entrance gates to the facility. Once I was sitting alone in my car, I closed my eyes and said out loud, "Yes, Dad, the questions would be answered soon, and today you felt was going to be the day. And so it was."

Afterword

September 12, 2010

This is my favorite time of day, when the sun is beginning to set slowly to the west and glistens over the water as if someone threw all the diamonds of the world across the top of the lake, sparkling beautifully. I am in my kitchen, a chilled glass of wine on the counter, the doors to the porch open, offering a clear view straight through to the water as I work on a bouillabaisse for dinner guests. The slap of the dog door closing means Spike has run outside for the thirtieth time today, and within minutes I hear the pad of feet on the outside walkway and then the slam of the screen door.

"Yoo-hoo, anyone home? It's just me!" calls out my next door neighbor, Jean Tallman, as she crosses the threshold from the porch to the great room of our beautiful new home. Seconds later I hear Spike return through his door, having run the length of the yard to determine who was coming for a visit and to scare off any squirrels that might decide to invade us.

"There you are, my sweetheart Spikie!" Jean chirps.

"Hello there," I reply as I stand stirring the pot as she approaches the island where I am working with fresh sunflowers from her garden in hand.

"You can't have a dinner party without fresh flowers on the table, now can you?" she says as we hug.

It has been so nice to have made this transition in my life over the past few years. I have everything that once only escaped me—love, a home filled with happiness, a family, and finally complete peace of mind.

When the Roberts Brothers purchased the Robinson-Cartwright acreage, they decided that the old cottage would have to go, and in its general location they created a narrow lane with three lots facing the lake, three across the street, and a park at the end of the road for the new community to have access to the lake called Baldwin Memorial Park. Glenn and I chose to purchase one of the lots, actually the very spot where the old cottage sat, and had this wonderful home built, along with a new pier and gazebo at the end of it. Jean purchased the lot two doors away to build her retirement home, which she shares with her friend Richard, and together we purchased lot in between and have gardens and a manicured area for playing croquet, my newest passion.

My home is quite simple but lovely. From the street it looks like a Cape Cod-style home, with the white picket fence and gate, brick walkways, cedar shake siding, and window boxes I fill each spring with flowers of vibrant colors. The house is actually two stories on the lake side. Inside, the main level offers a wonderful great room with a floor-to-ceiling fireplace flanked by bookshelves, Father's portrait over the mantel, and a full wall of french doors that miraculously open up like an accordion, offering a full open wall leading to the screened porch.

On the street side of the great room is the large kitchen, a room I never knew I would cherish so much, but I have learned so many good recipes from Jean's recently published cook-book. Also on this main level are two bedrooms, one for Dad, which overlooks the lake with a great big bay window, and one for his caregiver. See, Dad moved in with us after the house was built, and we share our days telling the stories of family and having fun, but very rarely do we speak of the academy.

Flanking the two-story wall is the open staircase up to our bedroom and an office. The house is filled with books, fresh flowers, and fine art, but mostly real love.

After making herself at home by pulling out the perfect vase from my cupboard, Jean sets the flowers on the dinner table set for twelve guests before she sits down on one of the overstuffed sofas with a glass of wine and Spike cuddling her. "Richard is over there snoring away, with the TV blaring on a Navy football game, so I thought I'd come around and see if you needed my help with anything," she says over her shoulder to me.

"Nothing whatsoever, Jean. Relax and enjoy yourself. I'm almost done, and we can sit together. Glenn will be back soon. He had to run some last-minute errands, and you know Grunt just had to be in the car with him; no matter where he goes, that dog is by his side. You would never know he was once my puppy before we met would you?" I chuckle as I pour a bit more wine into the large soup pot and head over to sit with Jean.

"I'm using your gran's recipe out of your book, by the way," I share as I settle in, and Spike lifts his head, looks over to me, and returns it to Jean's lap.

"I thought so, smells like our old house on Columbia Avenue all those years ago. Gran could make a pot of soup like no other," Jean says.

"Except me, of course!" I laugh.

A wonderful silence falls over the room. Father is taking his nap, and his caregiver, Lilly, is off for the day visiting family. We just sit and stare at the glistening water. "This is my favorite time of day, did you know that?"

Jean rolls her eyes as she says, "About a thousand times now. But I love to hear it from you, Rob. This is a good life we finally settled into and well deserved." Then, as she puts her glass back onto the coffee table, she shares, "And to think this beautiful view was wasted for so many years. No one to cherish it as we both do now."

"So do you want to hear who's coming for this Sunday supper? I've invited our dear friend Joano, since she is finally back in town from another one of her overseas trips chasing the location of the latest novel she read, and she is making her famous Caesar salad. Then there are your newest clients, Tom and that funny Nancy, who have yet to walk me through their new beautiful oceanfront McMansion, plus Mara and Bob are bringing one of her Italian dessert trays, and we might round the party off with Matt and Bill who will be heading to their Florida home for the winter next week. That's assuming they show up; you know with those two social butterflies, they might be elsewhere having a Sunday cocktail hour and will forget about our dinner!

"Last but not least, I set the table for the possible arrival of Betty and Mickey, but since they bought that damn motor home you never know where they'll be. I saw Mickey out there washing it down in their driveway when I came home from my run this morning. It might be a crowd or it could turn out to be more intimate. Just the usual fun members of our beach family," I tell Jean while she rubs Spike's belly.

"Sounds fantabulous! Just the perfect way to end this summer, not to mention the week," Jean says as Grunt and Glenn come into the house, his arms full of grocery bags and that winning smile, glad to be home.

After he puts the provisions away and makes a cocktail, he joins us on the two big sofas. "I got a call from my brother today while I was at Lingo's shopping. First, he sends his regards and will be in town to go fishing with us next weekend. Second, he said there's to be a story written of the entire Robinson mess that will become a screenplay and movie. Since Maria-turned-Laura-turned-Maria pleaded guilty and died while in the mental ward of the prison, there's no concern over a crazy person objecting, asking for the financial rewards, or using it to her advantage in a later reversal of her sentence. So what do you think of that?"

"I would say no one would believe the story. Sounds like something of a *Lifetime Movie of the Week!*" Dad says as he walks slowly toward us putting his weight on his new cane.

Acknowledgments

This book is clearly a work of fiction, and I sincerely hope that diehard Rehoboth Beach residents realize that I took the liberty of moving locations of certain landmarks, creating new ones, and having some fun with the landscape and description of this charming seaside town. It is true that Rehoboth Beach has been known as "The Nation's Summer Capital," and that dinner parties, art openings, and even lazy days on the beach are shared by conservative politicians next to gay and lesbian families—something that makes this charming town so fascinating and wonderful.

CAMP Rehoboth is a real place, with incredible ties to the community, and is a saving place for people of all ages and orientation. They have made incredible strides to add to the strength and the warmth of this town and its residents, guests, and visitors alike.

I have never written a novel before and would be remiss if I did not acknowledge the encouragement of several people who diminished my self-doubt and helped to make this dream come true.

First is my life partner, Glenn Randall. While Rehoboth Beach was a part of my past before we met, Glenn re-introduced me to it with a new set of eyes, and I fell deeply in love with the town. Without his encouragement I would have left those first chapters in a secret file on the computer for no one to read. I have never experienced the unconditional love and support that I receive from him, even when I know there are days…! His love for our small family, which consists of our real Scottish terriers Grunt and Spike, inspires me each day.

Mara Campbell enchanted me with her stories of her homeland, Italy, and guided me with the translations and the slang of modern-day Italian. *Thank you, Mimi.*

To Beth Horton, Mary Jane Stanton, and Joe Teixeira – Thank you for encouraging me to write, for reading my manuscript, and/or advising on characters and pointing out some flaws. I could have never done this without you. May you never be without a stack of books waiting your enjoyment.

Susanna Crowley, Pat Savani, Sophie Morris, and Eloise Bonney – Thank you for understanding that this work would take me away from the real job that pays the bills, and thank you for your continued support even though it may have caused me some lapses in recent business judgment.

This passion has been in my belly for many years, and I look forward to providing you with more stories that might tickle your funny bone or pull at your heart. Most importantly, I hope to make it hard to put the book down late at night. There is nothing more enjoyable than introducing yourself to a new world through the written word.

Last, I wish to thank Jean Tallman. She has been the friend who has stood by me the longest, has supported so many of my artistic ideas, and who taught me so much about life and about real estate. Not only is she one of my real-life cherished friends, she really was the finest real estate agent that existed.

Made in the USA
Charleston, SC
20 July 2012